DESIRES
AFTER DARK

What Reviewers Say About MJ Williamz's Work

Exposed

"The love affair between Randi and Eleanor goes along in fits and starts. It is a wonderful story, and the sex is hot. Definitely read it as soon as you have a chance!"—Janice Best, Librarian (Albion District Library)

Shots Fired

"MJ Williamz, in her first romantic thriller, has done an impressive job of building the tension and suspense. Williamz has a firm grasp of keeping the reader guessing and quickly turning the pages to get to the bottom of the mystery. *Shots Fired* clearly shows the author's ability to spin an engaging tale and is sure to be just the beginning of great things to follow as the author matures."
—*Lambda Literary Review*

"Williamz tells her story in the voices of Kyla, Echo, and Detective Pat Silverton. She does a great job with the twists and turns of the story, along with the secondary plot. The police procedure is first rate, as are the scenes between Kyla and Echo, as they try to keep their relationship alive through the stress and mistrust."
—*Just About Write*

Forbidden Passions

"*Forbidden Passions* is 192 pages of bodice ripping antebellum erotica not so gently wrapped in the moistest, muskiest pantalets of lesbian horn dog high jinks ever written. While the book is joyfully and unabashedly smut, the love story is well written and the characters are multi-dimensional. ...*Forbidden Passions* is the very model of modern major erotica, but hidden within the sweet swells and trembling clefts of that erotica is a beautiful May-September romance between two wonderful and memorable characters."
—*Rainbow Reader*

Sheltered Love

"The main pair in this story is astoundingly special, amazingly in sync nearly all the time, and perhaps the hottest twosome on a sexual front I have read to date. ...This book has an intensity plus an atypical yet delightful original set of characters that drew me in and made me care for most of them. Tantalizingly tempting!"—*Rainbow Book Reviews*

Speakeasy

"*Speakeasy* is a bit of a blast from the past. It takes place in Chicago when Prohibition was in full flower and Al Capone was a name to be feared. The really fascinating twist is a small speakeasy operation run by a woman. She was more than incredible. This was such great fun and I most assuredly recommend it. Even the bloody battling that went on fit with the times and certainly spiced things up!"—*Rainbow Book Reviews*

Heartscapes

"The development of the relationship was well told and believable. Now the sex actually means something and M J Williamz certainly knows how to write a good sex scene. Just when you think life has finally become great again for Jesse, Odette has a stroke and can't remember her at all. It is heartbreaking. Odette was a lovely character and I thought she was well developed. She was just the right person at the right time for Jesse. It was an engaging book, a beautiful love story."—*Inked Rainbow Reads*

By the Author

Shots Fired

Forbidden Passions

Initiation by Desire

Speakeasy

Escapades

Sheltered Love

Summer Passion

Heartscapes

Love on Liberty

Love Down Under

Complications

Lessons in Desire

Hookin' Up

Score

Exposed

Broken Vows

Model Behavior

Scene of the Crime

Thief of the Heart

Desires After Dark

DESIRES
AFTER DARK

by

MJ Williamz

2021

DESIRES AFTER DARK

ISBN 13: 978-1-63555-940-8

This Trade Paperback Original Is Published By
Bold Strokes Books, Inc.
P.O. Box 249
Valley Falls, NY 12185

First Edition: June 2021

Credits
Editor: Cindy Cresap
Production Design: Susan Ramundo
Cover Design By Tina Michele

Acknowledgments

First and foremost, I need to acknowledge Laydin Michaels, who is my inspiration, muse, everything.

Next, I want to thank my beta readers: Sarah, Sue, and Karen for keeping me on my toes and encouraging me to keep writing.

I can't forget to thank all the folks at Bold Strokes for believing in me for twenty books now.

And, finally, I want to thank the readers. Your warm reception for all my books is greatly appreciated.

Oh, yes—I can't forget to thank Tina Michele for the awesome cover.

Dedication

Dedicated to all vampire lovers and to everyone
who loves the mystery of New Orleans

CHAPTER ONE

The streets were crowded with people, mostly tourists on that balmy evening in December. The stores were decorated for Christmas and the sights, and sounds had my senses reeling. I felt alive, so very alive. The music pulsed through me as I watched the mortals milling about, watching the dancers perform a perfect tango, shopping at the tourist traps, and eating at the myriad restaurants.

Florida Street in Buenos Aires was my favorite haunt. And I'd had quite a few over the centuries I'd roamed the earth. I loved Buenos Aires. It had a European feel to it but was really an entity unto itself.

It was warm, and many of the women were scantily clad, which I loved. I loved women. All shapes and sizes. As I wandered the pedestrian street, I almost forgot my hunger as I admired all the beautiful mujeres. There were dark ones, light ones, and every shade in between. Perhaps I'd take one to my house in Recoleta later.

I kept a house in one of the most affluent areas of the city. It showed my vanity, to be sure. I was all about appearance. My house was ninety years old and designed to look like an old Argentinian palace. It was opulent, just the way I liked it. It had seven bedrooms, but I slept in the basement accessed by a hidden secret door in the floor in my study. No one was allowed in my study. Not even my housekeepers. I kept it locked at all times so no one could happen upon my lair. That could prove disastrous.

As I moved through the throngs, I kept my eyes and ears open for anyone who might be a good dinner for me. I needed to feed. And soon.

The music changed, and a techno beat floated on the air as I wandered down the street. The beat called to me, and I thought dancing would take my mind off my hunger. I followed the sound and came to a modern club. I was about to pay my cover charge when I heard a woman scream.

"He has my purse!"

I turned to see a man running in the opposite direction, jostling his way through the crowd. I used my preternatural speed to catch up to him. I dragged him off the main thoroughfare.

"Let me go. You don't know who you're messing with," he protested. But I didn't listen. I was on a mission.

Once off Florida, I found the nearest alley and carried him in. I shoved him against a wall and saw pure fury in his eyes. Too bad for him. I wasn't the least bit afraid. I unsheathed my fangs and his fury turned to disbelief and then fear. He started pleading for his life. Too late.

I buried my fangs deep and drank my fill. I drank until I felt his heart stop. Some vampires believed that it was dangerous to wait for the heart to stop, but I didn't hold stock in that. I wanted this deadbeat dead as dead could be.

Once he was gone, I licked his wounds to cover the bite marks, picked up the woman's purse, and began to cut through the crowds again. I sped up and made it back to the club where the woman was talking to a seriously disinterested policeman.

"I believe this is yours?" I held out her purse.

She snatched it from me and began looking through it.

"Is this the person who took it?" The cop began to unhook his handcuffs from his belt.

"What? No. This kind woman brought it back for me." To me, she said, "Thank you so very much."

"Everything should be there. I don't think he had anything on him."

"It all looks to be in order. Oh. Thank you again. How can I repay you?"

I looked at the blond beauty standing before me. She had wavy shoulder length hair and deep brown eyes. I thought of a million and one ways she could repay me.

"Don't worry about repaying me. I'm just happy you got everything back," I said.

She stared hard at me and then glanced at the club. Then back to me.

"At least let me buy you a drink," she said.

I smiled my best smile.

"A drink would be nice."

"I take it I'm not needed anymore?" I'd forgotten about the policeman.

"No, sir," she said. "But thank you."

We watched him walk off, then she turned to look at me.

"Come on, my hero. Or heroine. Let's get that drink. I know I could use one."

"Lead the way."

She paid our covers and we went into the darkened room with laser lights pulsating. The music felt like a living being. I wanted to dance so desperately, but I would first have a drink with my beautiful stranger. Not only was she attractive, but she had the most delicious accent. It was from the southern United States. I could figure that much out but couldn't pinpoint the exact whereabouts.

"What are you drinking?" she drawled.

"I'll have a Fernet and Coke." She arched an eyebrow at me. "It's practically the national drink here."

"Then I'll have one, too." She beamed at me, showing me perfectly straight white teeth. She was beautiful.

It was only nine thirty, so the place was still fairly empty. We easily found a table away from the speakers and sat down. She raised her glass.

"Here's to heroines."

I laughed but raised my glass.

"Here's to new friends."

"Oh. I like that," she said.

We clinked glasses and each took a sip. I watched her expression, as many people find Fernet to be quite bitter. She smiled.

"This is quite good."

"Excellent. I'm glad you like it."

Excellent was a word I used too often. I had only recently begun saying it. I picked it up in the nineties and it stuck with me. I hoped I didn't sound too old-school for my luscious date.

"Tell me about yourself," she said. "And tell me how you caught that horrible purse snatcher. I thought he was long gone with my information and money."

"I was a track star at university," I lied, "so he was no match for me."

"Well, thank you again."

"You're quite welcome. Tell me about you. Let's start with a name."

"My name's Martha."

"Nice to meet you, Martha."

"And you are?"

"I'm Alex."

"I love it. An androgynous name for an androgynous woman."

That was it. She'd won me over. She might have had an old woman's name, but she was anything but. She looked to be in her mid-thirties and was obviously open-minded. I settled in to enjoy our time together.

"Yes, ma'am. I'm androgynous. I'm glad that doesn't bother you."

"Heavens no," she said.

"And where are you from, Martha?"

"Georgia, in the US. What about you?"

"I'm from all over really. Though I was born and raised in Romania."

"Oh. How exciting. And enticing. Tell me, how did you end up in beautiful Buenos Aires?"

"I travel a lot. I came here once and loved it, so I decided to make it my home."

Martha sighed.

"Oh, how I wish I could make it my home. I love it here."

"How long have you been here?"

"Only a few days. In another few, it'll be time to head home. I'll miss this city."

"There is something so special about Buenos Aires," I said.

"It's definitely on my return to list."

As we talked, the music got louder, and people started filling up the place. I glanced around and couldn't help but notice that the patrons were all women.

"I think we may be in a women's club." I waited for her response. She glanced around.

"I believe you're right. Would you like another drink?"

That was nice. She didn't freak out or insist we leave or anything of the sort. She seemed to take it all in stride. I wondered if my sweet Georgia peach swung the same way I did. How fortuitous would that be?

"I'd love another drink. Allow me to buy this time," I said.

"Nonsense. I'm buying tonight."

She was back from the bar and must have noticed my toe tapping to the bass. She set the drinks on the table, then extended her hand to me. I looked at her, unsure what exactly she wanted. She motioned with her head to the dance floor. How could I say no?

I stood, took her hand, and we made our way to the center of the floor. The music took hold of my body and I moved this way and that. I jumped up and down with the others and only after the third song did I even remember Martha was there.

She didn't seem to have noticed. She had her eyes closed and was flowing with the music. It seemed a part of her and it was beautiful to watch. After five dances, she pointed to her open mouth and I agreed. It was definitely time for a drink.

I was parched and it was hard to simply sip my drink. I wanted to chug the whole thing but didn't want to look like a lush. So I sipped and sipped and sipped again. My respirations returned to normal and I glanced over to find her smiling at me.

"What?" I mouthed the word since I know my voice wouldn't be heard over the now blaring music.

She walked over to my side of the table and whispered in my ear.

"I'd love to see your house, Alex. I mean, this is fun, but I'm ready for some peace and quiet."

I was ready for that and oh so much more. I nodded, stood, took her hand, and guided her back out to Florida Street. It was almost midnight and the place was still teeming with people. It was a magical feeling.

We'd need a ride home, so I stopped her and pulled her into a space between shops.

"What are we doing?" She grinned at me.

"I need to call my driver," I hastened to explain. "Give me just a moment, please."

I told my driver to meet us at the south entrance of Florida Street and then stepped back among the masses with Martha in tow. We got to the entrance and there was no sign of a car.

"Are you sure he knew where to meet us?" Martha looked worried. I smiled at her.

"I'm sure. And look. Here she is."

The car pulled right up to us, and I held Martha's door as she slid in. I went around and climbed in, then asked my driver to take the long way back to the house.

"The long way?" Martha said. "Why?"

"I want to show you more of Buenos Aires. Remember I love my city. And I love to show it off. Relax and enjoy the champagne and the view."

We sipped champagne and I looked out the window with Martha, trying to imagine seeing the now familiar sights for the first time. Martha did not disappoint me with her reaction. It was obvious she was in awe.

A half hour later, my driver pulled up to the front door. I thanked her, then hurried around to open Martha's door.

"You're so chivalrous," she said.

"I like to think I know how to treat a lady."

"That you do."

I smiled broadly. If I had my way, I would indeed show her how a lady should be treated. In several meanings of the word. Once inside, I treated Martha to a tour of the house. She was duly impressed. The tour ended in the kitchen where I opened a bottle of champagne and filled two flutes.

"Where to now?" said Martha.

"Let's go up to the terrace. I love my rooftop oasis."

We took the stairs up and she gasped when she saw the luscious greenery that adorned the space.

"This is gorgeous," she said.

"You should see it in the daylight when everything is in bloom." Of course I had never seen anything in bloom, but I wasn't about to tell her that.

"Oh, wow. I bet it's breathtaking."

"That it is. Now come. Sit with me."

I led her to a white wrought iron table and chairs that overlooked the city. I moved my chair so I could sit next to her. I draped an arm across her shoulders, and she snuggled against me. I discreetly checked my watch. I had about four hours until the sun came up. I'd have to try to move things along.

"Well," said Martha, "this night certainly has turned out differently than I expected."

"Ah, yes. I know exactly what you mean. How lucky for us that thug stole your purse, huh?"

She laughed. It was a wonderful sound that was music to my ears.

"How lucky was I that you were there and able to come to my rescue?"

"I'm glad I was able to help."

It occurred to me that it would be odd for a woman to travel alone. Did she have a husband, wife, partner waiting for her?

"Who are you traveling with?" I asked nervously.

"Oh, a group of us teachers are traveling together."

I breathed a sigh of relief.

"Should you check in with someone?"

She laughed again. I felt my stomach flip. Other parts of me, now filled with blood from a decent meal, came to life as well.

"Oh, no. Today was do your own thing day. Tomorrow we have more tours."

"I see. And what time do those tours start?"

"Eight." She rolled her eyes.

"Should I get you back to your hotel then?"

"Alex, are you trying to get rid of me?"

"Au contraire. I don't want you going anywhere."

"Do you mean that?" said Martha.

"I do."

"May I ask a favor?"

"Anything."

"Will you kiss me, Alex? Please. I'm not usually this forward, but I'm dying to feel your lips on mine. We'll just say it's the champagne talking."

"No. We'll say it's Martha talking. And I'd love nothing more than to kiss you."

I looked into her pools of chocolate eyes and saw a longing there that I hadn't seen in far too long. I needed her and it seemed she needed me every bit as much.

Her full lips parted, and I lowered my mouth to hers. The first kiss was brief, hesitant, questioning. As I straightened, she looped her arms around my neck and pulled me back. I kissed her again, harder, and my breath caught when she opened her mouth. With a mind of its own, my tongue sought hers. I stroked over, under, all around her tongue and elicited wonderful moans of enjoyment.

I'm not sure how long the kiss lasted, but it seemed an eternity, and I was dizzy with need when it ended.

"May I show you my bedroom?" I whispered hoarsely.

"Dear God, please."

Chapter Two

We left our half full champagne glasses on the table, and I took her hand and led her back down the stairs to the master bedroom. Everything was black walnut, from the bed to the dresser to the desk. It had been stained dark, very dark so it was almost black.

My bedspread was green satin and the Egyptian cotton sheets were fresh. No one had been in this bed for a very long time, but the sheets were still changed regularly by the staff. They didn't know I didn't sleep there. How would I explain that to them?

Martha wandered around my room, running her hand over the bedframe, dresser, and desk.

"This is so you," she said. "So very you."

"I'm glad you like it."

I waited until she made her way back to where I was sitting on the bed waiting for her.

"I don't usually do this sort of thing," she said.

"Enjoy pleasure?"

"Not with complete strangers."

"Ah. But are we really strangers? I believe we're kindred spirits, Martha. Two souls on separate journeys whose paths crossed for a reason."

"I'll never see you again after tonight, will I?" She looked close to tears.

"I can see you every night you're in town. And after that, at least we can keep in touch."

"Would you do that, Alex? Would you stay in touch with me?"

"Of course, Martha. Of course I will."

I kissed her again. It was powerful, pressing, but close-mouthed. I didn't want to assume anything at that point. I needed to be sure she was ready regardless of the fact that I was beyond that point myself.

She ran her tongue between my lips, and I parted them to allow her access. As we kissed, I eased her onto her back and climbed on top of her. Supported by my elbows on either side of her head, I kissed her harder, more frantically. I needed her with every ounce of my being, and I wanted her to know it.

"Take me, Alex," she finally said. "My God, I need you."

I was happy to oblige. I kissed down her cheek and nibbled an earlobe. She smelled and tasted divine. I recognized her perfume but couldn't put my finger on it. I didn't ponder it too long as I had more important things to worry about.

As I sucked on her neck, I untucked her blouse, and together, we got it over her head. Her bra barely contained her voluptuous breasts. I kissed the top of each of them before lowering one cup and taking a hard nipple in my mouth.

Martha gasped and held my head in place while I played my tongue over her nipple. I sucked it deep and was rewarded with a low, guttural moan.

"You need to take this off," I said. "Please."

She removed her bra and lay back. As I continued to play with her nipples, she untucked my shirt and undershirt. She lifted them over my head and ran her hands over my belly and chest.

I was so thankful I'd fed. When I don't, I'm ice cold to the touch and that's a huge turn off to the ladies. But I was warm with all that blood in my system, so I didn't worry.

I sat up, then unbuttoned her shorts and pulled the zipper down. I was trying to go slowly. I sincerely wished I could just rip her clothes off and get to the heaven I knew awaited me. But I didn't. I went slowly and steadily, and soon Martha lay naked for my enjoyment.

"You need to get out of those slacks," she said.

I stripped and lay against her, skin to skin. The feel of her soft, silky skin against mine made my head spin. I kissed her on her mouth again, claiming it as my fingers found her hot, wet, throbbing center.

I entered her slowly, making sure not to hurt her. She arched off the bed and I plunged deeper. She felt amazing as she gripped my fingers and took me in.

Martha writhed on the bed under me and I became more aroused at her response. I tried to keep my focus on our rhythm, but it wasn't easy. My ability to concentrate was waning rapidly.

She wrapped her legs around me, and I could barely breathe. I was more excited than I'd been in a very long time. I felt her fingernails dig into my shoulders as she screamed, clamped hard on my hand, then relaxed on the bed.

Her breathing was labored so I rolled off her to let her catch her breath. I lay impatiently as I was beyond ready for her to have her way with me. My very core throbbed with unspent passion.

Often, simply pleasing a woman is enough to satisfy me, but such was not the case with Martha. I needed her. I put my hands behind my head lest I be tempted to take matters into my own hands.

Soon she was breathing normally and propped herself up on an elbow to look at me.

"You're amazing, you know that?"

"Thank you. So are you."

She blushed.

"May I ask you a personal question?"

"Sure."

"May I please you now?"

"I'd like that very much." I tried to sound calmer than I felt.

She smiled widely and looked up and down my body. She dragged her hand lazily up and down my thigh. Gooseflesh appeared where she'd touched. I was losing my mind. I could no longer think. I closed my eyes, spread my legs, and gave myself over to her.

I felt her breasts on my leg, soft and supple, and my insides clenched. Then I felt her wet center on my thigh and I almost lost it. When I felt her tongue on my clit, I clenched my fists and willed myself not to come too quickly. It was no use. My world exploded into tiny colorful pieces before coalescing into reality again.

As we lay together after, I glanced at the clock. I had forty-five minutes before I had to be in my coffin. I heard her breathing even out and knew she was asleep. Shit.

"Martha? Hey, Martha?"

"Hm?"

"Don't fall asleep. We need to get you home."

"Can't I stay here?" She pouted.

"You've got a tour in a few hours. I don't want your friends worrying about you. Now, get up and dressed and we'll drive you home. You'd better hurry."

"Oh, yeah." She bolted out of bed. "Oh, shit. I completely forgot. Thank you, Alex."

"My pleasure." I pulled on shorts and a T-shirt.

On the drive to her hotel, I handed her my phone.

"Enter your number, please," I said.

"Are you serious?"

"Dead serious."

She handed me her phone and I entered my number there.

"So maybe I will see you again?" she said.

"Text me when you're done with your tour. I won't be free until a little after eight, but maybe we can do something then?"

"I'd really like that. Like, big time."

I laughed. She was such a sweetheart. We reached her hotel, which wasn't far from my house. Thank God. I needed to hunker down. And soon.

Still, I walked her to the door of the hotel and kissed her cheek.

"I'll see you tonight," I said.

"Count on it."

I watched her enter the security of the lobby, turned around and walked as quickly as I could to the car.

"Let's get home," I said. "I'm exhausted."

The following night, I climbed out of my coffin at just past eight. I checked my phone even before I slid the trap door into place. There was a text from her.

Tour was great. Taking a nap. LOL Maybe dinner later?

Dinner? Shit. I didn't eat. I couldn't eat. But I could join her at a restaurant where I could have some drinks and enjoy her company. I texted her back.

Sorry. I just ate. But I'd love to buy you dinner. Can I pick you up in an hour?

The reply was instant.

I'll be ready.

Smiling, I took a long, luxurious, and completely unnecessary shower. Vampires don't sweat, so there's never any body odor. And even the pleasures of the early morning hours were gone as my body rebuilt itself in a manner overnight. But I liked my Axe body wash. It smelled outdoorsy. After my shower, I dressed in gray linen slacks with an emerald green shirt that I knew would bring out the green in my eyes. I was ready to go.

When we arrived at the hotel, Martha was waiting on a bench out front. She stood when we pulled up, and I marveled again at her figure as she was dressed in a body hugging short yellow dress. I got out and opened her door for her and was rewarded with a brief hot kiss. It only lasted a second, but it sent my head reeling once again.

"How was your meeting?" she said.

"Boring. But you said your tour was nice?"

"Very. Oh, Alex. I simply love this city."

My heart swelled with pride.

"I'm glad to hear that. I do hope you'll be able to return some day."

"I hope so too. But it's so expensive to get here. I doubt I'll be coming back any time soon."

"Yes. Traveling takes money. This I understand."

"Will you really keep in touch with me when I go back to the States?" said Martha.

"You have my word," I said solemnly.

"We could have a long-distance relationship."

I took her hand in mine.

"Martha, don't get me wrong. I really like you. But I'm not looking for a relationship. Especially not with someone thousands of miles away."

"So why see me anymore at all then?"

"Because I enjoy spending time with you. Why not see each other while we can?"

"I suppose you're right."

"Why the long face?" I asked.

"I don't know. I'm just not the type to do flings, I guess."

"My sweet Martha. We're not just having a fling. We're making memories. Memories no one can ever take away from us."

"Well...When you put it that way."

She smiled and leaned against me. I draped my arm over her shoulder and kissed the top of her head. She smelled of coconut and vanilla. She smelled good.

We arrived at a tourist destination, a little hole in the wall that I thought she would enjoy. And I knew I would. She could have dinner while we watched the dancers tango the night away.

She squealed when she heard the music.

"Oh wow," she said. "This is going to be amazing."

We were seated at a table in the front, and she sat mesmerized as the dancers made their seductive, precise movements. She ordered dinner while I sipped water. I hadn't fed so I didn't trust alcohol. Without blood in my system, food or drink could make me violently ill.

Since I was over six hundred years old, I didn't need to feed every night. I knew I might be cool to the touch later, but I wouldn't be morgue temperature at least. And I'd been in such a hurry to see Martha again that I hadn't gone hunting. Perhaps tomorrow.

"You're not drinking," said Martha.

"No. I want to be keen for later."

Her smile broadened, and I saw a faint color creep up her neck to her cheeks.

"I do like that idea," she said.

"Good. Now enjoy your steak and wine and the dancers."

The pulsing beat of the music had me pulsing all over. I spent more time watching Martha than I did the dancers. Her eyes shone in delight, and I was proud to have brought her such joy.

When she finished her dinner, she relaxed against me and we watched the dancers together. Their dances were so sensual, so seductive. And I wanted to take Martha out of there and have my way with her in an alley somewhere. My lust was carnal. I didn't long for the sweet lovemaking of the night before. I wanted to rip her panties off and take her. I took a deep breath and steeled myself against such thoughts.

After a bit, I felt her hand moving up my thigh. I knew she was as aroused as I was. I took her hand, leaned over, and whispered in her ear.

"Let's get out of here."

We climbed into the waiting car and snuggled on the way to my house.

"That was amazing," said Martha. "Thank you so much for taking me there."

"It was my pleasure."

She lowered her voice.

"But something about it has me thinking all sorts of inappropriate thoughts."

"Lucky for me."

Back at the house, I didn't waste time with champagne on the roof. I took her straight to my room, quickly undressed her, and made love to her. I was frantic in my need, and I'm sure it showed. I didn't take my time. I hurriedly devoured every inch of her.

I did have to pause once. When I had positioned myself between her legs, her femoral pulse pounded in my ears. My fangs unsheathed on their own and I had to wait a minute before the blood lust subsided.

"Are you okay?" she said. "Is everything all right down there?"

"Everything is wonderful," I lied. "I'm just admiring you for a moment."

When I could proceed without puncturing her, I did so. I brought her over the edge so many times, I lost count. She was a wet noodle when I final climbed up next to her.

"That was amazing," she said. "I don't think I've ever enjoyed myself that much."

"Mm. That makes me happy."

"Can we sleep now?"

I couldn't sleep. I was spent. And needed to feed. I had to get Martha out of there so I could hunt. The moment with her femoral artery had been a close call. Too close.

"Let's get you back to your hotel," I said.

"Why? Can't I spend the night with you?"

"I don't think that would be a good idea. Come on. Let's get dressed and I'll take you back to your hotel."

"Can't I at least please you first?"

"Trust me, my dear. Pleasing you was enough for me tonight."

We drove to her hotel in silence. I walked her to the door and she finally spoke.

"Tomorrow is my last day in town," she said. "May I spend it with you?"

"I'm afraid I'll be busy tomorrow, unfortunately. May I see you tomorrow night?"

She looked crestfallen. I lifted her chin with my finger.

"I'm sorry," I said. "But I planned these meetings months ago. Long before I knew I'd meet someone as enchanting as yourself. Please forgive me, but say I can spend time with you tomorrow night."

"How can I say no to you, Alex?"

"Excellent answer. Now, you sleep well and enjoy your last day in my city. I'll see you around nine tomorrow night."

"Good night, Alex."

"Good night, my dear."

I kissed her briefly, watched her enter the lobby, and got back into the car.

Chapter Three

My driver dropped me off in one of the many shantytowns in my beloved city. These were the slums where the roughest of individuals lived and hung out. I wandered through the streets unafraid as I knew I could take anyone who tried to start something with me.

The streets were dark, as most of the streetlights had long since burned out. I was looking for someone, anyone who I could feed off. I needed a meal in the worst sort of way. The need to eat every day was not something I was accustomed to. And I wasn't certain why I needed to feed that night. But I did. It might have had something to do with all the energy I'd expended with Martha. It might not. I wasn't in a state of mind to logically ponder it. I had to find someone. And fast.

As I walked, I became aware of someone following me. While there were people all around, milling every which way, this person was definitely on a mission.

"You lost, mister?" he snarled.

I knew he was speaking to me, which wasn't surprising, since I was taller than the average woman, had short hair, and carried myself with confidence.

Ignoring him, I walked on. An alley appeared on my right and I turned in. He followed. In no time, he grabbed my arm and spun me around. I saw the knife in his hand and hesitated only a brief second before I kicked it out of his hand and pulled him against me so I could drink my fill.

When I was satisfied I'd had enough, I licked his wounds and sealed them with my saliva. I walked out to the main street, found my car, and had my driver take me home. I slept hard that day. I was exhausted and needed my rest after such a filling meal. My eyes opened at precisely seven past eight, and I knew the sun had slipped below the horizon.

Humming a happy tune, I set about preparing to meet Martha. We pulled up in front of the hotel and there she was, looking ravishing in a pink sundress. I wanted to peel those spaghetti straps off and lose myself in her more than ample breasts.

"Are you ready for a big night?" I held her door for her.

"I was hoping for a quiet night."

"You were? But it's your last night in town."

"I've seen Buenos Aires. And while I love it, I'd rather just have some time with you."

"Are you serious?" I couldn't tell if she was joking.

"I'm dead serious. Let's go back to your place and sit on the roof and drink champagne. That is if you won't be too disappointed."

Her gaze bored into mine as if begging me to be okay with the concept. Truth was I was fine with it. Spending extra time with Martha sounded ideal to me. I sure would miss her when she was gone, but I'd been honest with her. I wasn't looking for a relationship. How could I be? My life would be one giant lie. And no woman deserved that.

"Sure," I said. "Let's go back to my place."

We took a bottle of champagne to the terrace and sat watching the people go by.

"I love it here," said Martha. "It's so peaceful. Like a little slice of heaven."

"I agree. I love my home."

We sat in silence for a few moments before she spoke again.

"Will you come to see me off tomorrow?"

"What time does your flight leave?"

"Nine. Please say you'll come."

I shook my head.

"How I wish I could. But I have a meeting tomorrow morning. I wish you would have mentioned it earlier. Perhaps I could have rescheduled."

"You certainly have a lot of meetings." I know she was trying to sound casual, but I didn't miss her wet eyes.

"I do. It's the price of doing business, my dear."

"And exactly what kind of business are you in again?"

"I'm in commerce. Not very exciting, but it's lucrative."

"Well, that's a good thing. I'll miss you, Alex."

"Oh, Martha. I'll miss you, too. And I promise to keep in touch. If I were looking for a relationship, you'd be the perfect woman. I promise. But I'm not. I can't right now. Please try to understand."

"I do. I mean, I don't really, but I do. I try to anyway."

I took her hand.

"Thank you for that."

The night wore on, and soon it was midnight.

"It's Christmas Eve," she said.

"Well, yes, it is. Shall we go to my room and celebrate?"

She laughed but nodded.

"That sounds wonderful."

It was our last night, and I wanted to make it as special as possible for Martha. I lit candles and put on soft music. I pulled her to me, and we danced for a bit before the feel of her in my arms was too much. I had to have her.

"May I take you to bed now?" I asked.

"Please."

I kissed her once, chastely, then walked her to the bed. Slowly and deliberately, I removed her clothes, kissing each inch of skin as I laid it bare. She was soft and silky and smelled divine. I couldn't wait to be naked with her.

With shaky fingers, she undressed me. We stood skin to skin and I thought I would self-combust. The heat between us was palpable. Gently, I laid her on the bed and climbed on top of her. We kissed for an eternity, our tongues frolicking together in their dance of lust.

I finally broke the kiss and made my way down her body, sucking and nibbling her heated flesh. I paused for a few moments to suck and lick her hard nipples, their peaks begging for attention. And I was happy to oblige.

When I finally reached the magical place where her legs met, I was aroused beyond measure. Still I stared at her beauty and inhaled deeply of the scent that was all Martha. When I could wait no longer, I lowered my head and took her in my mouth.

She was delicious. I lapped at her lips, her clit, every inch of her I could reach. She squirmed on the bed as she held my head in place. I focused on her nerve center and plunged my fingers deep, and in no time, she was screaming my name. I felt her clamp hard around me and buried myself as deep as I could while she rode out her orgasms.

Then it was my turn. Martha didn't miss a beat. As soon as I lay next to her, she moved between my legs. And when she worked her magic on me, I lost all coherent thought. I watched the light show explode behind my eyelids as I soared into oblivion and back.

We rested for a while and I heard her doze off. I was pumped, full of energy, and wanted to have her again. But I decided to let her sleep for a while. I put on a robe and went back to the terrace to sip some more champagne. I knew I should have stayed with her, should have held her while she slept, but I couldn't just lie there.

I was a night owl. And I lived in a city with an amazingly vibrant nightlife. I longed to be out among the throngs, watching people, mingling, hunting if necessary. I wasn't used to being home in the middle of the night.

Even on Christmas Eve. Especially on Christmas Eve. I loved the merriness and festivity in the air on this special night. I normally attended Midnight Mass. I was raised a Catholic and sometimes missed the pageantry and rituals of Mass. Not that I was a believer. But there was something about attending Midnight Mass that I loved.

I allowed myself to reminisce on the Christmases in my past, especially of my childhood, and was lost in thought when I felt a hand on my shoulder. I turned to see Martha standing there, bleary-eyed.

"I fell asleep and you were gone when I woke up," she said.

"I'm sorry. I was restless and didn't want to disturb you. Please, have a seat and I'll pour you some champagne."

She sat with me but didn't say another word. I wondered what she was thinking about and figured the only way to find out was to ask.

"What's got you so quiet?" I said.

She shrugged.

"I don't know. I guess I'm really dreading going home."

I took her hand.

"You shouldn't. That's where your life is. The center of your world. You should be excited about it."

"I wish you were in my world. Like, truly."

"And I'm sorry I won't be. Not physically anyway. But I'll always be your friend, Martha. You must never doubt that."

"How is it," she said, "that I finally find the perfect woman and she lives on another continent?"

"My dear, please. A pedestal is a far place to fall from. I'm far from a perfect woman. I have my flaws."

"Not that I've seen."

"Perhaps not. But you've only known me a few days."

"Still…"

I smiled at her.

"I appreciate the sentiment, Martha. I really do. And I'm quite fond of you. I suppose I'm just a tad more pragmatic than you."

"Perhaps."

I laughed at her pout.

"Please, let's enjoy our last night together instead of wondering what-if."

"Can we go back to bed then? I need you again."

I was more than happy to comply. I guided her down the stairs, peeled off her robe, and laid her on the bed. There I pleased her for hours until she pleaded exhaustion. I was satisfied from the act of making love to her, so I curled up next to her and cast a glance at the clock.

It was four thirty. I had about forty-five minutes before the sun rose. I hated to prod her but knew I must.

"Don't fall asleep, babe. We need to get dressed and I need to get you back to your hotel so you can get a few hours of sleep anyway."

"I don't want to go."

"I know. But you must. Come on now."

Our clothes were strewn all over the floor. I quickly dressed, then handed hers to her.

"Let's just pull an all-nighter. I can sleep on the plane."

"Ah yes. But I can't sleep in my meeting. Please, babe. Get dressed and let me take you home."

The tears she'd obviously been fighting cascaded down her cheeks. If I'd have had a heart, I do believe it would have broken a little.

"Fine," she said.

"Please understand. I want to have a few minutes with you at the hotel to tell you good-bye. So we should get going."

She dressed in silence then moved into my arms. I held her longer than was wise. I needed to get her to her hotel so I could get in my coffin before it was too late.

We arrived at her place and I got out and sat with her on the bench. I took her hand in mine and interlaced our fingers.

"Thank you for the past few nights," I said. "It's been truly magical."

"It really has. Thank you."

"You have a safe flight home. And take care of yourself once you're there."

"I will. Will you write me?"

"Text me your email address," I said. "I promise to keep in touch."

"I'm going to miss you, Alex."

"And I, you."

"Come up to my room with me?" she said.

"I can't do that."

"Can't? Or won't?"

"We both need our sleep. Please, don't tempt me."

"But I like tempting you."

"And you do it so well." I winked. "Now, come. Let me walk you to your door and we'll say good-bye for now."

"For now?"

"Who knows what fate has in store for us? Perhaps our paths will cross again sometime."

"Do you mean that? Would you come to Georgia to see me? Oh, please say you will."

I laughed.

"I don't know. But I certainly won't rule it out."

We walked to the front door where I took her in my arms and held her. The sky was lightening, and I could feel the first pricks of heat on my skin. I had to make this quick. I stepped back and tilted her face up to mine. I kissed her, softly at first, but then with passion. We were both breathless when the kiss ended, and she collapsed against me.

"Wow," said Martha. "Just wow."

"Just a little something to remember me by."

"I'll never forget you, Alex. I know I've said it before, but I want you to know I mean it."

"I believe you, my dear. Now, get inside before I change my mind and join you."

"I think I'll drag this out then."

I laughed.

"No, you won't. You'll go up to your room, sleep, and head home in a few hours. I'll be with you in spirit though, Martha. I'll always be with you in spirit."

"I guess this is really good-bye then?"

"It's farewell. Good-bye sounds so final."

She laughed.

"I like the way you think, Alex. Of course, there's not much about you I don't like."

"Please take care of yourself, Martha. I really must go now."

I could feel blisters forming on my arms and wanted to get away from her lest she notice. I kissed her one more time, patted her ass, and watched her enter the lobby. I got in the car and instructed my driver to hurry home.

"Would you like to go somewhere to view the sunrise?" she asked, but I knew she was joking.

"No, thank you. I'd like to get home."

The sun had crested the horizon as I got out of the car and let myself in my house. Even indoors, the heat was unbearable. And crippling. I staggered through the house, holding myself up with the walls. I was terrified that I might not make it. I had three minutes and I was moving slowly.

Why the hell did I have such a large house? Climbing the stairs was treacherous. Each step sent pain radiating through my body. I was in agony as I locked my study door behind me, and I was so weak it took several tries to open the trap door.

But I got it open and closed again. Then, with a minute left, I fumbled with my coffin lid. I finally got it open, fell inside, closed the lid, and let blessed sleep overtake me.

CHAPTER FOUR

Christmas Eve night. I'd been confused the night before thinking I'd missed Midnight Mass. I hadn't. I'd go that night. But first, I'd help decorate the large tree in the main hall. My servants were already hard at work on it as I walked in.

"This looks fantastic," I said. "But where are the tunes?"

I put a Christmas station on on my phone and we sang along as we placed ornaments and tinsel on the tree. It was a sight to behold, and I was just thinking something was missing when my maid handed me the star for the top. I climbed the ladder and put it in place. We turned on the lights and stood in awe at its glory.

"I think this is the most beautiful tree I've ever seen," I said.

My helpers beamed in appreciation. I really cared about my staff. They were good to me, didn't ask too many questions, and Lord, could they pick out Christmas trees.

As I looked around at them, I realized they were aging. I had been in Buenos Aires ten years, and it was time to realize that someone would soon begin to notice I hadn't aged. It was about time to think about moving on. The thought depressed me, but it was my reality.

Needing to cheer up and shake my dismal reality, I asked my driver to take me to the colorful neighborhood of La Boca. It was an old neighborhood that still had its Italian flair. The multicolored buildings were just what I needed to soothe my psyche and lift my spirits.

I wandered the main street, watching the people milling around. I made my way to a tourist shop and watched the shoppers ooh and ah over the selection of souvenirs. I smiled to myself. The pulse of the city beat within me. I was in heaven.

Making my way out of the main neighborhood, I ended up in a rougher location. Fewer people were there, and it was oddly quiet for that time of night. I chalked it up to Christmas Eve and was about to head back to the main drag when I heard yelling and grunting.

I followed the sounds and came upon two men in a knife fight. One appeared to be badly injured as he lay on the ground with blood oozing from his stomach. The sight of the blood made me dizzy. I hadn't fed in the past couple of days, and shouldn't have needed to that night. But the blood sent me into a frenzy.

With lightning speed, I picked up the standing man and drained him. Then I buried my face in the stomach of the man on the ground and drank some more. I was so close to killing him. I wanted to get every last drop out of him, but that wasn't fair. When I left, he was still alive. I called 911 to report the fight. I was told to remain on the scene until help arrived, but I couldn't. I needed to get away lest I be tempted to drain the poor surviving man.

Arriving back at El Caminito, I found a restaurant with outside seating. I sipped my Fernet and Coke and watched the passersby. Once again, I marveled at the mix of people on the little cobblestone walkway. There were myriad shapes and sizes, and I recognized at least five different languages.

A lovely woman who spoke Spanish approached me and asked me if the other seat at my table was taken. My libido kicked into gear, I smiled my best smile and told her it was not. She smiled back, took the chair, and moved it to another table where she sat with a group. So much for that prospect.

That was okay though. I didn't need a bedmate for the night. I had plans. I ordered another drink and smiled at the people walking by. Most smiled back, while some looked away. I had to laugh. What was so hard about smiling at a stranger? I shook my head. People were strange.

Soon it was time to have my driver take me to the Plaza de Mayo so I could attend Midnight Mass at the Metropolitan Cathedral. I stood in the plaza looking at the neoclassical style of the building. I admired the columns on display and wondered at the simplicity of the outside of the cathedral compared to the rich beauty I knew waited for me inside.

I crossed the plaza and joined the hundreds of others making their way into the cathedral for Mass. I braced myself for the overwhelming beauty of a church that was only a century younger than me.

The high ceilings and marble columns took my breath way, but it was in the stained-glass windows and frescoes on the walls that the beauty truly lay. The altar, done in Rococo style, featured not only the Holy Trinity, but also the Virgin Mary. She was my favorite. Always had been. My mother's name had been Maria so our family had worshiped her for as long as I could remember.

Mass was said in Spanish, so it was easy for me to understand. I spoke seven languages fluently and used Spanish most often. When it was time for communion, I joined the others in the queue to the altar, careful to keep my gaze away from the giant crucifix. I would decline the wafer but sip the wine. I wasn't a believer. I just liked the pageantry and tradition and wanted to be as much a part of it as I could.

Services ended and I felt empty as I wandered back out into the night. I was antsy, looking for something to do. I milled about the plaza engaging in people watching, one of my favorite pastimes, but soon grew restless. I had my driver take me back to La Boca where I sat at another outside table, sipping my drink, and enjoying the flow of foot traffic.

An attractive woman who looked to be in her mid-forties approached me. She spoke in German, which I understood.

"You shouldn't be sitting here all alone," she said. "It's a beautiful night, a magical night. It saddens me to see you by yourself."

I smiled at her and stood.

"I don't mind being by myself. Besides, I'm not truly alone. Look at all the people I'm surrounded by."

She laughed, a deep, soulful sound that warmed me to my core.

"You make a good point. But still…"

"Then will you please join me so I will no longer be alone? I'd be honored if you'd allow me to buy you a drink."

"That would be lovely."

She sat down and I took her order, then went inside to buy her drink. When I came back, I decided I needed to get to know this German beauty with the bobbed blond hair and pale blue eyes.

"I'm Alex." I extended my hand.

"Zelda. Nice to meet you." She took my hand in hers, and the feel of her soft skin made me warm all over.

"Where are you from, Zelda?"

"Bavaria. And you?"

"I'm originally from Romania."

"And now? Where do you call home?"

"Right here in Buenos Aires."

"Ah," said Zelda. "Lucky you. This city is beautiful."

"That it is. It's especially so tonight on Christmas Eve."

"Very true. I love how everything is decorated. I love the lights everywhere."

"I agree. There's magic in the air to be sure."

She arched an eyebrow at me, and if I had the ability to blush, I most certainly would have.

"And just how magical might this night be?" she said.

"You tell me."

She laughed again.

"Oh, no. Don't you put this on me. I want to know what your intentions are."

"My intentions?" It was my turn to laugh. "I would like to get to know you better. Is that an acceptable answer?"

"Is that all you want? Are you sure?"

"At this point in time. On this night, yes. Perhaps tomorrow you'll allow me to take you to dinner?"

"Dinner?"

"I'm sorry. Am I being to forward? I tend to be upfront. Shoot from the hip, as Americans say."

"Dinner would be lovely."

"Excellent. Tell me, Zelda, what brings you to my beautiful city on Christmas Eve?"

"We're on a cruise."

We? My chest tightened. Who was the other person she was with?

"We?" I held my breath and awaited her answer.

"My sister and mother. We're cruising around South America. Buenos Aires is our first stop, and I have to say, it has not disappointed."

I immediately relaxed.

"I'm so happy to hear that."

"Have you been to Florida Street?" I said.

"We were there this morning. We'll go back tomorrow. Mother loves to shop and plans on spending a small fortune there. I have to say, La Boca is more my style."

"Why's that?"

She shrugged.

"I don't know. The architecture. The people. It just feels real to me, more so than a tourist trap."

I laughed.

"You are a wise woman, Zelda."

"Thank you." She stood. "And now, Alex, I must bid you auf wiedersehen. I'm afraid if I don't get my beauty sleep, I'll turn into a pumpkin."

She made me laugh. That was a good thing.

"But dinner tomorrow?" I said. "Where shall we meet? Is eight thirty a good time for you?"

"That would be lovely. Why don't we meet here, then you can take me to your favorite restaurant? One perhaps that the tourists don't know of?"

"That would be perfect. I'll see who's open on Christmas and we'll go there. Have a good night, Zelda. I'll see you tomorrow night."

I watched her until I lost her in the crowd. When she was out of sight, I had another drink, my body humming with anticipation. I checked my watch when I finished, and it was four thirty-seven. Time to get home. I walked back to where I'd been dropped off and found my driver snoozing. I got in and asked to be taken home.

With time to spare that night, I locked my study door behind me and pulled up restaurants which would be open the following night. There were more than I'd anticipated, and that made me happy. Now to decide where to take Zelda.

I figured since she liked La Boca, she might like Italian. But then, a traditional Argentinian meal might be more fun. I chose La

Barrica Restaurant & Bistrot, one of my favorite places for steak and it had outdoor seating. A win-win.

I stripped down to my boxers and undershirt and climbed into my coffin, full of hope for the following night. The sun must have set at just past eight because that's when my eyes opened, and I climbed out. I stretched, pulled on a robe, and made my way to my bedroom to choose an outfit for the night.

Dressed and ready to go, I headed downstairs. There, by the front door, was a pile of presents. Damn. How could I have forgotten? I needed to deliver presents to the orphanage. Shit. Okay, okay. Zelda would just have to accompany me. We'd have a later dinner. I hoped she wouldn't mind.

She was waiting for me when I strolled up at eight thirty.

"I hope I'm not late," I said.

"Nonsense. You're right on time."

"Please forgive me," I began.

"Are you canceling on me?"

"No! No, no, no. But I forgot it's Christmas today. I have presents to deliver to the orphanage. I was wondering if you'd accompany me and then we'll have dinner a little later?"

Her eyes grew wide.

"You deliver presents to children? Why, Alex, I do believe I'm going to enjoy this night ever so much."

The presents dropped off, I had my driver take us to the restaurant. I took Zelda's hand as we entered.

"This place smells fantastic," she said.

"It's a wonderful restaurant. Come, I reserved us a table outside."

But I needn't have reserved anything. The place was almost empty. We sat, drank wine, and chatted while she waited for her dinner.

"I can't believe you're not eating," said Zelda. "I'm going to feel like a pig eating by myself."

"My dear, you are not by yourself. I'm with you. I'm just full from my own Christmas dinner at home. I ate early enough that I thought I'd have room for dinner. Alas, I have not."

"If you say so." She eyed me suspiciously.

"What? I'll be nothing but honest with you, Zelda. Please believe me." Well, that was a lie in and of itself. Oh, well.

"Fair enough. I'll trust you."

We made pleasant conversation as she ate her dinner and I sipped my wine.

"Tell me," I said. "How long are you in town for?"

"We leave tomorrow."

"That's a shame." I found that I meant it. Zelda intrigued me.

"Ah, yes, but we have tonight."

"That we do. What about the boat? Don't you have to be back by a certain time?"

"Not tonight. We just have to be there in plenty of time before it leaves."

"Well, that's a relief."

She beamed at me and I figured we were on the same page. I wanted to spend some intimate time with Zelda. Some very intimate time. I was starting to truly believe that's what she wanted, too.

After dinner, we strolled down the street hand in hand.

"What do you do, Alex? I mean, you must be fairly well off if you have your own driver."

"I'm in commerce. And I do okay."

"I'd say so. What about at home? Any staff there?"

I threw my head back and laughed.

"Yes. I admit I'm spoiled."

"Good for you. Someone's got to live the good life. It might as well be you."

"Well, thank you."

We stopped at a brightly decorated storefront to admire it. She looked up, tugged my hand, and pointed. Glancing up, I saw that we were standing under mistletoe. I looked into her eyes and saw a pleading. Far be it from me to deny a beautiful woman. I lowered my head and brushed her lips with mine. She shivered.

"Oh, my," she said. "That was nice."

"Yes, it was."

"May I see your house, Alex? Or am I being too bold?"

"I'd love to show you my house. Come on." I tugged on her hand and we walked back to the car. We drove home in silence, with Zelda craning her neck to look at everything we passed en route. I loved watching her. She was childlike in her fascination. While my thoughts were very adult indeed.

We drank champagne and she wandered the garden on my terrace, asking me about different plants. I finally got her seated at the little table and draped my arm around her. She leaned into me.

"This is nice," she said. "I love it here."

"As do I. It's my little paradise."

"Why do I feel this isn't the only paradise you'll show me tonight?"

I grinned at her.

"You've read my mind," I said.

CHAPTER FIVE

We finished the bottle and I escorted her down to my room. I watched as she admired it then pulled her into my arms. It was time to kiss her properly. I needed to taste her mouth, her neck, all of her. But I'd start with a kiss.

She kissed me back with a fervor that made my toes curl. She was a passionate woman and I was in for a treat. Merry Christmas to me.

I walked her back until she fell onto the bed. I disrobed her in record time, undressed, and climbed up with her.

"What kind of lover are you, Alex?" she said.

"You're about to find out."

"But I want to know what to expect. Are you a fast and furious lover? Or more slow and deliberate?"

"I like to be slow, but I'm so excited to have you that I might just be fast and furious."

"I understand," she said. "I'd like you to take me quickly. I hate, despise, abhor being teased."

"Duly noted. I'll do my best."

Keeping Zelda's wishes in the forefront of my mind, I kissed down her neck and chest and took one of her large nipples in my mouth. While I played over it with my tongue, I entered her with my fingers. I plunged two, three, then four fingers inside her. She arched off the bed and met every thrust.

I was kissing down her belly when I felt her quivering and knew she was close.

"My nipples. Play with them again," she breathed.

My pleasure. I kissed back up and suckled her again and she cried out my name. Before I could think of what to do next, she screamed again. Then again. Oh yeah, I knew she'd be fun.

"That's enough," she said. "That was amazing. Thank you."

"My pleasure."

"I'm hoping to show you what pleasure truly is."

"Be my guest."

I lay back, spread my legs, and hoped for a quick release. I was a wet, throbbing mess. She didn't disappoint. With no pretense, she climbed between my legs and I felt her talented tongue doing laps on me. She had me squirming on the bed, arching my hips, and pressing her face into me.

My stomach clenched. Every muscle in my body was taut, waiting for the inevitable. And it finally came. I finally came. White heat shot through my body, radiating out to my arms and legs and then to my fingers and toes. It was a powerful climax that left me struggling to catch my breath.

"That was fun," said Zelda.

"Yeah, it was."

"Thank you."

"Thank *you*."

"I hate to do this," she said. "But do you think you could get me back to the ship? Much as I'd love to sleep here with you and have a repeat in the morning, I can't miss the boat."

Relief flooded over me. There would be no awkwardness, no uncomfortable discussion about her leaving. She was ready.

"Certainly." I picked up her clothes and handed them to her before getting dressed. "I can do that for sure."

We sipped champagne on the way to the harbor.

"Thank you so much for making my stay in Buenos Aires even more enjoyable," she said.

"You're quite welcome. It really was a pleasure."

"That it was."

The harbor was not a safe place at that hour of the morning, so I walked Zelda to the gangway. I made sure she was safely inside before crossing back to the car.

Safely inside, I lowered the glass between me and my driver.

"Where to now, ma'am?" she said.

"Home, please. I have work to do."

"I'm surprised you have the energy." She winked at me in the rearview mirror.

"Energy is one thing I'm definitely not lacking."

In my study, I began the unpleasant task of deciding where to move. I thought I'd love to stay in South America, even Argentina. But there really was no point. Maybe Rio would be nice. I'd been on several occasions and had always enjoyed myself. But it wasn't calling to me. No place was really. I needed to make a decision.

Searching website after website, I looked for someplace, anyplace where I could feel at home. It needed to be a place with a bustling night life. Also, I preferred a place with a high crime rate where I could hunt and feed without suspicion.

I decided to check in the United States. I had no desire to go there. It had never called to me, but I decided to simply look. Los Angeles or New York were obvious choices, but New York got too cold and Los Angeles seemed too boring. I might have been wrong, but it was how I felt. I continued my search.

By the time I climbed into my coffin that morning, I had decided to move to the States. I had narrowed my choices down to Las Vegas and New Orleans. I'd make my decision when the sun went down.

The sun set and I rose no closer to a resolution. I gathered my staff together that night and told them my job was transferring me and I wasn't sure where. I explained that I wished I could take each and every one of them with me but that wasn't possible. I asked for their assistance in helping me get packed and assured them I'd pay them another month's salary but would not need their services after the first of the new year.

I listed my house as furnished, as I only planned to travel with my clothes, coffin, and a few necessities and treasures. I would buy a house furnished wherever I landed. I was still torn, so did some more research. The more I looked, the less decided I was. I had my maid blindfold me, spin me around, and let me throw a dart at the map of the US. My dart landed closer to Las Vegas, so it was there I decided to go.

It was with a heavy heart that I said good-bye to my staff. I kept my driver, who had discovered my secret years ago. She would fly first class while accompanying me in a coffin in storage. She would explain I had passed away and she was taking me home to Las Vegas. It would have to work. There was no other way for me to get there.

Las Vegas was cold when I finally got out of my coffin in my rented house. My driver, Shantay, had the heater on and a fire going.

"What is this fresh hell?" I asked. "Oh yeah. I forgot, deserts get cold, don't they? I don't know how long I'll last here."

"You mean you actually feel the cold?"

"Not like you do. But I still don't like it."

"You don't look good, Alex," said Shantay. "Do you need to feed?"

I nodded solemnly.

"I suppose I do. Where does one find people here?"

"That's easy. The Strip or Fremont Street. The Strip will probably have more people on it, to be honest."

"Let's go then."

She dropped me off in front of the Venetian. The bright lights called to me, tantalized me, but first things first. I needed to find a meal. I wondered if I could find someone inside the beautiful hotel with its Italian flair. No, I needed to walk the streets to find an easy target. Someone who wouldn't be missed.

There were people everywhere. I was jostled to and fro as I tried to make my way along the Strip. I noticed people handing out cards right and left and took one out of curiosity. It had a scantily clad woman on it and was advertising a show at another hotel.

I pocketed the card. Who knew? Maybe I'd be interested in some entertainment a little later.

"Watch where you're going!" Someone bumped me with their shoulder. Instinctively, I checked for my wallet. It was gone.

I spun around and went after the bastard. I found him, grabbed his arm, and pulled him down a side street. But there were people there, too.

"Let me go," he screamed.

I ignored him. It was time for dinner, and he would be perfect. My anger flared at him for trying to rob me, my hunger had me barely able to concentrate. We happened upon a gas station and I took him behind it and feasted. The blood pumped through my veins, and I felt like a new woman. I sealed his wounds, took my wallet, and strutted back to the Strip.

The sounds of all the people talking and the sight of all the bright lights were much easier to bear since I'd fed. It was no longer a cacophony, but a rather pleasant experience. As with Buenos Aires, several different languages floated on the air. Most I could understand. Some I could not. I found my way back to the Venetian and went inside. The whirring and clanging of machines made me smile. I hadn't gambled in far too long and perhaps it was time to place a bet or two.

I found the card tables and settled in for a night of winning. And I did win. I won big. It was a nice experience. I chatted amicably with the other players and the dealer. There was a very attractive older woman at the table, and I was just about to sit next to her when a very butch looking older woman walked up and rested her hands on the first woman's shoulders. Ah. So she was taken. It didn't dampen my mood.

After several weeks in Vegas, I was feeling restless. It was a nice place with lots to do. I tended to cruise the Strip in search of a meal then wander Fremont Street to people watch and gamble.

It wasn't a bad life, really. And no one expected me to be up before sundown which was a nice change. But something didn't feel right. Try as I might, I couldn't make myself feel like I was home. I decided to see what Shantay had to say.

"What do you think of Las Vegas?" We were on our way home early one morning.

She shrugged.

"It's okay."

"Just okay?"

"I'm not a big gambler," she said. "So after I drop you off for the night, there's really not much for me to do here." I nodded, which of course she couldn't see. "What about you, Ms. Bogdan? Are you enjoying your new home?"

"Hm. That's just it. It doesn't really feel like home."

"Shouldn't you give it time?"

"I'm not sure time will help. I don't think this is where I'm meant to be."

She glanced at me in the rearview mirror as if she'd see my reflection.

"Perhaps you need to find a woman to spend some time with."

I exhaled loudly.

"I don't even think that would help. I really feel like it's time to move on. Time to try our luck somewhere else."

"You're the boss." It was one of her favorite expressions. It was true, but I often treated her more as a friend than an employee.

"I suppose I am."

I was tired, the sun would be up any minute, and I was cranky. I'd wake up that night and make some decisions. I hated moving though I'd done it so often over the centuries. It was necessary. I couldn't get close to people and that meant I couldn't stay in one place for too long. Buenos Aires was the longest I'd ever stayed in one city. And I missed that city. So very much.

So there I was in Las Vegas which was teeming with people all night long. There was no shortage of delinquents on whom to feed. There were women, all kinds of women, everywhere. So why didn't it feel like home to me?

The thoughts crashed through my mind, colliding and bouncing off each other until I closed my eyes and gave myself over to the sleep of the dead. The thoughts were back when sundown arrived, and I opened my eyes to face another night. Another boring night.

I went downstairs and found Shantay playing cards with the rest of my staff, most of whom should have gone home to their families by then. Shantay stood when I walked in.

"You need to go somewhere, Boss?"

I sat heavily in an empty chair.

"No. I don't want to go anywhere. Not here anyway. I think I'd like to talk to you in my office if you don't mind?"

"I don't mind at all." She threw her cards on the table. "Let's do this."

Shantay and I had a wonderful relationship. We could talk about anything and everything. At first, when she put two and two together and confronted me about being a vampire, I denied it. But she wouldn't let it go, and I finally told her the truth and made her promise not to tell anyone under penalty of death.

She was filled with questions and we spent many hours at my casa in Buenos Aires going over my history, where I'd lived, what I'd done, whom I'd met. She was fascinated by the whole concept. I'd half expected her to ask me to turn her during those early talks. But she hadn't. And now I needed to talk to her again.

"What's up, Boss?" she said as I closed the door behind us.

"I'm bored."

"So let me take you out to find a woman."

"It goes deeper than that," I said.

"What do you mean?"

"You're going to kill me. Or you would if I wasn't already dead."

"You're scaring me, Ms. Bogdan."

I forced a smile, though my heart wasn't in it.

"No need to be scared. And don't you think it's time you call me Alex?"

"I'm not sure that would be right."

"I think it would and I'm the boss." I laughed.

She laughed with me.

"Okay, Alex. What's up?"

"I'm afraid it's time to move again."

"Again? We just got here."

"We've been here a month. I'm not happy, Shantay. I don't think I'll be happy here."

"Maybe you just miss Buenos Aires," she said.

"I do. God, how I miss it. But this is more than that. I don't want to spend another night here. I really want to get away. Will you make the necessary arrangements?"

She looked like she might argue. Then her face smoothed out.

"If that's what's necessary, that's what I'll do."

"Thank you."

She walked to the office door, but before she opened it, she looked at me.

"I'm curious. What's next on our journey around the world? Paris? Venice?"

"Oh, how I'd love to revisit those places. I miss them. This is true. But I've already lived there. I'm looking for something new."

"Fair enough. Will you tell me where it is so I can make the necessary arrangements?"

"Of course. We're going to New Orleans."

CHAPTER SIX

My eyes opened and I checked my watch. It was just past five thirty. Why was I awake so early? Fear gripped me. I shouldn't be awake when the sun was up. It would be deadly for me. I closed my eyes and tried to go back to sleep but it was fruitless. Sleep would not come back.

I eased my coffin open, preparing myself for the burning heat that was sure to come. But it did not. Instead, I was in a dark room that I didn't recognize. It took me a moment to realize that I wasn't in Las Vegas anymore.

The room was not furnished. It was small with the curtains closed. It was very dark, and I inhaled, but didn't smell the dank, musty smell of earth that I was used to smelling upon awakening. Which meant I wasn't in a basement or crawl space. What the hell was Shantay thinking putting me in a regular room? Did she not understand the danger?

Then it all came back to me. I was in New Orleans. There were no basements in the city. Hell, even the cemeteries were above ground. Resolved not to chastise Shantay, I wandered around the tiny space. I came across a small table along one wall. There I found a set of keys. Perfect.

I unlocked the door and stepped into a long hallway. My room was at the far end. I locked my door behind me and followed the hall until I came to a gorgeous spiral staircase. When I reached the bottom, I found Shantay and several others seated around a small table in what appeared to be an entryway. Shantay stood when she saw me.

"Boss," she said. "You're up. How are you?"

"I'm fine. Though I'm hungry."

A woman with smooth dark skin stood.

"I'm not a cook, but I'll be happy to make you something to eat if you wish."

"Thank you, no." I smiled. "I'd like to explore my new city and taste its offerings. I do appreciate the offer, though."

"Let's get you out and acclimated," Shantay said. "I'll get the car and meet you out front."

I looked cautiously through the windows in the front door, still unconvinced it was safe to be awake. But only the moon shone through. There was no sun. I wondered when the sun would rise but knew Shantay would let me know. Not that I needed a schedule. My skin, my whole body would let me know when the sun was about to rise.

Stepping outside, I was in awe of the wraparound porch. It appeared to encircle the whole of the house. It was beautiful with intricate wrought iron. I noticed a swing in front of large windows that I surmised led to the living room. There were several small wicker tables with matching chairs spread out across the porch.

There were five small steps leading to the driveway where Shantay waited for me.

"This place is beautiful." I slid into the back seat. "Absolutely gorgeous."

"We're renting now with the option to buy. Let's see how you like New Orleans."

But I already loved it more than Las Vegas. The temperatures felt to be in the sixties, so chilly, but not cold. And the scent of the night blooming jasmine on the air comforted me. Not to mention the gorgeous house. Yes, I was sure I'd like New Orleans.

"What section of the city are we in?" I asked.

"The Garden District. I'll take you to the French Quarter where you'll find gobs of people."

"Thank you, Shantay."

"Is there any place in particular you'd like me to drop you off?"

"That's a really good question. I suppose Bourbon Street will be my destination. However, I've always wanted to see Jackson Square. Why don't you drop me off there? I can walk the French Quarter from the Square. I'll text you when I need you again. Will you be enjoying the sights and sounds as well?"

"I believe I will. I've never been to New Orleans. I'd like to check it out."

"Sounds good. Be safe, Shantay. Text me if you need me."

"Yes, ma'am."

Jackson Square did not disappoint. It was teeming with life. People in all shapes and sizes, social statuses, and colors wandered around the square. I joined them and was completely enthralled at all the art on display there.

The need to feed was growing, however, and I knew I'd have to find a victim soon. I wondered where I'd find someone. The Saint Louis Cathedral called to me. I couldn't resist the call of a beautiful Catholic church.

Tamping down my hunger, I entered the holy building. The scent of burning candles was the first thing I noticed. A sound like jingling coins was next. I looked to my left and there was an older gentleman trying to break open the box where people placed their money to light a candle. Who would rob from a church?

Anger washed over me, and without thinking, I flung the man to the ground. He looked at me, terror showing in his eyes. Anger quickly replaced fear and he rose. He came at me and tried to push me into the rows of lit candles. I held my own. Foolish mortal.

I looked around and saw no one else in the cathedral. I dragged the would-be thief to the confessionals and drained him. Down to the last drop. His thieving days were over.

Satiated and ready to check out the famed French Quarter, I exited and wandered down Chartres in search of Bourbon Street. I heard music to the north, so turned on St. Louis Street. Two blocks later, I was surrounded by people, bars, and music. I had found Bourbon Street.

I wandered up and down the street, checking out the shops and bars without paying much attention to the people. I wanted to acclimate to my new city. A voodoo shop caught my attention and I strolled inside.

There was an amazing array of goods in the store. I noticed many candles, along with bags of gris-gris, voodoo dolls, and even some pralines for sale. I bought nothing but looked at everything. I lost track of time and was looking at various charms when I heard a most delightfully accented voice in my ear.

"Are you looking for anything in particular?"

I turned to see a beautiful woman with short blond hair and more piercings than I could count.

"No." I laughed. "I've just always been intrigued with voodoo. So, I'm just kind of taking everything in."

"Well, my name's Patricia and I'm here to help you. May I ask what it is about these charms you find so fascinating?"

I chose a charm I found particularly amusing and showed it to Patricia.

"Do these work?"

"What do you think?" said Patricia.

"I don't know. It says they ward off vampires, yet I thought there was no such thing."

"Then they must work. They're warding them off, yes?"

I laughed. I was holding one in my hand and it had no effect on me.

"I suppose you're right." I set the charm down. "Thank you for your time, Patricia. I'm sure I'll be back."

"Ah yes," she said. "The music and alcohol calls to you, does it? You must heed the call. I understand."

"I'm not a big drinker. Though I confess, the urge is there to sit and listen to jazz. Real jazz."

"New Orleans Jazz. There's nothing like it."

"When are you off, Patricia? Would you like to listen to music with me?"

"I'd love that… I'm sorry. I didn't catch your name."

"Alex."

"I'm not off until ten. So that's a couple of hours yet."

"I'll be back," I said. "Shall we call it a date?"

She beamed at me.

"We shall."

I kissed her hand and left the store. I made my way farther down Bourbon Street until the crowds thinned and the bars were darker. I turned and walked in the other direction and was soon back in the middle of it all.

Crowds ebbed and flowed around me, people jostled me, but left me alone. I wandered in and out of bars, listening to a few strands here, a few more there. It wasn't until I was about halfway up the street that the sound of laughter and music drew me into a rundown establishment.

The bar could have been there since the city was founded, but it was welcoming. It was comfortable and cozy, not large, but there was enough space that you weren't right on top of another patron.

I sat at the bar and ordered a hurricane. Drink in hand, I turned to survey the dance floor. There were several couples on the floor. Mostly men and women, but the occasional two-woman couple was out there as well.

Good. I'd be able to dance with Patricia without asking for trouble. I studied the dancers, determined to learn how to dance to jazz. I'd spent most of my centuries on foreign soil where jazz wasn't anywhere near as popular.

I had three drinks, felt comfortable enough to dance, and checked my watch. I had ten minutes until Patricia was off work. I walked back to her store.

"You're early." Her face lit up when she saw me.

"Better than being late. I'll wait outside for you to close up shop."

"I'll be right out."

True to her word, Patricia met me out front a few short minutes later.

"Where to?" She laced her fingers through mine.

"Come on. I found a place I love."

We talked about nothing as we walked toward my newfound bar. When we arrived, she laughed.

"This is like my favorite place."

"Excellent. Let's have a drink, listen to music, and dance the night away."

She got us a table as I ordered our drinks. When I joined her, she asked a logical question.

"So, where are you from, Alex? I don't recognize your accent. And I like to think I'm pretty good with accents."

"Originally I'm from Romania, but I've most recently lived in Buenos Aires."

"And now?"

"Pardon me?"

"Where do you live now?"

"Oh. I've only just moved to your city."

"Is that right? Does that mean I'll be seeing more of you?"

"If you'd like," I said.

"Oh, I'd like." She winked at me.

We chatted for a while, danced for hours, and finally, it was time for me to say good night.

"I've had a marvelous time tonight," said Patricia. "Thank you."

"Shall we do it again tomorrow night?"

"I'd love that."

"Great. I'm afraid, I must get going for real now. Is there somewhere I can walk you?"

"I live above the shop, so I'll be fine. Thank you though. I do appreciate the offer."

"Good night then, Patricia. I'll be at your shop at ten if not before."

"I'm looking forward to it."

I kissed her cheek and watched her walk off until I lost her in the crowds. I texted Shantay that I was ready to head home, then walked back to Jackson Square.

Shantay was waiting for me the next night when I awoke.

"Where to today? Back to Bourbon Street?"

"I would love to go back to Bourbon Street," I said. "But I think I should like to walk tonight."

Something passed in Shantay's eyes, but I couldn't quite catch it. Disappointment perhaps?

"I'll give you the night off. Unless I stay out too late and require a ride home. Please, take the night and enjoy yourself."

"Yes, ma'am."

I walked up Phillip Street, where my house was located, across Prytania, to St. Charles Avenue. I followed St. Charles to Canal Street, then turned east onto Bourbon. The walk was pleasant, and I admired the large, plantation style houses on my route. The walk took less than an hour and my body hummed as I approached Bourbon Street proper.

Patricia was in front of her shop as I passed, so I stopped to chat with her.

"Business slow tonight?" I asked.

"The night is young." She smiled. "How are you this evening?"

"I'm wonderful. I've just had the loveliest walk."

"Really? Where did you go?"

"I walked here from my house on Phillip Street. It was glorious. I love the architecture of New Orleans."

"It's quite a hodgepodge isn't it?"

"It really is." I'd never heard the word, but determining its meaning wasn't difficult. "And you? How's your evening going?"

"It just got tons better."

"Thank you. I'm glad you think so."

"May I be bold for a moment?"

"Certainly," I said. "What's on your mind?"

"Can we forego the bar tonight? Could we maybe just have some wine at my place and listen to music?"

"That would be delightful. I'd enjoy that very much."

A customer entered her store.

"Great," she said. "See you in a few hours."

"Yes. Yes, you shall."

I leisurely meandered up Bourbon until I came to the bar I'd discovered the night before. The place was fairly empty at that early hour. I took my seat at the bar and ordered my hurricane.

"You really put those away last night." The bartender laughed at me. "And what would have knocked grown men on their asses didn't seem to affect you."

"I have a high tolerance."

"Apparently so. Well, here's your drink. Enjoy."

I checked out the other patrons and saw nothing to catch my interest until I saw a table in a far, dimly lit corner. I'd know that person anywhere. I took my drink and crossed to the table.

"Is this seat taken?" I said.

Shantay looked up and smiled at me.

"Please, ma'am. Have a seat."

"Alex," I said. "Please call me Alex."

"Yes, ma'am."

We both laughed.

"What are you doing by yourself? There are tons of people milling about. You'd make friends very easily."

"I just wanted to be alone. I have a lot on my mind."

"Like what?"

"I don't know. Just stuff."

"Well, if you need a sounding board, I'm always here for you."

"I appreciate that. Do you think you'll need me here, Alex?"

"Of course. I need you no matter where I am."

"But, like tonight for instance, you walked rather than let me drive you."

"That was a one-off. I need to get the lay of the land. Well, maybe not a complete one-off. I may walk occasionally. But I need you to drive me home. Especially, God forbid, if I stay out too late."

"Thanks. I feel better. I just don't want to lose my position with you."

"You? Lose your position with me? That'll never happen, my friend."

"Phew. I can breathe easier."

"What are you drinking?" I said.

"Rum and Coke."

"May I buy you another one?"

"That would be awesome," said Shantay.

"Great. You stay put. One more rum and Coke coming up."

CHAPTER SEVEN

We finished our drinks and I offered to buy her another one. "That depends," said Shantay. "Will you need me later?"

"I will indeed. I'll need you to pick me up and drive me home."

"Then I'd better switch to tea."

I smiled at her.

"That's very responsible of you."

"I try."

As much as I was enjoying my time with Shantay, it was soon nine forty-five and I needed to make my way to Patricia. I stood.

"I must take my leave now. I'll text you where to meet me later."

"Sounds good. Have fun. Thanks for hanging with me for a bit."

"Believe me. It's been my pleasure."

Bourbon Street was overflowing with people as I wandered toward Patricia's shop. I noted the cross street and texted it to Shantay. Patricia saw me and came outside.

"How was your night?" I said.

"Good. It got really busy for a while. Let me lock up and I'll join you in a minute. If you want to wait for me back by the stairs, that would be great."

I did as she asked and stood in the alley for only a matter of minutes before she showed up.

"Is this alley safe for you?" I was concerned about the darkness and emptiness.

"Of course. I've lived here for years. No one has ever bothered me. Now, come on up."

I thought carnal thoughts as I followed her up the stairs. Her body was beautiful, if a little slight for my taste. But she was tight, and her ass didn't jiggle in the slightest as she walked up the stairs. Rather, it swayed temptingly from side to side and I felt my pulse race in anticipation of what the night might hold.

She opened the door and stepped out of the way to let me enter. I felt like I was in another decade. She had colorful scarves pinned to the ceiling, billowing in the breeze. There were at least four lava lamps at first count. And the posters on the wall were of Janis Joplin and Jimi Hendrix.

"What do you think?" she asked.

"I love it. I absolutely love it. It's so you."

I crossed the room to the bookshelf, which held books by Anne Rice, books about Marie Laveau, and several books, which made me uneasy, about Van Helsing. I also spotted quite a few other books on vampires.

"Interesting collection," I said.

"I love to read. I'll read anything I can get my hands on."

"It appears you have an affinity toward vampires."

"Vampires and voodoo." She laughed. "Those are my favorites."

I refrained from asking her if she believed in either for fear of insulting her. Instead, I went back to the couch.

"Shall we sit?" I said.

"Let me pour us some wine first. Do you prefer red or white?"

"I much prefer red, thank you."

"Great."

She brought two glasses and set them on the ebony coffee table.

"You ready for some music?" she asked.

"Sure. What kind of music are we listening to?"

"I thought we'd start out with some local jazz musicians, followed by some blues, and then your choice."

"Excellent," I said. "I love music."

Her music selection was fantastic. We listened, we danced, we finished a bottle of wine, and opened a second. I was having the time of my life.

She played Dr. John, a local celebrity and I thought my legs would give out from moving and grooving with her. We sat back on the couch and she slowed the tempo down. I draped my arm across the back of the couch, which apparently, she took as an invitation to snuggle close to me.

"I'm having so much fun," she said. "Thank you for agreeing to do this, Alex."

"It's my pleasure."

"What do you do, Alex? What brought you to my city? And how is it you can wander around at night? Do you not have a job?"

"To tell the truth, I'm retired."

"You seem awfully young for that."

"I inherited some money." That part was true. "And I've dabbled in commerce. So I made some money there. Now that I'm in the States, I plan to play the market. I keep myself occupied."

"You're a fascinating woman."

"Thank you. I would say the same of you."

"Alex?"

"Mm?"

"Will you kiss me? Please?"

I looked into her hazel eyes and saw a pleading that matched her words. Her full lips were parted and, though I tried to draw it out and add a little tension, I was unsuccessful. I lowered my mouth to hers and kissed her.

The kiss, while chaste at first, soon deepened, and in the next minute, Patricia was on her back on the couch and I was on top of her. I dragged my free hand over Patricia's body, exploring everywhere and frustrating me. I needed to touch Patricia's skin. I craved so much more, but if this was all I would get, I would make the most of it.

We continued to kiss and gyrate against each other for hours. The confines of my clothes only serving to irritate me further. I wanted to rip off my own clothes and tear Patricia's off her and get naked. But Patricia didn't seem too inclined to do that.

Eventually, I managed to get under Patricia's T-shirt and clasp her firm breasts. She arched into me and I could feel the heat coming from the seam of her shorts. I brought my knee against her and she moved against me, rubbing back and forth until I thought my head would explode from the blatant animalistic need she showed.

I reached under her bra and teased a nipple until it could have cut glass. I longed to suck it, but when I lowered my head, she grabbed me firmly and pulled my mouth back to hers. Confused, and horny as hell, I accepted that we weren't going any further that night.

She kissed down my cheek and sucked my earlobe. My center was on fire. She nibbled my neck and I turned my head to allow her more. It was then I saw the clock on the wall. It was five thirty. I didn't feel the sun yet but knew I should get home. Just to be safe.

Regretfully, I sat up and pulled her up with me.

"I need to go, Patricia." My breath still coming in fits. "I'm sorry."

"No. It's fine. I should get some sleep myself. Would you like to stay?"

"I think it's best if I head home."

"I understand. Maybe tonight I can see your house?"

"That would be wonderful. We'll plan on it."

"Good night, Alex."

"Sweet dreams, Patricia."

"Thank you."

She walked me to the door, and I took the stairs carefully as I did not fully trust my legs. I texted Shantay that I was ready, and she texted back that she was already there. I climbed into the car and she drove us home.

"The sun won't rise for another hour," said Shantay. "What would you like to do?"

"Why don't you give me a tour of the house? I don't really know my way around and plan to have company tomorrow night."

"Is that right? Good for you. Come on. I'll give you the grand tour."

We went upstairs where she showed me my master bed and bath. It was a huge room, done in dark mahogany. I loved it. She showed me the four other rooms up there, including my office, which was modern chrome and glass.

The downstairs tour was enlightening. I was particularly enamored with the ballroom and its grand piano. Next, we stepped onto the deck in the backyard where I fell in love with the hot tub. I also admired the gazebo in the middle of the yard, surrounded by what I assumed were native plants.

One plant in particular caught my attention.

"What is this?" I asked Shantay.

"It's called a skullcap. Beautiful isn't it?"

"It really is."

It was then I noticed the sky lightening and bid adieu to Shantay.

"I'll see you tonight," I said.

"Sleep well."

My stomach fluttered as I climbed out of my coffin. I was filled with hope and anticipation for my night ahead with Patricia. The previous night's make out session had been most enjoyable, but it had also flipped a switch inside me. I needed more than simply kisses from the lovely Patricia. I needed all of her. In every way. I hoped that night would bring relief to my frustration.

Unfortunately, I'd need my strength if that was going to happen, which meant I had better feed. It had been a while since I'd needed to feed as often as I had been, and I hoped it wasn't a harbinger. I didn't want to have to feed frequently again. I preferred going weeks on end without taking a life. But such was not the case at the moment. My hunger overwhelmed me. I went downstairs to find Shantay. She needed to take me to my meal.

"You okay, Boss?" She stood as I came down the stairs. "You don't look too hot."

"I've been better. Come on. A drive will help."

Once in the car, Shantay turned to face me.

"What's going on, Alex?"

"Nothing. I just need to feed. And that disgusts me."

"But..."

"No buts. Regardless of what I am, it disgusts me to have to feed all the time."

"Right. You hardly ever fed in Buenos Aires."

I sighed heavily.

"That's correct. I don't know what's going on now, but I need to find a meal. And soon. Where shall we go?"

Shantay looked at her phone, apparently found a place, and turned to start the car. She drove me out of the beautiful Garden District and past the French Quarter. I closed my eyes and let my new city pass by. I was startled when the car stopped.

"We're here, Alex. I'll wait right here. You go do your thing."

I got out of the car and started down the street. The boarded up buildings and graffiti on the walls told me I was in a rough area of the city. I walked along the streets, ignoring the curious stares of the people I passed.

"You lost, lady?" A large man with a giant beer belly approached me. "We don't like your type around here."

Attempting to ignore him, I continued looking straight ahead and walking in that direction. He grabbed my arm, which led to guffaws from a group of onlookers.

"I'm talking to you, bitch."

His scent was strong and repulsive. But the blood pumping through him called to me, begging me to drink it. The crowd of onlookers had closed in around us, though. I couldn't just drain him right then and there. I needed to get him behind one of the abandoned buildings.

"What the fuck's the matter with you? You deaf?" He spit in my face.

"I'm not deaf." I'm sure my calm voice frustrated him. I wasn't scared. I could take the whole lot of them if I had to.

"You know what you need, tough gal? You need a man who'll teach you not to be a rug muncher."

His intent was clear, and I swallowed my laughter. He couldn't teach me anything. Tougher men than he had tried. I was stronger than any mortal and wasn't fazed. My thoughts must have shown on my face though as his face turned beet red and he leaned even closer.

"You think that's funny? You won't be laughing when I'm through with you."

"Do it!" the crowd chanted.

I pulled my arm away and headed between two buildings. I wanted to get away from the crowd lest there be witnesses. I knew he'd follow me and try to take me. It would be the last thing he ever did.

"The lady wants some privacy," he sneered.

I heard his footsteps behind me as I found a dilapidated building to hide behind.

He was on me then, holding me on the ground. He was fumbling with my pants when I unsheathed my fangs and buried them deep within his carotid artery. He never knew what hit him. He collapsed on top of me and I rolled out from under him, straightened my clothes, and continued walking down the alley until I reached Shantay.

"Where to now, Alex?"

"St. Louis Cemetery."

"Which one?"

"There's more than one?" That seemed odd to me.

"Yes, ma'am."

"Let's go see Marie Laveau's grave."

Shantay pulled out her phone, did a quick search, and put it away.

"Right you are. Coming right up."

We walked together through the cemetery until we found the Voodoo Queen's grave. There were x's all over it and I asked Shantay what that meant.

"Apparently if you ask her for something, you leave an x. If you get what you asked for, you circle the x."

"What shall I ask for, Shantay?"

"Whatever you'd like. I think I'll ask for something, too."

We stood silently for a moment then each marked an x on Laveau's grave.

"What did you ask for?" I said.

"I'll never tell." She smiled.

"Fair enough." I laughed. "That's totally fair."

"And you?" she said.

"Nothing too exciting. Now, let's see if she delivers. We should get home. I need to shower."

"You're the boss.'

I was showered and feeling better having washed off the essence of the man. I dressed in jeans and a hoodie and went back downstairs. Shantay was waiting for me.

"Back to Bourbon Street, Boss?" she said.

"Indeed. Let's go back to that pub and have a few drinks."

"I'll find a place to park and we can do just that."

We laughed and chatted and drank until Shantay switched to tea. I loved how responsible she was. She was a smart one. That was for sure.

"Dance with me, Boss?"

"Are you serious?"

"Sure. I love this music."

The music was different that night. More upbeat and lively. The sign in front of the band said, "Zydeco." I'd never heard of it, but had to admit, it had my toes tapping.

We danced a few songs then sat back down.

"Must be nice." Shantay wiped the sweat from her face.

"What's that?"

"Not to sweat."

"Ah, yes," I said. "It's one of my favorite perks."

"Lucky you."

I checked my watch and told Shantay I needed to go.

"Where will I meet you? And when?"

"Same as last night and a little after ten."

"That's right," she said. "You'll have company tonight."

"That I will. And I'm both nervous and excited." I chuckled.

"You? Nervous? Never."

"I would say I'm only human, but I'm not."

"No, ma'am. You're definitely not. Okay. You get going and I'll meet you in a few minutes."

I made my way down Bourbon Street until I was in Patricia's shop. She saw me and crossed the store to give me a hug.

"Alex," she said. "It's so good to see you. Give me a few and I'll meet you out front."

"Take your time," I said.

I was sure she'd be worth the wait.

CHAPTER EIGHT

Patricia soon joined me, and I admired how she looked in black skinny jeans and a rock and roll T-shirt featuring a band I'd never heard of.

"You look adorable," I said.

"And you look delectable."

I laughed. Interesting choice of words, but I'd take it. I was glad she found me attractive. I was hoping she found me delectable enough to go to bed with. Only time would tell.

"Are you ready to see my humble abode?" I asked.

"I am. Let's do this."

She took my hand, and I led her to the cross street where Shantay was waiting for us.

"Nice ride," she said.

"Thank you. I'm not much into driving myself. This works just fine."

We arrived at my house, and when she saw it she let out a low whistle.

"These are sweet digs," she said.

"It's home." I added a modest shrug. "Ready to see the inside?"

"I suppose. Though I could sit on this porch for days."

"Ah, yes. It's a great place from which to watch the world go by."

She followed the porch around to the back where she saw the deck.

"Is that a hot tub?"

"Yes, it is."

"Is it working?"

"I suppose so," I said. "I have yet to use it."

"Can we go in? Right now?"

"Did you bring a suit?"

"Do I need one?"

The look she gave me told me I was indeed in for a most enjoyable night.

"I don't suppose you do," I said.

She stripped and I admired her wonderfully naked body as she climbed the steps then submerged herself. I took my clothes off and joined her. The water felt great and the sight of her breasts floating just below the surface made my mouth water.

"Can we turn on the bubbles?" she said.

"Sure." I pushed a button and the bubbles came. I could no longer see her body, but that was okay. It was there and I knew it.

She stayed across the eight-foot tub from me which only served to heighten my desire. A nice game of cat and mouse to whet my appetite always enhanced the end result. I relaxed and let the water beat my body. I had a jet pointed directly at my lower back and it felt amazing.

We sat in silence. Her head was back as she seemed to be admiring the beautiful night sky. I joined her. There were stars twinkling and a full moon was on display. I loved the nighttime. Obviously.

Finally, Patricia looked at me.

"This is wonderful," she said. "Thank you for indulging me."

"Your wish is my command."

She stood, breasts on display, nipples hard in the cool night air. She crossed the hot tub and sat next to me. She rested a hand on my thigh and my whole body came alive.

"Tell me your wishes, Alex. Tell me your deepest, darkest desires."

I swallowed hard.

"I don't have many. I do as I please for the most part. My desires are mostly of the flesh if you must know."

"Ah. I must know. And if I let you have my flesh, how would you please me?"

"With you? My dear Patricia, I do believe I'd tease you. I'd be slow and deliberate and tease every inch of you until you could take no more."

"I love the way you talk," she said. My libido slowed a bit.

"How so?"

"You talk, I don't know. So properly. I love it. You don't use much slang. Which is cool."

"Good. I'm glad it's not a problem for you. You must remember, English is not my first language."

"But you speak it so well. Anyway, you were teasing me, remember?"

She moved her hand closer to where my legs met. I held my breath in anticipation, but she moved it back and rested it on my knee.

"I would love to tease you, Patricia. And please you. If only you would allow me to."

"I think that would be awesome. You keep me primed. That's for sure. And that kissing we did last night? I was still breathing heavily when I woke up this morning."

I laughed.

"Is that right?"

"Mm." She nibbled my neck and my core twitched.

"Perhaps we should go inside," I suggested.

"Patience, Alex. Anticipation. Besides," she whispered against my ear, "we have things we need to discuss."

"We do?" What the hell could we need to discuss? "Are you into kink or something?"

She laughed.

"Nothing like that." She turned so she was facing forward and clasped her hands in her lap. "I like you, Alex. You are a really neat person. And a wonderful kisser. But I must be completely honest with you."

"What? You're not a lesbian?"

She laughed again.

"Oh, I am most decidedly a lesbian."

"Well, that's good."

"It's just that… Well, the truth is… I'm not looking for a relationship. I'd love to enjoy all you have to offer and have you take me to the moon repeatedly, but you must understand, I don't want to get involved."

"That's all you had to tell me?" I breathed a sigh of relief. "That's fine. We could be friends with benefits. Or we could be a one-night thing. Either way would suit me."

"Thank you for understanding."

"You're quite welcome."

"Great. Now, I'm turning into a prune. Let's get inside."

"We can't just walk in naked," I said. "I don't live alone."

She raised her eyebrows at me.

"You have roommates?"

"No. I have staff. My driver and housekeeper live onsite. I'll grab us some towels."

There was a stand next to the hot tub filled with fluffy blue towels. I took two and handed one to Patricia.

"Wrap this around yourself and we'll go on up to my room."

She dried off, got her towel situated, and smiled at me.

"Lead the way."

Once in my room, we dropped our towels and came together in a soul searing kiss. Patricia moaned into my mouth as her hands roamed my hair, neck, back, and ass. I moved my hands all over her body as well, careful not to land on her inviting breasts. I'd save that for when we were horizontal.

"I need you," Patricia breathed. "Take me, Alex."

She lay on the bed and I lay on top of her. I kissed her mouth, her neck, her chest, and finally closed my mouth on her nipple. She groaned in delight as my tongue played over the hard peak.

"Don't tease me," she said. "I need you."

I slid my hand between her legs and found her hot, wet, and ready for me. I entered her and she arched off the bed.

"Yes! That's what I need. Give me more."

I added another finger, then another and watched as she threw her head back, clearly enjoying herself. Her other nipple called to me, so I moved my mouth to it, all the while plunging deep within her.

Her walls quaked and I knew she was close. I pressed my hand as far as it would go and felt her insides collapse around my fingers as she cried my name loud and long.

She crumpled in a heap on the sheets, but I wasn't through. Far from it. I had other plans for Patricia. I got out of bed and walked to the dresser.

"Where are you going?" Her voice was weak.

"Stay there. I'll be right back."

I fastened the harness and slid a dildo in place. Certain she would enjoy this, I climbed back in bed. I was greeted with wide eyes and even a wider smile.

"Oh, Alex," said Patricia. "I do like the way you think."

Before I could properly position myself over her, she rolled me onto my back and climbed on top of me. She slowly and deliberately lowered herself onto my cock. She ground into it, smearing her essence all over me.

I grabbed her and suckled her as she moved up and down on me.

She arched back and continued bouncing. At that angle I could see her swallowing the dildo and had a lovely view of her swollen clit. I wanted to taste it, to suck it, to feel it pulsating against my tongue.

Soon my view was obscured as she placed her hand on herself and rubbed until she cried out again and again. She fell forward and covered me with her lithe body. My whole body hummed with desire after what I had just witnessed.

"Are you ready to climb off?" I said.

"No." She laughed. "But I should. Go ahead and take that off and let me have a go with you."

The harness fell off me but before I could toss it on the floor, she was putting it on.

"What are you doing?" I said. I was so horny I'd go for anything, but I was used to driving.

"It's your turn to enjoy this in all its glory. Now, get on all fours."

My arms shook so badly I didn't know if they would support me, but I managed. I was on my hands and knees and she was behind me. I braced myself for entry but gasped when she entered me all the way with one thrust. Once the surprise wore off, I felt amazing. She moved in and out of me so deeply I could feel her thighs slapping the back of mine. Never before had I felt so completely full. I rocked into every thrust and was teetering on the edge when she reached around me and pressed into my nerve center.

My whole body shook as I left it and soared into orbit. Colors burst before my eyelids and I lost all conscious thought. I floated back to myself and she was still inside me.

"Do you need more?" she said. I shook my head, not trusting my voice. "I'm coming out then."

I heard her exit then collapsed on my stomach. I had indeed had all I could handle. And Patricia had proven to be most fun in bed. I would have loved to have another go at her, but it was getting late and I needed to get her home. She snuggled into my arms and I stroked her silky shoulder.

"Hey, Patricia?"

"Hm?"

"We need to get you home."

"Yeah," she said. "I suppose you're right. Thanks for the fun tonight. It was even better than I'd fantasized."

"I'm happy to hear that."

We got dressed in silence, then I took her hand and we went downstairs. Shantay was in the living room.

"Hi there," I said. "We need to give this lovely lady a ride home."

"I'm on it, Boss. I'll go get the car."

I walked Patricia down the alley to her stairwell.

"Thanks again for a wonderful night," she said.

"Thank you."

"Don't be a stranger, okay, Alex? I'm thinking friends with those kinds of benefits could work for me."

I laughed.

"Sounds good to me. I won't be around for a while, but I'll definitely be back. Even if we don't end up in bed together."

"Oh, Alex. If you stop by, we'll end up in bed. I guarantee it."

"Sounds good," I said. "Take care, Patricia."

I kissed her cheek, watched her safely enter her place, then walked back to the car.

"Good night tonight, Alex?" Shantay said.

"Mm. The best."

"Right on. Welcome to the Big Easy, eh?"

"No doubt."

"So, who was she? Are you serious about her?"

"I don't have it in me to be serious with anyone, Shantay. So, no. That was all for fun."

"But she lives here in town. Your paths may cross again. That could be awkward," Shantay said.

"Nah. It'll be fine. If our paths cross again, we'll probably just end up in bed again."

"Good for you."

"Indeed.

Back at the house, I cleaned up the mess we'd left in the bedroom, put the dildo away, and checked the time. I still had about an hour until sunup. I thought about the gazebo in the backyard and contemplated how nice it would feel to sit there and relax.

Shantay was there when I got there.

"I'm sorry," I said. "I didn't know you'd be here. I certainly don't want to intrude."

"No intrusion at all, Alex. Have a seat. I find this place to be most peaceful."

"I worry about you, Shantay."

"How so?"

"You're always at my beck and call. And while you never complain, I have to wonder what it's like to live such a lonely existence. Surely you'd like to meet some nice man...or even woman...to spend time with?"

"Woman. No men for me. I'm like you that way. And I don't get lonely. I love my life."

"Still. Why don't you take a few days off so you can get to know the city? Meet people? Maybe make a connection."

"I'm not looking for a connection. I assure you. But if you're trying to get rid of me..."

"Not at all," I assured her. "I enjoy being selfish with you."

"Good. Then forget about time off. If I decide I need it, I'll ask for it."

"Fair enough."

We chatted about the differences and similarities between Buenos Aires and New Orleans. We talked about our favorite parts of both cities. She told me she'd been in contact with my housekeeper from Buenos Aires who'd taken a vacation to Rio de Janeiro after we'd left.

"That's great," I said. "I hated having to let them go, but it was necessary."

"Why? What made you decide at that moment?"

"I'm never going to age, Shantay. And after ten years, it becomes fairly apparent that I still look the same. I can't have people asking questions. Worst-case scenario, they get too close to the truth and I'd have to dispose of them."

"You didn't dispose of me."

"I didn't perceive you as a threat."

"Good. Because I'm not a threat. I couldn't threaten you."

"Excellent. Then you can stay with me until you no longer want to. Then I'll see to it that you're well taken care of in your golden years."

"I appreciate that. I really do. I can't imagine not driving you around, Alex. I love it."

"Thank you. That means a lot to me."

I felt the burning just as she motioned to the east.

"Sun's coming up," she said. "You should get to sleep."

I stood.

"I'm on my way. I'll see you tonight."

The sun set that night and I awoke with memories of Patricia and the night before flooding over me. How I'd love to go by and pick her up for another night of pleasure, but I couldn't do that. We needed some time apart. Besides, I didn't want to seem desperate.

I climbed out of my coffin, dressed, and locked the door behind me, wondering what earthly pleasures awaited me that night.

Chapter Nine

S hantay dropped me off at Jackson Square, where I marveled at the sheer number of people milling about. The place was packed. I studied people and admired art for a while before making my way to Bourbon Street.

The place was a madhouse. I could barely squeeze through the crowds as I fought to get to my favorite bar. When I finally reached it, I couldn't get in. Patrons were overflowing onto the street. What the hell was going on?

I continued to be jostled as I struggled to move farther down the street. I came to a gridlock and was delighted to see several women with their tops pulled up, exposing lovely breasts to the crowds. They were looking up and I followed their gazes to see men on a balcony with different colored beads. They tossed them to the women who jumped and cheered.

I had no idea what bacchanalian ritual I'd stumbled upon, but I wasn't complaining. Young and old crowded the street. The smell of horse manure was strong, and I saw no less than five mounted policemen in that block alone. Crowd control. That made sense.

Music of all sorts blared from the bars and the apartments along Bourbon Street. People danced in the street, on the balconies, and in the bars. The festive air was contagious, and I soon found myself moving to the music as well.

More women had their shirts up. Women with all sorts of figures were lifting their shirts for beads. I wished I had some beads to offer them. I was definitely a breast woman and would have loved to have tops lifted for me.

The crowd pressed into me and I rode the wave down the street. Soon I was in front of Patricia's Voodoo shop. I fought through the crowds to get in. Patricia was behind the counter ringing up one of the many customers in line. I stood at the back of the line and waited my turn.

Finally, Patricia looked up and saw me.

"Alex," she said. "I didn't expect to see you so soon."

"Forgive me," I said. "But I needed some sanity. Can you tell me what in the world is going on out there?"

"Mardi Gras." She beamed. "Only the biggest night of the year for New Orleans."

"Ah, yes." It all made sense. "I hadn't realized. Thank you. I'll leave you now. Good luck with sales."

"We've already made more than we do in a month. Thanks though, Alex. Enjoy Mardi Gras."

"Thank you. I will."

The crowd enveloped me as I stepped back out onto the street. I made it to the west end of the street where there were much fewer people. I took a deep breath and began my way the other direction, determined to find a place to have a drink and watch the crowds from a slight distance.

The people pressed into me and again I could sense their pulses. I could feel their blood pumping through their veins. It was tempting, oh so tempting, to take a bite out of everyone. They probably wouldn't notice. I fought to keep my fangs sheathed so I wouldn't drink from any of the innocent party goers.

Bar after bar, I entered, but each was filled to capacity. I noticed an establishment with a balcony across the street, so I went up there and was able to sit and watch the insanity from a distance.

As I sipped my hurricane and watched the crowds below, I wished I had beads to throw in exchange for glimpses of myriad breasts. But I didn't have beads, so I simply observed and enjoyed.

My waitress, Bijou, approached and asked me if I wanted something to eat.

"No, thank you. I'm happy to simply drink tonight. You look tired. Would you like to sit and join me for a moment?"

Bijou had rich, dark skin and expressive brown eyes. Her full lips begged to be kissed and, for some reason, the need to claim her consumed me. She laughed.

"I wish I could. We're much too busy for that." She turned to leave.

"Later then?"

"I'm sorry. We're open all night. And when this night is over, I'll go straight home and to bed. But thank you."

"Fair enough," I said. "What about tomorrow? May I see you after work tomorrow?"

"I don't work tomorrow. But if you're here Thursday at two, I'd be happy to go out with you."

"Thank you. I'll see you then."

Bijou was beautiful and when she spoke, her voice was lilted with a lovely accent that I couldn't quite put my finger on. She was back later to ask if I'd like another drink.

"Yes, please," I said. "And may I ask you where you're from? Your accent is melodious, but I can't put my finger on it."

She smiled at me.

"I'm from Haiti. I've lived here twenty years. You'd think my accent would be gone by now."

"It's not. It's quite lovely."

"Thank you. I'll be back with your hurricane."

I fantasized about Bijou as I continued to watch the crowds. More shirts were lifted, more beads were tossed. I'd love to see Bijou without her shirt. Her breasts were ginormous, and I wanted to love on them in the worst sort of way.

The night wore on into the morning. I checked my watch and knew I needed to get back to the house. I found Bijou, handed her a fifty-dollar bill as a tip, and told her I would see her Thursday.

The crowds were still thick, and I should have taken that into consideration. There was no way I was going to make it back to Jackson Square in time. I cut over at the first side street and wandered down Royal until I finally arrived to find Shantay pacing by the car.

"You're late," she said.

"I'm sorry. The crowds—"

"You can explain in the car. We need to get you home."

She held my door for me, and I slid in. The sky was lightening at an uncomfortably fast pace, and I was scared. Obviously, she was too.

At the house, she held my door for me to get out.

"Are you going to be able to make it up the stairs?" she said.

I nodded, as I had no energy to speak. I went inside and dragged myself up the stairs. I was in so much pain. The agony tore through me with each step. Damn. I needed to be more careful.

The struggle to keep my eyes open was real. They wanted to close as they automatically did at sunrise. I fought through, though, and fumbled with my keys to unlock my secret room. I finally found the lock and hurried inside. I climbed into my coffin, fully clothed, and welcomed the sleep of the dead.

Thursday night, I woke with a smile on my face. I was going to take Bijou out. I wondered what kind of music she liked. Would she be happy listening to jazz? Or would zydeco be more to her liking? Or maybe blues? Rock? EDM? I had no idea. I would find out soon and I couldn't wait.

I took a shower and dressed in fresh clothes, gray linen slacks and a black button-down shirt. I would have checked myself out in the mirror, but I had no reflection, so there was no point. I gelled my hair in a spiky fashion and was ready for my night.

Shantay was waiting for me downstairs. She stood when I approached.

"Where to, Boss?"

"I think I'd like to just relax in the gazebo for a bit. I don't have to be anywhere until two."

Shantay raised her eyebrows.

"You have somewhere to be? Another date, perhaps?"

"Indeed. I have a date with a beautiful woman at two."

"Be careful," she said. "That doesn't leave you much time."

"Thank you for caring, Shantay. And I will be careful. Would you care to join me in the gazebo?"

"Sure."

We sat in silence, lost in our own thoughts. She finally spoke. Her voice was quiet, barely a whisper.

"What's it like?" she said.

"What's what like?"

"Living forever."

"It's both a blessing and a curse."

"Can you expand on that for me?" she said.

"It's exciting to see all the changes in society. It's difficult to get used to all of them, but it's exciting. And, of course, not have to worry about dying is wonderful. I can do as I please with no concerns except being in my coffin on time."

"That makes sense." She nodded. "I bet it would be awesome."

"It's quite nice." I laughed.

"And you said it's also a curse. How so?"

"I don't age, Shantay. I never will. Yet people I care about get old and pass on. Or, as was the case in Buenos Aires, they age and I don't, so I need to move before someone notices I haven't gotten the least bit older. I loved our staff in Buenos Aires. I loved the city. I miss all that. But I couldn't have stayed. So, it's a curse."

"Right. I miss Buenos Aires, too. We had some good times there."

"That we did," I said.

She grew silent again, yet I could see in her eyes she had more to ask. I let her form the questions in her own time. I was enjoying the peaceful stillness of the night.

"May I ask you another question?" she finally said.

"Of course."

"What's it like? To kill someone?"

If I'd had a heart it would have sunk. I didn't know how to answer the question. It wasn't something I thought about. It was just something I had to do. I pondered for a while and chose my words carefully.

"It's awful, if you want to know the truth."

"Is it? You don't enjoy it?"

"I loathe it. With every ounce of my being. I'm so glad I've evolved to the point where I don't have to feed often."

"I'm glad to hear that. You're so kind and gentle, Alex. I can't imagine you taking someone's life."

"It's something I must do, though."

"Do you have to kill people? Couldn't you just drink and let them live?"

"And have them recognize me? Be able to identify me? Have them understand what happened to them? Most people don't believe in vampires. And that works for me. I couldn't feed and let them survive. It would be too dangerous."

"I understand. You said you've evolved. How often did you feed when you were first made?"

"I fed uncontrollably and randomly. I'd feed several times a night. The draw was unbearable. When the need to feed comes upon me, I'm of a single mindset. I can't concentrate on anything but meeting that need."

"I don't think I could drink blood. Or kill someone. But I sure wouldn't mind living forever."

"It sounds wonderful, doesn't it?" I sighed. "But, as I've mentioned, it has its drawbacks as well."

"Do you ever get lonely? What will you do after I die? I know you'll get a new driver and move on, but don't you miss having a confidant to share your life with?"

"I surround myself with people I enjoy. Yourself included. I know it's all temporary though. I keep that in mind. It doesn't make it any easier. That's for sure."

"It's eleven o'clock." She abruptly changed the subject. "Would you like to head toward the French Quarter now?"

"Sure." I smiled at her. "Will you join me for a few drinks?"

"Of course." She smiled back. "I'd love that."

She parked the car and we found Bourbon Street much tamer than it had been two nights earlier. There were still people everywhere, but the sheer madness had ebbed. We found our way to the bar with ease and went in to drink and listen to the music.

There was a zydeco band playing again and I had to admit, I preferred it to the jazz bands I'd heard. The music was upbeat, happy, and decidedly New Orleans. Shantay and I drank and danced and drank some more. She switched to iced tea and I checked my watch. One thirty.

"I should get going," I said.

"Okay. Text me where you want me to pick you up."

"Will do."

I found myself outside of Bijou's restaurant with ten minutes to spare. I went inside to order a drink and wait. She saw me and favored me with a warm smile.

"Hello, stranger," she said. "You're early."

"I thought I'd have a hurricane and wait."

"Hold that thought. We're slow. I'll see if I can leave early and we'll get out of here."

"Very well. I'll wait."

She was back a moment later, sans apron, carrying her purse.

"Shall we?" she said.

"But of course."

"I'll drive you to my neighborhood, if you don't mind. I'd like to show you a different side of New Orleans."

"That sounds wonderful. I have a driver, if you'd rather."

"No, thanks. Come on. I'm parked not far from here."

I could have listened to the soft lilt of Bijou's voice for hours. I was hoping to do just that. She drove us to a brightly colored neighborhood and parked in the driveway of one of several rowhomes.

We got out of the car and she walked around to my side.

"Where to now?" I was half hoping she'd invite me in. I could have spent the next few hours enjoying her body. But she motioned down the street with her head.

"This way. There's a bar I'd like you to see."

The bar was fairly empty, and I looked around, admiring the art on the walls.

"These are beautiful," I said.

"All Haitian artists."

"Wow."

"I'd like to order you a drink. Do you trust me?"

"I have no reason not to."

"Have a seat," she said. "I'll be right back."

She brought back drinks that I could taste had condensed milk and rum in them. I also tasted almonds. It was quite delicious.

"What is this called?" I asked.

"Kremas. It's a Haitian cocktail."

"It's delicious."

"So, mystery woman," she said. "Do you have a name? I must admit you intrigue me, but don't even know what to call you."

"I'm Alex."

"Nice to meet you."

"And you." I raised my kremas. "To new friends."

"Mm." She clinked my glass then took another sip of her drink. "Tell me about yourself, Bijou."

"What would you like to know? Where do you want me to begin? I grew up in Haiti and now I live here."

I laughed.

"Surely there's more," I said.

She shrugged.

"I suppose there is. Why don't you tell me about yourself?"

"At the risk of sounding childish, I asked you first."

She laughed.

"Oh, Alex. I've so much to tell. I feel like writing a book about my life. It hasn't always been easy, but I'm where I belong now."

"I'm so glad you're happy," I said. "And I'm sorry for anything that's ever made you sad."

"You're very kind, Alex. I think I'm going to enjoy getting to know you."

"And I you, Bijou. And I you."

Chapter Ten

It's getting late," said Bijou. "I'm afraid I must call it a night and get home now."

"I'll walk you to your house."

In front of her house, we stood, me with my hands in my pockets to avoid the temptation of touching her. I wanted to. God, how I wanted to. But she hadn't indicated my touch would be welcome, so I refrained.

"Thank you for a lovely night," she said.

"Believe me, it was my pleasure."

"Will I see you again?"

"Whenever you'd like."

"I'm sorry I'm not inviting you in," she said. "I'm just still exhausted from Mardi Gras."

"Understood. No apologies necessary."

"At the risk of sounding too forward, can we do this again tomorrow?"

"I tell you what. I have a hot tub and champagne at my house. Why don't we plan to go there after work tomorrow night?"

Her whole face lit up.

"That would be wonderful. I'll bring my suit to work and you can pick me up at two again."

"Sounds great," I said. "I'll see you then."

She stood on her tiptoes and kissed my cheek. It was brief but said so much. I longed to kiss her properly but knew I'd have to wait. We'd see what the following night brought.

"Good night, Alex."

"Sleep well, Bijou." I liked the feel of her name on my tongue. I was sure I'd like the feel of everything about her on my tongue.

When she was safely in her house, I walked to the nearest cross street. I texted Shantay the address.

Please hurry. The sun will be up soon.

I'm on my way.

I waited impatiently, but Shantay was there in just a few minutes.

"That didn't take you long." I got in the car.

"I was sort of in the neighborhood. I was just driving around checking out the city when you texted."

"How fortuitous for me."

We started the drive home, and I was beginning to feel the heat of dawn approaching. I'd have to figure out a way to see Bijou earlier. I didn't think I could properly please her in the few hours between the time she got off work and when the sun made its appearance.

"How was your night?" said Shantay.

"It was quite nice. Oh, that reminds me. I need a favor of you, please."

"Anything for you, Alex."

"Will you pick up some champagne and chill it for me? And get me something that would be appropriate to wear in the hot tub?"

"Like a swimsuit?"

"I suppose. But not a woman's. I'm not sure what I want. I'll leave it to your discretion."

"I'll take care of it."

When I woke that night and went to my bedroom to take a shower and get ready for my night, I found a pair on long legged swim trunks on the bed with a matching muscle shirt. I smiled. Shantay had done well.

The clothes fit perfectly, but I felt a bit underdressed. I never went out in public dressed like that. But it was for a good cause, and not having to change when we got back to the house would definitely save time. Time that would hopefully be spent with Bijou in my arms.

I went downstairs to show off my outfit and thank Shantay for a job well done, but Shantay was nowhere to be found. Normally, she was waiting for me in the expansive entryway or in the library.

Occasionally, I'd find her in the living room, but she was in none of those places. Oddly disappointed, I went out onto the deck to check that the hot tub was ready for use. It was then I saw Shantay in the gazebo. I crossed the yard to join her.

"What are you doing out here?" I said. "And do you mind if I join you?"

"I wish you would."

"Great. Why are you sitting out here by yourself?"

"I love this gazebo. It's so peaceful. Besides, I knew you'd be up soon, and I really enjoyed just hanging out with you last night."

"That was nice, wasn't it?" I said. "Do you have any more questions for me tonight?"

"Alex, I'm sure I have a million questions for you. It's just a matter of where to start. Also, I don't want to offend you."

"My dearest Shantay, you could never offend me. We have a few hours to kill, so ask away."

"How old were you when you became a vampire?"

"When I was made? One doesn't simply become a vampire. One is made. I was thirty-two."

"Was it a willing thing?"

"Yes and no."

"How so?" said Shantay.

"I was attacked by a group of vampires. Back then, vampires ran in packs for the most part. There were many more of them. They each drank from me and I was weak and begging for my life. It's kind of a blur still to this day, but the leader asked if I wanted to live. Of course, I said I did. He asked if I wanted to live forever. I said I didn't care about that, I just wanted to live. He slit his wrist with his fangs and put his radial artery up to my mouth. He told me to drink if I wanted to stay alive. So I drank. The rest, as they say, is history."

"Did his blood taste like regular blood?"

"Yes and no. It had that familiar copper taste to it, but it was rich and creamy. It wasn't bad, to be honest."

Shantay nodded and sat there in silence, obviously absorbing what I'd said.

"What was your life like back then? Before you were made?" she said.

"I was the spinster daughter of a blacksmith."

"Why were you a spinster?"

"Even then I knew I liked women. I was introduced to the joys of lesbianism by a neighbor. She was older than I and married. My father sent me to her house one day with a delivery. I was sixteen. We visited for a while, most of the afternoon, then she kissed me. It was the most marvelous thing that had ever happened to me. I went over the next day and she made love to me. And I to her. A whole new world opened before me, and I understood why no male suitor did anything for me. And none ever would."

"You're a very fascinating woman, Alex," said Shantay.

"I'm just me." I shrugged.

"How did the vampires find you?"

"I'm sorry?"

"The ones who made you. How did that happen? How did a whole pack of vampires happen upon you?"

"I had been at the marketplace two towns over. I met a lovely young woman there and we snuck off for some private time, so I was late getting home. I was almost to our town when they surrounded my horse. I thought they were robbers, simply after what I'd bought in town. Obviously, I was wrong. So very wrong. The leader reached up and pulled me off my horse. I fell to the ground with a thud. I was sure my ribs were broken, but that was only a minor thought in the back of my brain as I feared for my life. Rightly so. I thought I'd be gang raped. I'd heard of that sort of thing by hanging out in the smithy and listening to my father talk with his friends. I was sure that's what was going to happen. But again, I was wrong. The leader lifted me up and bit my neck, taking a large drink off me before passing me to another. I went around the circle and then was thrown back to the ground. The leader must have liked something about me because he picked me up and made me a vampire."

"Did you join them then? Did you become part of their gang?"

"Their coven. Yes, I did. What choice did I have?"

"And when did you feel comfortable with being a vampire? I mean, did you ever resent them? Or was it okay from the start?" Shantay was indeed full of questions.

"I hated it. I hated having to drink blood to stay alive. And I had to drink so frequently. They had dens in the mountains surrounding our town. They lived in caves. We lived in caves, I should say. When we were in the mountains, I drank from bears, wolves, anything I could get my hands on. But it wasn't very satisfying. They kept me alive, to be sure, but I needed, craved human blood."

"When did you get your first taste of human blood?"

"Not long after I was made. We traveled to another town and I met a beautiful woman. We hit it off and I was about to take her to bed when my cravings got the better of me. I was between her legs and her femoral artery pulsed in my ear. My fangs came out, I turned my head, and drank her dry."

"How did that feel?"

"Awful," I said. "Well, conflicting. I felt terrible at having taken an innocent life, but the blood… Oh, the blood. I felt all powerful. I felt invincible. It was a remarkable feeling that I wanted to feel over and over again."

"And now?" said Shantay. "When you feed, do you still feel all powerful?"

I shrugged.

"I don't know. I feel that way all the time, really. Because, for the most part, I am invincible. I drink now because I have to. Not because I want to. But I'm picky about who I drink from. No more innocent lives for me."

"I have another question."

"Go for it."

"Have you ever made a vampire?"

This brought up horrible memories for me. I remembered the pressure from the coven, the jeering, teasing, taunting.

"No," I said. "They wanted me to. They told me to. They brought me a strapping young lad who they said they wanted in our coven. I drank from him, as instructed, but when it came time to let him drink from me, I couldn't. They were pissed. They shoved me, yelled at me, beat me, but I wouldn't turn him. So one of them did. I was kicked out of the coven."

"For not making a vampire?"

"Exactly."

I looked at my watch. It was midnight. We'd been talking for hours. It was nice, but I wanted to get to the French Quarter.

"We should get going," I said. "I'd like to listen to some music and have a few drinks. Will you join me?"

"Of course. Let's go."

We sat in our usual bar. The bartender had seen us come in and had our drinks waiting for us when we arrived. There was a jazz ensemble playing.

"So what are your plans for tonight?" Shantay said.

"I'm bringing a new friend over to sit in the hot tub."

"And?" She grinned at me.

"We'll see. I only know we're hot-tubbing."

"Fair enough. Where shall I meet you?"

I gave her the cross street next to Bijou's place of employment.

"We should be out a little after two."

"Sounds good. I'll be there."

A little after two, Bijou and I rode to my place mostly in silence. I wondered if she was nervous, scared, or a combination of the two.

"Are you okay?" I asked. "You're awfully quiet."

"Just winding down. I promise to be better company later."

"Fair enough."

Shantay pulled up in front of the house and opened Bijou's door for her.

"Your friend is very nice," said Bijou.

"Yes. Yes, she is. Would you like to unwind some more or are you ready for the hot tub?"

"I'd love a soak in the tub."

"Let's do it then."

I led her to the back deck and pointed to the small changing room.

"You can change there," I said.

"Thank you. I'll be right out."

She emerged a few minutes later looking absolutely stunning in a one-piece bathing suit. Her voluptuous breasts were barely contained by the flimsy material and once again I found myself longing to feast on her.

We got in the hot tub and Shantay came out with champagne for us.

"Thank you," I said.

"This is wonderful," said Bijou.

We sat back and sipped champagne and gazed at the stars.

"Would you like bubbles?" I asked.

"No, thank you. I'm enjoying this just the way it is."

"Excellent. I'm glad you're enjoying yourself."

"I truly am. Let's play getting to know you again. This is a nice house. I have to believe since we met on Mardi Gras that you're a tourist. Is this an Airbnb?"

I laughed.

"No. I live here. This is my home."

"And you have servants? Or is that woman your roommate?"

"I have servants. Shantay is my driver and right-hand woman. I also have a housekeeper."

"Must be nice."

"It is."

"Well, if you live here, why on earth were you on Bourbon Street during Mardi Gras?" She laughed.

"I've only just moved to town. I didn't realize it was Mardi Gras. But I'm glad I was there, or I wouldn't have met you."

"You say such sweet things, Alex."

"Well, I mean them." I picked up the bottle of champagne. "Would you like a top off?"

She handed me her glass, which I filled.

"You must be very well off," she said. "What do you do for a living?"

"This and that. I must admit, I inherited a great deal of my wealth. I've invested wisely so I have money to spare at this point."

She sighed.

"I wish I had that kind of money. I love my job. Don't get me wrong. It's just that, as I get older, those trays get heavier."

"I'm sure."

"Alex?"

"Hm?"

"May I come sit by you?"

"I wish you would."

"What is it that you want from me?" she said.

"What do you mean?"

"We are from different worlds. Yet you're so kind and sweet. Are you in the market for a girlfriend? Partner? Part-time lover?"

"My darling Bijou. I want to be perfectly honest with you. I'm not in the market for a partner. But in the vein of truthfulness, I'd love for you to be my lover."

"For how long?"

"Tonight? Tomorrow night? As long as you'd like."

"Not tonight," she said. "For one thing, I'm not that easy. For another, I'm tired after my shift."

"When is your next night off? And I wouldn't presume to think you're easy, Bijou."

"My next night off is tomorrow. Why don't we go on a date? You can take me to dinner, and we can go from there."

"That would be wonderful. I'll pick you up at six thirty."

"I'll look forward to it."

I draped my arm over her shoulders and pulled her close. She snuggled up against me and the feel of her full breasts pressing into me almost weakened my resolve not to take her then and there. But I was strong. I could wait. Bijou would be worth it. I was sure of that.

CHAPTER ELEVEN

Dinner was an amazing experience. Bijou suggested a restaurant within walking distance of my house that was decorated like a shipwreck. Beams of wood stuck out this way and that, and there was a giant aquarium so we could watch the fish as we dined.

I paid little to no attention to the fish, however. My attention was on Bijou. She was so beautiful and shy, and she intrigued and attracted the hell out of me. Her brown eyes were soulful and expressive, and I easily lost myself in them.

Bijou told me stories of her childhood in Haiti. It seemed to be a happy one even in the poverty in which she was raised. Her father worked on a sugar plantation. He worked from sunrise to sunset and she remembered many days where she wouldn't get to see him at all.

Her father was a strict man, and her mother picked up where he left off. But she never felt anything but love from them. They immigrated to New Orleans when she was a teenager, hoping for a better life. They moved into the house Bijou now owned. She bought it from her mother after her father passed. Her mother lived with Bijou until her final days.

"You haven't touched your dinner," Bijou said as she pushed her empty plate away.

"I don't suppose I have. I was too enthralled with your story. That's okay though. I'm not really hungry."

"That's too bad."

I shrugged.

"It is what it is. I'll be fine. What would you like to do now?"

"Shall we walk through a cemetery? Telling my story made me miss my parents. I'd like to visit them."

"Of course, Bijou," I said. "Let's do that."

She took my hand and we strolled to Lafayette Cemetery Number One. I was at once at peace. I loved cemeteries. They were filled with nonliving beings such as me. I remembered years of living in cemeteries when I was a young vampire, after I'd been cast out of my coven and learned of the draw of bigger cities. It was a dangerous existence, I suppose. But it worked for me.

We found her parents' graves and she knelt and pulled some weeds, brushed dirt off the headstone and became still. I was happy to give her this time. I could only imagine how nice it would be to visit the graves of one's parents. I supposed I could have gone back to my small village in Romania and looked for my parents, but I didn't even know if my village still existed. That was ancient history.

When she had prayed, mourned, or whatever she was doing enough, Bijou stood and wiped her knees. She stood proudly and turned to me.

"Okay," she said. "The rest of the night is yours."

"Are you okay?"

"I'm fine. I appreciate you letting me pay my respects."

"Of course, Bijou." The feel of her name on my tongue still exciting me. "I would never deny you anything."

She looked at me questioningly.

"What is it you want from me, Alex?"

"What do you mean?"

"You are so kind. And you've been so patient. I think we both know where this night will end." That excited me and I fought not to break into a wide smile. "But after that? What do you want? We are from two different worlds. I like you very much. But I'm quite settled in my solitude."

"I understand," I said. "I'll take whatever you want to give me."

"Will one night be enough?"

"As long as after one night, we can still see each other occasionally. As long as I can still call you friend."

"Oh, Alex, my dear. You'll always be able to call me your friend."

I bent to kiss her. It was a brief meeting of lips, yet I hoped it conveyed all my wants and desires. She kissed me back, her lips sucking on mine and keeping them in place.

"Shall we head back to my place?" I said.

"What shall we do there? It's early yet."

I took a deep breath. Obviously, she wasn't ready to go to bed yet. I wondered what sort of lover Bijou would be. I suspected she'd be a pillow priestess and I longed to worship at her altar.

"We can sip champagne in the gazebo. It's my favorite place to relax and unwind."

"That sounds lovely. Let's go."

We stopped in the kitchen to get some champagne and flutes, which I carried out to the gazebo. When we got there, Shantay was relaxing with a book.

"We should go someplace else," Bijou said.

"No, that's fine. I'll leave," said Shantay.

"Please don't. Join us."

Shantay looked from Bijou to me and back again.

"Go grab a glass and another bottle," I said. "You're welcome to join us."

Shantay disappeared into the house and returned a moment later with a glass, a bottle of champagne, and a bucket of ice.

"Well done," I said. "Bijou, this is my dear friend Shantay. Shantay, meet Bijou."

"Your friend? Is she a roommate?" Bijou obviously wondered at our relationship.

"I'm her right-hand gal," Shantay said. "Driver, confidant. You name it. I'm in her employ though, so not really a roommate."

Bijou simply nodded. Was it my imagination or were sparks flying between them? Had I made a mistake asking Shantay to stay? Would I strike out after all?

I needed to shake off that way of thinking. Bijou was there to be with me. Shantay was a wonderful person and obviously Bijou could read that.

"How was dinner?" Shantay said.

"It was delicious, and the company was fantastic." Bijou smiled. "Though Alex didn't touch her etouffee."

"She's often too distracted to eat," said Shantay.

"She needs more meat on her bones." Bijou was voluptuous and obviously thought me too thin. But I was a normal weight for my height. I'd never been heavy and, of course, was still the same size I was when I'd been made.

"I'm right here." I laughed.

They laughed too. We filled our glasses and Bijou and I sat on one bench while Shantay sat opposite us.

"This is nice," said Bijou. "This champagne is delicious."

"Drink up," I said. "We have two bottles to get through."

We drank and chatted, and the night was passing most pleasantly. We were well into the second bottle of champagne and I was getting antsy to take Bijou upstairs. But she didn't appear to be in any hurry, so I relaxed and enjoyed the conversations.

Finally, Shantay looked at her watch.

"It's been very nice getting to know you, Bijou. But it's time for me to turn in. Y'all enjoy the rest of your evening."

My pulse raced. It was almost time to take Bijou to bed.

"Don't go," Bijou said. I looked at her, dumbstruck. "Please join us? That is, if it's okay with Alex?"

"Bijou," I said, "if you want Shantay, you may have her. No hard feelings."

"I want you both."

Shantay looked at me and I smiled. I'd always found her attractive. And she meant the world to me. What would it hurt to sleep with her?

"All in fun?" I said to Shantay.

"Of course. I'm happy to play."

My stomach was in knots as we climbed the stairs. What would happen with Shantay after this? Would we, could we, go back to the way things had been? I certainly hoped so. I didn't want to lose her. She was a faithful companion as well as a wonderful employee.

In my room, I pulled Bijou to me and kissed her hard. I made no pretense of tenderness. I wanted her to feel all the passion that burned within me. Shantay pulled me away from Bijou and kissed me. The flutters in my stomach surprised me. I was more aroused than usual by that simple kiss. Any worries flew. I couldn't wait to get the two of them into bed.

"Everyone lose their clothes. Now." I breathed.

We all stripped and climbed onto my king-size bed. There was plenty of room for all of us and, as I looked hungrily at Shantay and Bijou kissing, I wondered where to start.

Bijou's breasts called to me. They were huge and I couldn't wait to get my hands and mouth on them. I took one in both hands and suckled at her large nipple while Shantay did the same with the other.

The sight of Shantay, eyes closed in pleasure, nearly sent me over the edge. I moved one hand from Bijou's breast and ran it down Shantay's arm. She winked at me, then closed her eyes and seemed to focus on Bijou. But suddenly I was hungry for Shantay. Hungrier than I could ever remember being. I leaned over and kissed her, and when our tongues met, my chest tightened. I was ready for her, I realized. Just as ready as I was for Bijou.

Kissing lower on Bijou, I made my way to where her legs met. I breathed in her heady scent before taking her in my mouth. I was focused on her flavor, her texture, her being, and was startled to feel Shantay's tongue on me.

Shantay knew what she was doing. Of that there was no doubt. I ground into her face, needing more of her, craving a release I was so close to.

Bijou was moaning softly, and I knew she was close. I replaced my tongue with my fingers and took her swollen clit in my mouth. I sucked on it and her moaning grew louder. Shantay was wreaking havoc on my own hormones. I fought to focus on licking Bijou, and she finally screamed just as Shantay took me over the edge and into oblivion.

When I came back to my body, I found Shantay and Bijou kissing again. It was my turn to please Shantay and I couldn't wait. I saw her moving her hand in and out of Bijou and my insides clenched. I wanted her again. But first, I needed to please Shantay.

I held her lower lips open with my fingers and licked between them. She tasted marvelous. Musky and salty and delicious. I slid inside her with my fingers, and she pressed into me. I swirled my tongue around her throbbing nerve center, and she closed hard on my fingers as she cried out her pleasure.

Bijou's eyes had closed. She looked like she'd had enough, but I was just getting warmed up. I kissed her again, but her response was flat. She was almost asleep. I looked at Shantay.

"I don't think she has anymore in her," Shantay said. "I guess that just leaves us. Unless you're too tired yourself?"

"I'm just warming up," I said. "Come here."

She climbed over Bijou's sleeping body and kissed me. We dragged our hands over each other as the kiss intensified. I rolled on top of her and brought my knee up to her hot, wet center.

"No," she said. "Roll onto your back."

I didn't want to. I wanted to stay right where I was, but if she had other ideas, why not let them play out?

Once on my back, she climbed on top of me and rested her wet pussy on my face. She leaned over and started to devour my own wetness. She had an amazing flavor and I was thoroughly enjoying tasting her.

Until I started to quiver and quake. I was close to an orgasm, yet she hadn't indicated she was anywhere near that point.

"Come for me," she said against me. "Please come for me."

"You first," I said.

"Not gonna happen."

I felt her tongue swipe over my clit, and my world split into a million tiny pieces, before it coalesced again, and I was able to finish her off. I was rewarded with a muffled yell as she still had her face buried between my legs.

"You're quite a lover, Alex," she said.

"You're not so bad yourself."

"Are you tired?"

"Not at all. What time is it?"

"We have an hour and a half."

I knew we'd have to wake up Bijou soon to get her home and have me back safely. But I needed Shantay again. I kissed her, then worked my way down to her pert breasts. Her nipples were small but reactive, and they hardened as I licked them.

"Shit," she said. "I can't believe what you make me feel."

"Go with it. Relax and enjoy."

She reached between us and slid her fingers deep inside me. I returned the favor. We moved in and out of each other in time until we both slid our hands over each other's clit. We rubbed softly at first then with more pressure and soon we cried out and collapsed together.

We lay like that for a few moments, neither of us in any apparent hurry to stop touching the other.

"I'd better get dressed and go get the car," she said.

Reality was back. I wasn't particularly pleased with it.

"I'll wake Bijou."

"I'll see you out front in a minute."

"Wait. Shantay?"

"Yes?"

"May I kiss you again before you go?"

She smiled at me.

"Of course. I'd like that very much."

We kissed for an eternity before she finally stepped back.

"We need to get going. Or I'm going to lose you. And I don't think I could handle that."

Her words hit the very essence of my being. She didn't want to lose me. And, God knows, I didn't want to lose her either. Especially not now.

"Okay. I'll wake her up."

When we got home from dropping a very disoriented Bijou off, the sun was just beginning to crest. I wanted to talk to Shantay. I needed to discuss what had happened. But there was no time.

"Get to your room," she said. "Do you need help up the stairs?"

"I do."

Arm in arm, we took the stairs. She stood outside my door.

"I'll see you tonight, Alex. Rest well."

"Mm." Was all I could manage.

The following night, I awoke and relived the pleasures of the night before in my mind. But I was torn. On one hand, I couldn't wait to see Shantay. On the other, I was afraid it would be awkward. But I couldn't hide in my coffin all night, so I climbed out and went downstairs.

I found Shantay in the gazebo.

"This place is magical, isn't it?" I said.

"It truly is."

"Should we talk about last night?" My stomach was in knots, but I felt we needed to clear the air.

"Sure. If you want."

"What are your thoughts?" I said.

"It's more what are my feelings."

"Really? Okay. What are your feelings?"

"I'm not really sure I can put them into words," said Shantay. "I just know I've never had feelings like these before in my life."

"For Bijou? Or just post coital? Or?"

"For you, Alex. I have feelings for you."

CHAPTER TWELVE

Her words hit me like a freight train. Suddenly, nothing else in the world mattered. Shantay had feelings for me. My feelings were reciprocated. But was that possible? Was it healthy? I sat on the bench next to her, rested my elbows on my knees, and hung my head.

"That's not good," I said.

She shrugged.

"It is what it is. And you? Are you gonna tell me you didn't feel anything last night?"

"Shantay. We can't…"

"Why not?"

I exhaled heavily.

"I can't be in a relationship with a mortal. I won't age and you will, for starters."

"I'd break up with you before then." She laughed. "But seriously, aren't we getting ahead of ourselves? Why not just enjoy what we're feeling? Why not explore what might be there?"

Damn, but she made sense. I longed to take her in my arms, to promise her the moon. But was that fair? To either of us?

"Shantay, I have to be honest. I felt wonderful things when I was with you last night. I feel wonderful things just sitting with you. But I'm scared. I just don't see this happening."

"I'm here. I'm not going anywhere. Why not just up the ante a little? We have feelings for each other. Feelings, apparently, we've both tried to fight. Let's just let it happen, Alex. Let's see where it goes. We may find we're not even compatible."

"Oh, babe. You know we'll be compatible. It was like fireworks last night."

She smiled at me.

"Yes, it certainly was."

I moved so I could sit next to her. I wanted her again right then. I wanted her fiercely. But I had other needs. Realistic needs. I had to feed. It was time.

She moved into my arms and I held her. I was acutely aware of her scent, her shampoo, her body wash. I was more aware of her carotid artery, which pulsed with desire I was sure. Or maybe because I was so hungry, it felt like her artery was pulsing loud and strong. I released her and stood.

"That was abrupt," said Shantay.

"I'm sorry. But the reality of what I am has reared its ugly head."

"How so?"

"Come on. We need to go for a drive."

"You're pale, Alex," she said. "I understand. Where shall we go?"

"I don't know." My brain felt fuzzy and I felt weak. I was hungrier than I had been in a very long time. "Let's just drive and we'll figure it out."

For the first time, I sat in the front seat with Shantay as she drove through the city. We drove through the Central Business District, around the French Quarter, and finally to the outskirts.

My stomach ached from the need. I was cramping up and was scared I wouldn't be able to overpower anybody.

As we drove through some shadier neighborhoods, I saw two men fighting. My keen eyesight told me there were knives involved. Someone would die or be seriously injured. It was my moment.

"Drop me off here," I said. "Drive around the corner. I'll meet you in a few."

I waited until she was gone before I made my way to the men. One ran off as I approached, and I saw the other lying on the ground, bleeding out. I went after the runner and soon caught him.

Terror showed in his eyes as I unsheathed my fangs. I watched his mouth open, but no sound came out.

"You'll pay for what you did," I said. They were the last words he ever heard.

Shantay was in the car right around the corner. I slid in feeling wonderfully human, if that was possible. At any rate, I felt alive. I was bursting with energy and ready to take on the night.

"Where to?"

"I want a drink or two. Fancy a trip to our favorite club?"

"That would be nice."

She parked the car down by Jackson Square and held my hand as we made our way through the crowds. Bourbon Street pulsed with life, and activity and I loved every minute of it. Our favorite bar was filled to overflowing so we moved past it. We found another place, smaller and darker, with no live music, that wasn't crowded at all.

"I don't know," said Shantay. "It doesn't look very safe."

"You're with me. Nothing bad could possibly happen to you."

We had a few drinks and talked about us and me and life.

"How do you decide?" she said.

"Decide what?"

"Who to… You know…"

"Ah. I try to get the bad guys, Shantay."

"And if you couldn't have found a bad guy tonight?"

"I would have. It's not like the early days when I had little or no control. I can be patient when I hunt." She nodded but said nothing. "Do you worry I would turn on you?"

"No! Of course not. I just wonder what would happen if we couldn't find someone for you."

"There will always be people for me. Don't you worry. And you're not an option, Shantay. You're never an option."

"That's good to know." She laughed dryly.

I moved my chair so I was right next to her.

"This is important," I said. "You need to understand and believe me. I would never feed off you nor would I lie to you. I've always been extremely honest with you. Ever since you first figured me out. That's not going to change now. I need you to believe that. Especially if we're going to make an attempt at a relationship."

She brightened visibly.

"So you're willing to try? We can really make a go of it?"

"Sure. Why not? It'll be tricky. But I think we can make it happen. You just have to trust me, Shantay. Please say you'll trust me."

"I will, Alex. I promise."

I stood.

"I want to celebrate. I want to listen to music and dance. Let's get out of this dive."

"I read of another area in town that has live jazz. I think we should check it out."

"Let's do that," I said.

She drove us to the Faubourg Marigny neighborhood where we strolled around listening to the live music coming from just about every establishment. We stepped into one and found a seat in the back, which was the only table available. I ordered a drink and Shantay had an iced tea. I loved that she didn't drink and drive. She was so very conscientious.

I watched Shantay watch the musicians, and something deep inside me roared to life. It had been dormant for hundreds of years but had awakened somewhat the night before. At that jazz club, however, it was alive and well. I was crazy about Shantay. It wouldn't last forever, as my forever and hers were quite different. But I had to give it a chance. I couldn't have denied it if I tried. And God knows I'd tried.

"Would you like to dance?" Shantay said.

"Certainly."

We danced and swirled and tore up the dance floor. There weren't a lot of dancers, so we had plenty of room to move and groove. Shantay was a lovely dancer who followed my lead quite naturally.

Before I was ready, last call was announced. We took our leave and walked back to the car, the music still playing in my head.

"What shall we do now?" I still had a few hours before I had to be asleep.

"Let's head home. We can sit in the gazebo and talk some more."

"Or," I said. "We could go to bed. Just the two of us this time."

She blushed, which I hadn't thought possible. She was so down-to-earth that I didn't think she'd get embarrassed at anything.

"That would be wonderful," she said.

We took our clothes off and climbed into bed. I wanted to have her every which way I could. But I didn't know what she was into and, as this was more than a one-night thing, I wanted to be sure I pleased her any way I could.

We lay on top of the covers admiring each other's bodies. I finally kissed her, and the blood raced through my body. It pounded in my ears as the kiss intensified. The next thing I knew, she was lying on top of me, breasts pressed into me, and I thought I would short-circuit from the simple feel of that.

She sat up, leaving a wet trail on my stomach.

"Tell me your fantasies," said Shantay. "Tell me your deepest desires."

I laughed.

"My dear Shantay, I have so many. But I've lived most of them. What about you?"

"I've always wanted to be tied up and taken. I've never trusted anyone enough though."

"Do you trust me?" I said.

"Implicitly."

I lifted her off of me and grabbed some silk scarves from my nightstand.

"Are you sure about this?" I was serious.

"Please, Alex. Let me live out all my fantasies with you."

I tied her arms and legs to the bedposts.

"You okay?" I asked.

She nodded.

"Now for the pièce de résistance."

I blindfolded her with the last scarf and stood looking down at her luscious naked body. I moved to the foot of the bed where I could admire her glistening center. She was obviously turned on, and that, in turn, aroused me to the point of pain.

There was one more thing I needed from my nightstand, and I took it out and rested it on my pillow.

We started slowly enough, with me kissing her again. She struggled against her restraints as she tried to arch into me, to press her body against mine as our tongues frolicked together.

I kissed down her neck to her breasts, which I sucked and licked until I thought they'd be raw.

"More, Alex. Please don't deny me."

The vibrator that sat on my pillow called to me. I turned it on by her ear and she smiled.

"Oh, God, yes. Please."

I rubbed the vibrator over her taut nipples, pressing into each one. She cried out once, then again.

"Oh, my God. That felt good. I've never come from nipple play before."

"Ah, yes. Let's hope it'll be a life of firsts for you, my dear."

I pressed the tip of the vibrator into her as I moved it lower on her curvy body. I finally buried it inside her, and she seriously struggled against the scarves. I turned the vibrator on high and plunged it in as deep as it would go. I held it there before slowly sliding it out and then driving it back in.

She was beautiful. I watched as she swallowed my toy. The evidence of my arousal ran down my inner thighs. It was tempting to use the vibrator on myself, but I didn't. This was for Shantay. It was her time.

I dragged it out of her and pressed the tip into her clit. She screamed loudly as she found her release yet again.

"No more," she whispered.

I turned off the vibrator and set it on the nightstand. I untied Shantay then removed her blindfold.

"Well?" I said. Though I knew she'd enjoyed it.

"That was magical. It was hotter than I'd even imagined."

"Good, sweetheart. I'm glad you enjoyed it."

I lay down and pulled her close. When her breathing returned to normal, she glanced at the clock.

"We don't have much time now, Alex. May I make love to you now?"

"Please do."

I didn't care that the sun would be up soon. I needed relief from the throbbing between my legs. Relief only Shantay could give me.

With no foreplay, Shantay climbed between my legs. The feel of her mouth on me made my chest tighten. I was already so close. She slipped her fingers inside and moved her talented tongue to my needy clit.

One, two, three swipes was all it took to send me out of my body and into another dimension. I drifted back to earth to find Shantay still pleasing me. I tried to fight it, to hold out as long as I could, but it was no use. She brought me to another climax more powerful than the first.

When I was back in touch with reality, Shantay was snuggled against me on the bed. She felt so right in my arms. I wanted to stay like that all day. But the sun was cresting. I could feel it. Heat seared my skin and threatened my very existence.

"I need to go," I said.

"I understand. May I sleep in here?"

"Of course." I kissed the top of her head. "I'd like that."

That night, we started our evening in bed, then relaxed in the hot tub where I pleased her yet again. I couldn't get enough of Shantay and was so happy we'd decided to take the next step in our relationship.

We showered together, which resulted in me feasting on her again and again until she begged me to stop. We dressed and sat at the hall table.

"What would you like to do now?" I said. "Where shall we go?"

"I'm famished," she said. "I'd love to get some food."

"Great. Let's go out to dinner. I'll drink while you eat."

"Excellent. There's a restaurant we can walk to from here. It's a steak house. Let's check it out."

Dinner was fun. Shantay told me stories about her childhood and how much trouble she used to get into in her hometown of Chicago and of running away to Rio de Janeiro as a teen. She'd been quite a delinquent.

"I so wish I could have known you then," I said.

"Just as I wish I could have known you before. Although I don't know that I would have wanted to know you as a mortal."

"Why's that?"

"I don't think I could have handled life back them. I'm much too modern. I just can't fathom small town living. Much less without modern conveniences."

"It was different," I said. "It was very different."

"Do the memories fade? You've lived through so much. I'm curious if some of the memories disappear to make way for the new ones?"

I shook my head.

"No. I remember my childhood as clearly as you remember yours. I remember modern inventions as easily as you remember the streets of Chicago. They don't fade. No, they're all there."

"What was the most awesome invention you remember?" said Shantay.

"There have been so many. Running water. Flushing toilets. But I think the grandest invention of my time would have to be electricity. Things you take for granted, I lived without for hundreds of years."

"You fascinate me, Alex. You must have been so resilient."

"I lived the way everyone lived. Sort of. With a few exceptions. We never had electricity, so I didn't miss it. You know?"

"I suppose that makes sense. So you lived by candlelight?"

"Exactly. Then gas lanterns."

"Wow."

"Speaking of candlelight, let's light some candles and go to bed."

"I'm with you, Alex. I'm always with you."

CHAPTER THIRTEEN

Days turned into weeks and weeks into months. I was so happy with Shantay. I'd never been happier. We spent our nights exploring New Orleans and our early morning hours exploring each other. Never had I felt so complete, so accepted, and so loved.

We hadn't said those three words to each other, but the feelings were definitely there. For me at least, and I could only assume she felt the same. She seemed to.

One night, about six months after we had gotten together, Shantay was waiting for me downstairs as usual. There was something different about her, though I couldn't quite put my finger on it. She looked seductive sitting there in her khaki shorts and baby blue golf shirt. It wasn't necessarily how she was dressed, though. It was more the way she looked at me. And it made me melt inside.

"Hello, beautiful," I said.

"Greetings, handsome." She stood and kissed me full on my mouth. My toes curled and I grabbed her hand, heading toward the stairs. I was as ready as she apparently was. But she didn't move to follow me.

"What's up?" I said.

"Not yet. I want to wander around. I want to go back to Marie Laveau's grave."

I arched an eyebrow at her.

"That's an odd request."

"Please?"

"You know I'll never deny you."

The drive took less than ten minutes, and Shantay easily found a place to park. She took my hand and we wandered through the cemetery, checking out the old headstones, slowly making our way to the voodoo queen's grave.

There were several people around the tomb, but we walked up and joined them. I looked over at Shantay who had a smirk on her face. I couldn't understand why. I knew not what she was thinking but was oh so curious.

She took my hand and slowly backed away from the grave. I went with her as she led me behind another tomb a row away. She shocked me by taking off her shirt.

"What are you doing?" I whispered.

"Take me, Alex."

"Here? Now?"

"Here. Now."

I looked around, but there was no one in sight. That didn't mean no one would show up any minute.

"Are you sure?" I said.

"Remember when we first got together? You asked me about my fantasies? Well, one of them has always been to be taken in public. I need you to fulfill that fantasy for me."

Coherent thoughts flew from my mind. All that mattered was Shantay needed me and apparently quite desperately. I tried to block out the sounds of the tourists walking by as I backed Shantay against the tomb and kissed her.

She kissed me back with a fervor I hadn't known she possessed. And I knew she possessed a lot. She seemed frantic, almost desperate as we kissed. She pulled me closer, pressing me into her then took my hand and slid it under her bra to find her soft breasts.

Shantay moaned into my mouth as I kneaded her flesh and pinched her nipple. We continued to kiss as she pushed my hand downward. With shaking hands, I unzipped her shorts and slid my hand inside.

I was pleasantly surprised to find she had on no underwear. I was free to make my way to heaven. I entered her with my fingers and pressed my palm against her slick swollen clit.

She quit kissing me and buried her face in my shoulder. She was moving her hips in time with my thrusts, and I didn't know which of us was more aroused. I was lightheaded I was so turned on.

I continued plunging in and out until she bit my shoulder and I heard her muffled cry. She collapsed against me, and I slowly and regrettably withdrew my hand.

"That was so fucking hot," she said.

"Yes, it was. Very."

"Thank you."

"My pleasure," I said. "We can do that whenever you want."

"Next time it'll be in the gardens of Jackson Square."

I laughed.

"I love it. That will be incredible. Now put your shirt on, sweetheart."

"Oh, yeah." She got herself situated and leaned against me. "Thank you again so very much."

"You're more than welcome." I needed my own release, but that moment was all about Shantay. "Where to now, my sweet vixen?"

"Bourbon Street. I need a drink and I think I'd like to dance."

"Sounds good to me." I swallowed hard, willing the throbbing between my legs to cease.

We went to our usual spot and took a table in a corner, away from the stage, so we could talk while we drank.

"So tell me, beautiful, what other fantasies do you have?"

She blushed, looked down, and stirred her drink.

"I don't know."

"Yes, you do." I laughed. "You can tell me anything."

"It's embarrassing."

"Why? It's just me. And I'd almost guarantee it won't be anything I haven't done before."

She arched her eyebrow at me.

"Have you had sex in public before?"

I nodded.

"I suppose so. I've had sex with other vampire women in graveyards. Not that I'm proud of that. But it's happened, although not when anyone else was around really."

"Okay. So tonight was kind of a first for you as well."

"Pretty much. I suppose it was. And I loved it."

"Well, finish your drink. We're going to cruise Bourbon Street looking for ways to fulfill my next fantasy."

"Mm," I said. "Now you're talking."

We were walking along when I heard a voice I recognized.

"Alex? How are you?"

I looked to my left and saw Patricia.

"Patricia. Good to see you. How have you been?"

She glanced from my eyes to my hand, clasped with Shantay's.

"So this is why I haven't seen you in a while," Patricia said.

"Patricia, you remember Shantay?"

"Of course. Congrats. I'm so happy for you both."

"Thank you."

"If you ever want someone to spice up your night. You know, make it a threesome, let me know."

"What are you doing right now?" Shantay shocked me.

Patricia laughed.

"Not a thing. Why?"

"Come on. Let's go have some fun."

My sweet Shantay never ceased to amaze me. Although I knew she liked threesomes, as that was how we ended up together. And another night with Patricia certainly didn't sound like a bad idea to me. Though I didn't need anyone but Shantay, Patricia would add a bit of taboo excitement.

"You're so wet already." Patricia rested her hand on Shantay's crotch when we arrived at the car.

"My woman already took care of me once tonight," Shantay said.

"Do tell."

"She took me in Lafayette Cemetery Number One."

"Ooh," Patricia squealed. "I love it. That's hot."

"It was indeed," I said. "Now, can we stop talking and get home?"

We took the steps slowly, the anticipation building. I hoped I could pay Patricia enough attention. Shantay was my prime interest. But then I remembered the night I'd spent with Patricia and those memories fueled my desire.

The three of us took turns kissing each other, and soon, I was shaking I needed them so desperately. We tried to undress each other, but hands just got in the way.

"Okay," I said. "This isn't working. Let's each undress and get in bed."

"Do you have your friend still?" Patricia said.

"My friend?" Then I remembered I'd used my strap-on with her. "Oh, my friend. Of course I still have it."

"Can we play with it?"

"What friend is that?" asked Shantay.

"You haven't shared with her?" said Patricia.

"Not yet."

They lay on the bed kissing while I got my harness on and put the dildo in place. When I climbed onto the bed, Shantay's eyes grew wide.

"Oh," she said. "I like that. I like that a lot."

She grabbed me by the dildo and positioned me over her.

"Yes," said Patricia. "I want to watch you fuck her with that."

She got on her knees so she could watch Shantay swallow my cock with her pussy. Shantay wrapped her legs around my hips, pulling me deeper. I moved in and out of her while Patricia kept a commentary going.

"This is so fucking hot," she said "Look at her. She's so wet. And listen to the sound you make. This is such a turn-on."

She leaned into me and rubbed my clit, which was swollen to the bursting point. I closed my eyes, tried to keep my rhythm, and fought hard not to come before Shantay. Shantay finally called my name, her legs still wrapped tightly around me.

I lost all ability to think and soon found my own release, then collapsed onto Shantay.

"My turn," Patricia said. "When you're ready."

I gently slid my cock out of Shantay and knelt in front of Patricia, who surprised me by bending over and licking my dildo.

"You taste divine, Shantay," she said. "Though I knew you would."

She licked the tip over and over, eyes closed, obviously savoring my girl's flavor. It was such a turn-on watching her that my clit was soon throbbing yet again. But nothing could have prepared me for Patricia's deep throating me. I watched her swallow my cock, and it took every ounce of energy to remain upright.

Shantay must have seen my reaction because the next thing I knew she was kneeling next to me, sucking on my tender nipples. My whole body shook with unspent passion. I needed to take someone and be taken. And soon.

"Lie back," I finally said to Patricia.

"Oh, no." She got on all fours. "Now you may enter me."

I swallowed hard as I looked at her glistening beauty, but before I could enter her, Shantay licked the length of her, from clit to cunt, and back again.

"Oh, shit," Patricia said. "Please, Alex. I need you."

I gently moved Shantay aside and plunged my rod into Patricia. I buried it as deep as it could go. She moaned and rocked against me. Shantay reached around her and rubbed her clit, and in no time, Patricia let out a guttural moan and collapsed, face down on the pillow.

With shaking hands, I unfastened my harness and threw it on the floor. I lay on my back with my legs wide, ready for either of them to grant me my release.

They were kissing though, and running their hands over each other. The sight frustrated me and aroused me even further. I was about to masturbate to get off when they broke their frenzied kiss and turned their attention to me.

Patricia suckled at my breasts while Shantay licked between my legs. I thrashed my head on the pillow from side to side. I was close. So close. Shantay focused her attention on my clit while Patricia buried her fingers inside me. Together they took me to such a powerful climax that I forgot where I was for a moment. I left my body, soaring high in the atmosphere before slowly drifting back to myself.

They didn't stop though. I lost track of who was doing what, but they took me to three more orgasms, each more powerful than the one before.

When they'd clearly had enough of pleasing me, they went back to kissing, which I watched lazily. I glanced at the clock on the other side of them and realized we needed to end this gig soon. Or I wouldn't live to see another night.

I regretfully tapped Shantay on the shoulder.

"Hm?"

"We need to get Patricia home."

"Why?"

"Shantay, please."

She seemed to come to her senses, because she sat up and looked at the clock.

"Oh, yeah. Come on, Patricia, we should get dressed."

We dropped her off and returned to the house. It had been a night to remember and I filed Patricia in my memory banks for possible future reference.

"Did you enjoy yourself tonight?" I asked Shantay as we lay together on the bed.

"I did. Did you?"

"Very much."

"Good. Patricia was a lot of fun."

"That she was." I felt the heat start beating on me through the curtains. "I need to get to bed, Shantay. You rest well and I'll see you tonight."

"Good night, Alex."

She kissed me and I stumbled down the hall and into my coffin.

The next evening when I awoke, the previous night came back to me the minute I opened my eyes and I was ready to take Shantay again right there. I climbed out of my coffin and headed downstairs. It was then I remembered Shantay saying something about another fantasy. I wondered what that was.

"You look quite chipper tonight," Shantay said.

"I'm feeling quite chipper. How could I not after everything that happened last night?"

"Last night was wonderful. It was amazing. From beginning to end."

"So what are your plans for me for tonight?"

"I don't know. I'm hungry so I'd like some dinner. How are you feeling, hunger-wise?"

"I think I'm okay for now. Though last night took a lot out of me. I think I'll be okay tonight. I'll probably have to feed tomorrow."

"Fair enough. Let's go down to Bourbon Street."

"Hoping to see Patricia again?" I laughed. She did too.

"No. Just want food, drink, and to explore."

"What are we exploring?" I said.

"You'll see."

After dinner, drinking, and dancing, Shantay took my hand and led me back out to the throngs on Bourbon Street. It was as if her head was on a spinner as she looked left and right and left again as we walked along.

"What are you looking for, exactly?" I said.

"You'll see."

I walked along beside her, waiting to see what had her so excited. I was patient and knew I'd find out in time.

"Here." She pulled me up on the sidewalk.

I glanced up and saw that we were standing in front of a sex shop.

"Oh my." I laughed. "I've used my vibrator and dildo on you already. What more do you want?"

"You'll see."

Her mysterious air amused me. She was like a little kid as she wandered the aisles. The store was bigger than it looked from the outside, and we spent quite a bit of time simply looking around.

"Here." She stopped, and I looked at the row of butt plugs and anal beads.

"Oh, yeah," I said. "I learn yet another fantasy of my baby. Which one do you want?"

"I don't know," she said. "I've never had anal sex before. Which one is for a beginner?"

I held up a link of gigantic beads.

"Okay. Definitely not these."

"No." She laughed. She picked up a small butt plug. "What about this?"

"That looks to be about perfect for a beginner." I picked up a tube of lube. "Can't forget this."

We paid and went back to meander the street.

"Did you want to go home now?" I said. "You want to try out your new purchase?"

"Not right now," she said. "I'm happy just knowing we have it."

Chapter Fourteen

The next few weeks continued to be the happiest of my existence. I couldn't get enough of Shantay both physically and emotionally. She was such an exciting lover and proved to be up for anything.

Though try as I might, she continued to say she wasn't ready to try the butt plug yet. Fair enough. I wasn't in any hurry. I'd be ready when she was. She carried it with her wherever we went. She always had it in her pocket and I always wondered what night would be the night. I continued to wonder.

The days were growing longer, which meant our time together was shorter. I was half tempted to move to the southern hemisphere for the next few months but didn't want the hassle. So we enjoyed what time we did have.

One night in the middle of July, I awoke filled with wonder of what the night held in store. I found Shantay in my bedroom and my strap-on laying on the bed.

"What's this about?" I said.

"I want you to wear this."

"Okay. So we're not going out tonight?"

She grinned at me.

"Oh yes, we are."

"And I'm to wear this? Out?"

"Please."

As usual, I couldn't say no to her. I dutifully put on my harness and dildo then slipped on slacks and a green golf shirt.

"You look delicious," said Shantay. "I could eat you up right now."

"I wouldn't object."

She laughed.

"I'm sure you wouldn't."

"And where are we going with me all equipped and whatnot?"

"Jackson Square."

"Your wish is my command," I said.

We parked and walked toward the square. I felt overly aroused with my dildo slapping my leg as we walked. I was sure I'd get to use it that night and that thrilled me. I loved burying it deep inside Shantay and watching her grind into it.

We used it frequently, as it was a favorite of both of us. We arrived at Jackson Square and she headed straight for the gate to the gardens. It was locked.

"Shit," she said. "It closed at seven."

"Is it imperative we go in there?"

"Yes. I need to be in the garden."

"If you insist."

I broke the lock and eased open the gate to let us in. I closed it and arranged the lock so it looked untouched. I took her hand and she guided me through the garden. We walked along the paths and stared up at the statue of General Jackson.

Eventually, she dragged me to one of the clumps of palms. She looked at me, longing in her eyes.

"What's up?" I said.

She dropped her shorts and faced the tree, legs spread.

"Take me, Alex," she whispered.

Hotter words had never been spoken to me. I dragged my fingers along her opening before thrusting inside. She was hot and wet. Oh, so wet. I unzipped my slacks and pressed against her.

At first, I simply ran my cock along her, allowing the tip to tease her nerve center.

"No more," she breathed. "Don't tease me."

But I couldn't help myself. I slipped just the tip inside her. She leaned back to get more, but I pulled out. After several times doing this, and seeing her attempting to take all of me, I thrust the whole unit inside her.

"Yes," she said. Loudly. I looked around, but no one else was there.

I continued to move in and out of her until she leaned back against me, shuddered, and moaned. I waited a few moments before I slid out of her and zipped my slacks.

"That was amazing," she said.

"I certainly enjoyed myself."

"Good. Thanks for being such a good sport."

"Always."

"Let's go get a drink. I need one."

We wandered Bourbon Street in search of a hole in the wall. Throngs of people lined the streets, and most of the bars were filled to overflowing. We finally happened upon a dive toward the west end of the street, just past Iberville. There was no live music, but it was dark and relatively empty. We sat at a table in the corner sipping our drinks.

"What other treats do you have in store for me tonight?" I said.

"I don't know. That was pretty much a fantasy come true. It was dangerous and hot and felt fucking fantastic. I don't know that I have anything else up my sleeve for tonight."

"Then we shall just relax and chat and enjoy each other."

"That sounds marvelous," she said.

"I would like to take another trip to the toy store."

Her eyes widened.

"You would, would you?"

"Mm. I have dirty thoughts of my own, you know."

She laughed.

"Oh, that doesn't surprise me at all."

We had our three drinks then wandered back up Bourbon Street until we came to the sex shop. There were very few other customers in it, and we cruised the aisles unashamed.

"What are you looking for?" said Shantay.

"I'll know it when I see it."

"Fair enough."

We ended up in an aisle of dongs.

"Would you like me to buy a bigger one?" I asked.

"Sure. I think I could take more."

"Choose one. I'll keep looking around."

I found myself in an aisle of battery-operated devices. I found a vibrator that was very slim. It was hardly thicker than my finger. Satisfied, I took it to the cashier where Shantay was waiting for me.

"What did you find?"

"It's a surprise," I said. "Now please wait for me out front."

She left and I paid for the supersized dildo and the thin vibrator. What an interesting combination. I met her out front.

"Are you ready to head home? I don't have much time left before sunrise."

"Sure. Let's do it."

Back in my room, I pulled Shantay against me and kissed her full lips. She was so beautiful and so sexy and so fucking desirable. I needed her again and she seemed to be thinking the same thing.

I quickly removed her clothes before stripping and climbing on the bed with her. We kissed and kissed and kissed some more. Her tongue was demanding as it sought mine. And when they met, my world tilted off its axis.

"All fours," I breathed. "Now."

She got on her hands and knees, and the sight of all her holes on display made my insides clench with desire.

I took the thin vibrator and used the tip to tease around her lips. First her outer lips, then her inner lips.

"Inside," she begged. "Please."

I slid it inside and she looked back at me.

"That's not enough. It's tiny. Give me more. Please."

"Patience, my dear."

I moved it around inside here, coating it with her juices. Then I withdrew it.

"Do you trust me?" I said.

"Always."

I pressed the tip of the vibrator against her puckered nether hole. She jumped, then seemed to relax slightly.

"I'm not going to do anything you don't want," I said. "Do you understand?"

She nodded and I pressed the tip inside.

"Oh fuck," she said. "That feels so fucking good."

I slid my cock in her pussy, and she rocked back against me as I slid the vibrator in another centimeter. I longed to bury the vibrator deep but knew I had to be cautious. She'd never been penetrated there before, and far be it from me to violate her trust.

It wasn't easy to fuck her pussy and focus on her ass, and I struggled as my own arousal reached dangerous heights. My hand shook as I eased the vibrator a little farther inside. Concentration was hard to come by and, rather than do something we might regret, I tossed the vibrator on the bed and finished her off with my cock.

When she was lying face down on her pillow, I lay next to her and kissed her neck and back.

"Are you okay?" I said.

"Never better."

"Good."

She rolled over and looked at me.

"That vibrator felt wonderful," she said. "Why did you stop?"

"I was losing my ability to think and worried I would just bury it inside you before you were ready."

"I think I was ready."

"Duly noted."

"It really turns you on to make love to me, doesn't it?"

"Words cannot express."

With no pretense, she climbed between my legs and brought me to one powerful orgasm after another with her talented tongue.

We lay cuddled together in silence until I began to feel the burn.

"Babe?"

"Hm?"

"I need to get to sleep."

"Already?" She pouted.

"I'm afraid so. If I wait much longer, I'll sleep here and that would be the end of me."

"Do you need me to walk you to your room?"

"I think I do."

We dressed quickly, and I leaned heavily on her as I limped my way down the hall. It was with great relief that I fell into my coffin and closed the lid.

When I woke the next night, I found Shantay dressed in a tan denim miniskirt with a short-sleeved pink-and-white broad-striped shirt. She looked like something from days gone by.

"What's up with the outfit?" I kissed her hello.

"There's an eighties party tonight. I want to go."

"What do you remember about the eighties?" I laughed.

"Not a thing. I was just a little one in that decade, but I've heard stories of how fun it was to have grown up then. What do you remember?"

"Cocaine," I said. "Everyone was using it. I used it. I enjoyed it. But mostly I remember the flavor of it in the blood I drank."

"Really? You could taste it in the blood?"

"I could indeed. And it kept me hyped up. I loved the eighties." I laughed.

"Can we go to the party?"

"Have I ever denied you?"

"Not yet."

"Where did you find that outfit?" I asked.

"I found it at a thrift store."

"It looks great.

"Thanks. Do you have anything from the eighties you can wear?"

"Probably. Let's go look through my clothes."

We settled on tan slacks and a mint golf shirt under a pink golf shirt. We starched the collars of both shirts and popped them. Shantay crossed her arms and laughed.

"You look so totally eighties," she said.

"Good." She kissed me. "Do that again and we won't be going anywhere."

"Oh no, you don't. If you get too hot, you'll wilt your collars."

It was my turn to laugh. I realized then how often Shantay made me laugh. And how good that felt. I was crazy about her. Simply crazy.

The party was a house party. Very eighties. The house was dimly lit with mirrors laid out on every surface. It was very amusing. Posters of *The Breakfast Club* and other popular movies lined the walls.

Everyone was dressed in character. There were about a hundred people there, and they all looked authentic. Ages ranged from people who had obviously lived through the decade, to people Shantay's age, and even younger.

Duran Duran blared from the speakers, and Shantay pulled me to the center of the living room to dance. The Cars came on next, and as we were dancing, Shantay started laughing uncontrollably.

"What's so funny?" I said.

"You know every word to every song."

"Heck yeah." I wasn't embarrassed. "That decade had the best music."

When she'd tired of the music, we made our way to the kitchen where there was a keg as well as bottles for mixing drinks.

"What would you like to drink?" I asked.

"Let's keep it authentic." She moved to the keg.

We filled our cups and went upstairs to see what was going on up there. There were two pool tables and a wall of video games like Pac-Man and several pinball machines.

"Let's play pinball," I said.

"I don't know how."

"I'll teach you."

"Don't you two look adorable?"

I turned to see Patricia standing there.

"Hi," I said. "Shantay, you remember Patricia, don't you?"

"Of course." She smiled. "Good to see you again."

Patricia was wearing high-waisted shorts, a Depeche Mode T-shirt with her sleeves rolled up, and green high-top Reeboks. She was stunning.

"You look every bit the eighties girl," I said.

"I tried. It was either dress like this or try to dress like Madonna."

"There are plenty of Madonnas here," Shantay said.

"That there are. Would you mind if I joined you?" Patricia asked.

"That would be great. We were just about to start a new game."

"I've never played pinball before," she said.

"It's not hard," said Shantay. "Once you get the hang of it."

Watching them shake their asses as they used body English to try to get the ball to the right slot had my palms itching and my clit twitching. I was ready for more games with these two. Pinball was a nice warmup, but I wanted more.

At one point, Shantay was taking her turn and I was sipping my beer when Patricia leaned into me.

"There are lots of bedrooms up here," she said.

"That there are."

"I wonder if we could sneak into one."

"You do, do you?"

"Your turn," Shantay said.

Patricia winked at me and took her turn.

"What were you two talking about?" Shantay asked me.

"She was just wondering if we could all sneak into a bedroom."

"Oh, shit. That would be fucking awesome. Can you imagine? A threesome surrounded by all these people?"

"I suppose you'd even want to leave the door unlocked?"

"Sure. If someone happened upon us it would be off the charts."

I laughed.

"I love you and your exhibitionist side."

"Thanks. I love being a semi-exhibitionist."

I kissed her and was soon lost in the kiss. I cupped her ass and ground her pelvis into mine. We kissed so long I forgot where we were. Soon I felt lips on the back of my neck and moaned into Shantay's mouth. My nipples tightened and I shivered as the second pair of lips found my earlobe.

Finally, I broke the kiss with Shantay and stepped away from Patricia.

"We need to find a room. And fast," I said.

They nodded their agreement and we started down a long, dark hall with eight doors lining it. Each door was locked. Were people already in there? Or were they locked because they were off limits? My libido was in high gear and I had to find a room to share with Shantay and Patricia. I wouldn't give up.

I saw light at the end of the hall and followed it to a bathroom. That would do.

"Come on, you two," I called.

"Not the bathroom," Shantay said.

"Why not?"

"That would be rude. People will need it. Let's find someplace else."

"There is no place else," I pleaded.

"There has to be. What's that door there?" She motioned to a door on the right side of yet another hallway.

I followed her and Patricia opened the door to a nice size walk-in closet.

"This will do," said Shantay. "This will do just fine."

CHAPTER FIFTEEN

As soon as the door closed behind us, we were in each other's arms. We kissed, our hands roamed, partners were swapped. After a few minutes of this, Shantay pulled away from us.

"Where are you going?" I asked.

She didn't answer, but flipped the switch on the wall, flooding the small room with light. At first it was painful to me, but I quickly grew accustomed to it.

"Was that necessary?" Though I knew the answer. She simply smiled at me and took her shirt off.

"Are we getting naked in here?" Patricia sounded nervous.

"I'm not," I said. "But Shantay obviously is."

Shantay lay on the hardwood floor, naked as a jaybird, legs wide, knees bent, putting herself on display for both Patricia and me. My mouth watered at the sight of her wet lips begging for attention.

Before I could act, Patricia was between her legs feasting on Shantay's deliciousness. I lay next to them and slipped my hand down Patricia's jeans. I pulled her thong to the side and buried three fingers inside her.

I heard her moan against Shantay and found myself more turned on than I had been in a long time. Which was hard to believe because Shantay kept me aroused beyond measure. I found Patricia's clit and gently stroked it. She arched into me, gyrating her hips against my fingers and she continued to devour Shantay.

Shantay let out a scream I'm sure the whole house heard, and Patricia collapsed as well. The ladies had had their fun. That was good, but I was still needing their attention.

"Please get naked, babe," Shantay said. "I want at all of you."

I stripped and lay back. Patricia kissed me, sharing Shantay's unique flavor with me. I ran my tongue over hers, savoring every drop. Shantay was between my legs, teasing me with her tongue.

Patricia moved to my breasts, which she sucked and bit, causing me to arch my hips and force my wet center into Shantay's face. Shantay slid her fingers inside me and sucked my clit. Between the two of them, it took no time for my world to splinter as I rode the crest of the climax.

I dressed quickly, but Shantay didn't seem to be in any hurry. I was ready to get back to the party and see what was going on. Shantay began to stroke herself between her legs, and I couldn't resist. I lay next to her, sucked her nipples, and used my fingers to coax another orgasm out of her.

Patricia just watched, lids at half mast, obviously aroused.

"Do you need another turn?" Shantay asked her.

"No, thanks," Patricia said. "I'll save some for later."

"Later?" I said.

"Why not?" said Shantay.

"Later indeed then. Come on, beautiful, get dressed."

Shantay dressed and we went back downstairs to get more beer. We danced to the Go-Gos, Dexys Midnight Runners, Michael Jackson, and more Cars.

The three of us were inseparable for the rest of the night. We drank, danced, and teased each other until the wee hours of the morning.

"Let's go back to my place," Patricia finally said.

We parked our car and found her waiting at the top of her stairs.

Inside, she pulled aside the beads hanging at one end of her living room and invited us into her bedroom. We all disrobed and found space on her double bed. We tangled tongues and limbs as we prepared for yet another glorious escape.

I found myself on top of Shantay and wasn't complaining, until I noticed Patricia was absent. She returned with lined handcuffs and fastened Shantay's hands to the headboard. I knew Shantay would be in heaven and watched as Patricia tied her feet, spread-eagle, to the foot of the bed.

"We're going to make you feel things you've never felt before," Patricia said.

"I'm up for that." Shantay was all smiles.

"Where to start?" I was practically drooling as I looked at Shantay all spread out and vulnerable.

"Anywhere, please," said Shantay.

I kissed her and cupped a breast, kneading it as our tongues played over each other. Patricia had disappeared again, and I only vaguely wondered where she was. I was perfectly content with Shantay, my woman.

Patricia returned this time with a flesh colored dildo that was almost as big as the one Shantay had picked out from the toy store. Shantay lifted her head off the pillow and her eyes grew wide.

"Is that going in me?"

"You'd better believe it," said Patricia.

I smiled down at Shantay before lowering my mouth to lick her breasts and suck her nipples. Patricia surprised me by lying next to Shantay. She lay on her back and buried the huge dildo inside herself.

I couldn't resist. I reached a hand out and massaged her clit until she came. Then, with no down time, Patricia slid the dong to its hilt inside Shantay. I heard it enter her and my own clit swelled.

One eye open, I watched Patricia fuck her as I continued to tease Shantay's nipples. I had to force my tongue to move and lick and play as I was totally into watching Patricia.

I kissed down Shantay's belly until I could smell her essence. I looked at the dildo as it slid out covered in her juices. Patricia buried it to the base and pressed and released, pressed and released as if trying to drive it farther than it could possibly go.

Shantay was ready for release, and I dragged my tongue over her throbbing clit until she screamed, louder and longer than I'd ever heard before. Clearly, she was satisfied.

I lay back, craving my own satisfaction. I needed one or both of them to take me to the other side of the moon. Before either of them touched me though, I felt the burning, the searing of my skin and knew I had to hurry.

"Come on, Shantay. We should get home."

"So soon?" said Patricia. "We're just getting started."

"Raincheck?" I handed Shantay her clothes, found mine, and quickly put them on. Shantay helped me down the stairs and to the car. The windows were tinted but provided little protection against the light of the rising sun.

She helped me to my room, and I fell headfirst into my coffin, dead to the world.

"This morning was a close one," I told Shantay that night.

"I'm so sorry. I completely lost track of time."

"As did I. We won't make that mistake again."

"No," said Shantay. "We won't."

We walked out to the gazebo in silence and I tried to think of something to say but couldn't concentrate on anything but the gnawing in my gut.

"What would you like to do tonight?" she said.

"I'm sorry, baby, but I need to feed. It's been too long, and the sun did a real number on me. I need blood to get my strength back."

She stood.

"Let's go then. We'll find you a meal."

"Thank you."

I stood on shaky legs. I felt weak, fatigued. It wasn't a good feeling. I liked being strong, self-assured, confident. I'd feel better soon. I knew I would.

"Where to?" Shantay started the car.

"Anywhere. Just get me somewhere quickly please."

"Could you feed off me?" she said.

I was shocked and appalled.

"I don't want to kill you."

"But couldn't you drink a little? Just for sustenance."

"Thank you. I appreciate that. I really do. But that's not a good habit to get into."

"Okay. Just thought I'd offer."

She stopped the car in a neighborhood whose streetlights were all burned out. People were milling in and out of establishments, mostly rundown, dimly lit bars.

"Park the car around the corner," I said. "Keep your doors locked and your windows up."

"I will. I won't let anything happen to me. I promise."

I wandered in and out of the bars, looking for someone who deserved to die. I hated thinking like that, but it was part of my makeup. I had to accept it. There were lowlifes and derelicts by the dozen, but none struck me as trouble.

At the final bar, a fight broke out. A group of men were hitting each other with pool sticks and barstools. The fight flowed out into the street and I followed. Punches were thrown and people were collapsing.

Finally, it was down to two men. One swung at the other and missed. The second pulled a switchblade. Before he could drive it into the unsuspecting first man, I grabbed his arm.

"Let me go," he slurred.

"Not a chance."

The first man fell to the ground and passed out. I dragged the man with the knife around the building. Behind it, in the darkness, I bared my fangs and drank my fill. I closed the wounds and left the lifeless man in a heap. I straightened my clothes and found my way back to Shantay.

"How was it?" She put the car in drive.

"Satisfying."

"Good. Where to now?"

"Let's go soak in the hot tub," I said. "I'm really wiped out still. I think a quiet night will do me good."

"Okay, Boss."

We sat in the bubbles quietly, each of us relaxing. It felt good. The jets on my shoulders were working their magic. I opened my eyes and chanced a glance at Shantay, whose eyes were closed, and head was back. I took in her arched neck and, without thinking, crossed the tub to nibble on it.

"Mm. That feels good," she said.

"I'm glad." I found her center. She wasn't quite ready for me, but I was sure that would soon change.

"I thought you were too tired," she teased me.

"Never for you, my dear. Never for you."

I kissed her mouth gently, lovingly. We kissed like that for a few moments before she shifted to face me. She pressed her voluptuous breasts into mine as her mouth opened and we kissed as lovers do.

As we kissed, I dragged my hand along her inner thigh. I felt it quivering and knew she would be close. I tested the waters again and found her ready for me. I entered her, and she threw her head back and let out an animalistic cry.

"Already?" I said.

"I'm not through," she whispered.

"Good."

I pleased her for hours and finally she said she'd had enough.

"I'm ready to go inside."

"What would you like to do?" I said.

"Explore every inch of you."

"Now there's something I can agree to."

We rinsed off in the shower then dried each other. When we were dry, we lay on the bed, me on my back and her resting her head on my chest. I'd thought she had plans for me and made myself wait patiently until she was ready. I was beyond ready, having never quite finished the night before.

Eventually, Shantay dragged her hand down to rest it on my belly. My muscles rippled at her touch. I took her wrist and placed her hand on my wetness. Her hand came alive and her fingers poked and prodded. She was inside me and on me and around me and I was so close to release I could taste it.

She continued to please me, and my world went black before it exploded into bright colors as I shivered my release. I lay catching my breath, barely aware that Shantay had left the bed. I looked at her when she made the mattress shake by climbing back on.

I saw the mischievous grin on her face then looked down to see the harness around her legs with my dildo sticking straight out.

"Is that right?" I said.

"May I?"

"Of course."

"I...well...that is... I've never worn one of these before. What do I do?"

"Lay on your back," I said.

She did so and I climbed on top of her. I held myself up then guided myself back down on top of the toy.

"Oh, fuck, that's hot," she said.

"Yeah?"

"Oh yeah."

I buried the dildo as far as it would go and moved around on it, loving the feel of it hitting everywhere inside.

"Oh, shit," she said. "You're getting me wet."

I climbed off and turned around, facing her feet. I climbed back on and moved up and down, easing it in and out. Shantay was gripping my ass cheeks like her life depended on it. I finally buried the dildo all the way and ground into it again.

I buried my fingers in her hot, tight center which excited me even more than being filled with her cock. The angle wasn't ideal, but I finger fucked her as best as I could. When I was teetering near unconsciousness, I used one hand to rub her clit, and the other to rub my own. We cried out simultaneously as our bodies rocked on the waves of orgasms.

"That was so fucking hot," she finally said. "Like, beyond."

"Mm. I agree. I'm going to climb off now, okay?"

"Okay. Will you put it on then?"

"If that's what you want."

"I do."

We got the harness off her and got me strapped in. She bent over and took me in her mouth. It was the hottest sight I'd ever seen. She licked me like a popsicle before deep-throating me.

"You taste so good. Like, you're indescribably delicious," she said.

"I'm glad you think so."

She used her mouth on me until I could stand it no more.

"Lay back," I said. "Spread your legs for me."

She did so and I guided my cock inside her. At first, I entered with only the tip, but she begged me for more. I entered halfway.

"Please," she said. "Give it to me, Alex."

I slid the whole thing in, withdrew it slowly, then slammed it back in deep. She arched off the bed, meeting every thrust. She was moving quickly, up and down and around and I continued my rhythm knowing she would get herself where she needed to be.

She got there, calling my name into the night as she came. When she was coherent again, she took the dildo out of the harness and entered me. I spread my legs wide and welcomed her. She fucked me royally until I felt my world crumble as I lost touch with reality, then came to to find her lying next to me, smiling.

"What's up?" I was still breathing heavily.

"We have so much fun," she said. "You're a fun playmate and an excellent lover."

"I could say the same about you."

"Thank you."

"Mm. My pleasure. Now let's shower again and hit the road. I'm ready to party."

"Party? I don't know that my legs will hold me at this point."

I laughed.

"Give them a try. Surely a few drinks and some music sound good to you."

"If they sound good to you, then they sound good to me."

"That's what I like to hear."

I helped her off the bed.

CHAPTER SIXTEEN

August meant slightly shorter days, but not by much. Still, any extra moment with Shantay was a blessing to me. I took her out to dinner in the middle of the month and sat watching her enjoy her plate while I sipped my wine.

"Do you ever miss it?" she said.

I had no idea what she was talking about.

"Miss what?"

"All the women?"

I straightened in my seat and looked her dead in the eye.

"Nope. You're woman enough for me, baby girl. Besides, we've been known to bring other women to bed with us."

She shrugged.

"Sure we have. But you were quite the womanizer."

"And how did that make you feel?" I said.

"What do you mean?"

"I mean, assuming you had feelings for me back then, how did it make you feel to see me with a different woman almost every night?"

She carefully chewed her mouthful, took a sip of wine, and looked into the distance.

"I suppose I was jealous. But not necessarily of them."

"How do you mean?"

"I mean, I don't think I realized that I had feelings for you. I think I was just jealous that you were constantly getting some while I had settled into pretty much a celibate existence."

I smiled at her. That had to have been so hard for her. I hadn't ever considered her needs. She was always just my faithful driver at my beck and call. I didn't think she'd ever had a night off while in my employ.

"I've not treated you very well, have I?" I said.

"You treat me wonderfully."

"Sure, now that you're my partner. But not while you were my driver."

"I'm still your driver, aren't I? And is that what else I am? I've moved up from girlfriend?"

"Yes, my dear. I consider you my partner. I want to spend as much time with you as I can. And maybe I shouldn't continue to employ you. Maybe I should give you enough to retire. Would you stay with me?"

"Of course. I'm not going anywhere. And you can pay me or not. I can't remember the last time I've spent a dime of my own."

"Okay. That settles it. You're fired."

"Thank you."

"But seriously, you'll need your own spending money. I don't want you to be totally reliant on me."

"I have plenty of money. You've always paid me well, and I've never had time to spend any of it. So I have a nice nest egg."

"Great. That makes me happy."

She finished her dinner and we walked through the neighborhood. The old houses were beautifully kept up, and I loved each one of them. Shantay stopped in front of one and took a picture. The house was old and dark with lots of plants in the front yard.

"What's so special about this house?" I asked.

"It was the inspiration for a bunch of books."

"Yeah? What were the books about?"

"Vampires," she said.

"Vampires? You've read books about vampires?"

"I have. Though I didn't believe in them."

"Ah. So I wasn't your first?" I laughed.

"You're my first and my last."

"Good answer."

We strolled farther and finally ended up at home. She got her keys out of her pocket.

"Are we going somewhere?"

"To the French Quarter."

"Sounds good to me."

"I thought we'd have some fun."

"I'm always up for fun," I said. "What sort of fun did you have in mind?"

"You'll see."

She parked next to Jackson Square and I smiled, wondering if we'd be breaking into the garden again. As we walked past though, she stopped among a group of people.

"What are we doing?" It was then I saw the sign a young man held.

Vampire Tours, it said.

"Are you serious?" I was amused and somewhat irritated.

"Sure. I thought it would be good for a laugh."

"Okay. As long as you're not looking to learn more than I could teach you myself."

"Relax, you. This is all in fun."

And fun it was. "True" stories filled the heads of all these tourists and had them gasping. Several people started checking over their shoulders as we walked on. It was all fun and games as we made our way through the French Quarter.

Until we came to the convent. Our tour guide told us how the caskets found in the abandoned third floor were supposedly how the first vampires came to the new world. She droned on about how, even today, one needed special permission to be allowed to enter that floor.

My skin prickled and the hair on the back of my neck stood up. I could sense others. Beings like myself had definitely been there. Were they still there? I struggled to sense something, anything that would let me know, but I couldn't be sure. One thing I did sense was danger. Whoever had been there, or whoever was still there, was definitely foe, not friend.

The tour moved on, but I stayed glued to my spot, staring at the third floor.

"Are you okay?" Shantay said.

"I don't know."

"What's going on? You don't look like you're having fun anymore."

"They were here," I said. "They may still be here. This part's not bullshit."

"Oh fuck. Are you serious? Are you sure?"

"Dead sure."

"Do you want to look around? Or should we join the group?" said Shantay.

"No. Whoever's here is dangerous. We need to get out of here."

We joined the group at the "vampire bar." It was a lovely dark bar with dark oak walls and ceiling. Everyone was in a joyous mood, and I tried to join in but couldn't quit thinking about the convent.

"Did y'all enjoy yourselves?" The tour guide had made her way over to us. "What was your favorite part?"

"It was all fun," Shantay said. "It was a great way to spend an evening."

"Fun?" said the tour guide. "So you're not a believer?"

"We believe," I said. "And I really think there was something to your story about the convent. I'll be doing some research on it to learn more."

"That's great. I'm glad we got under your skin. At least a little." She cast a sideways glance at Shantay, who laughed.

"I'm a believer," she said. "I believe vampires still roam the earth to this day. I just don't know how much I believe about the vampires who supposedly lived here."

"Well," said the guide, "you do your research like your friend here. I think you'll be surprised."

"Oh, I will."

"Great." The tour guide walked off to mingle with some others and Shantay turned to look at me.

"Are you really okay? You look a little pale."

"I'm still shaken. I haven't felt vibes like that in decades, possibly longer. It was unsettling to be sure."

"And you're sure you don't want to go back there? We could look around. They wouldn't hurt you, would they?"

"'They' being the key word. If there's a coven there they could easily overpower me. I'm strong, very strong due to my age. But who knows how old they are? And how many there are? I could be committing suicide by looking around there."

"But if they were here, wouldn't you have sensed their existence before? Like wouldn't you have run into them by now?"

"I haven't been here that long, really. And who knows where they roam? Where they hunt? If they need to hunt? I don't know, Shantay. It's very nerve-wracking to think of."

"Sounds like it. Should we get you home now?"

"I think I'd like another drink, if you don't mind. And then I'm feeling the need to hunt. I'm sorry. I just need to keep my strength up."

"Don't apologize, Alex. You never need to apologize to me for being who you are."

I wanted a kiss. I needed to kiss her. But I couldn't. Not in that vampire bar surrounded by redneck-looking tourists. I did, however, squeeze her hand before going back to the bar to get us a couple more drinks.

Most of the tourists had departed by the time we finished our drinks.

"You ready to get out of here?" said Shantay.

"Yeah. Let's hit the slums."

She drove us to the worst part of the city where crime was rampant. I admonished her, yet again, to keep her windows up and doors locked as she waited for me. Then, I went in search of a donor.

I wandered past an alley where I heard a muffled scream. A woman was pressed to the ground by a large man who had one hand over her mouth and the other unzipping his fly. I sped down the alley and pulled him off of her.

"Run," I said. She ran. As fast as she could.

When she was out of sight, I held the man up against a wall by his neck.

"What the fuck do you think you were doing?" I was seething. I looked into his eyes which shone with terror.

"We were just having a little fun. She wanted it."

"Bullshit."

I bent his head to the side and drank. When his body no longer contained life, I dropped him in a heap and went in search of Shantay.

She was parked just where she had said she would be but when I arrived, the car was surrounded by three men. Two had baseball bats and looked like they were ready to beat my car. I was not amused. Fury tore through me when I thought of how terrified my Shantay must have been.

The men turned their attention to me as I approached. They circled, surrounding me. I wasn't worried. I knew I could take them. And, having just fed, I knew my gifts were at an all-time high.

"Why don't y'all mosey on back to where you came from?" I tried to keep my voice calm.

"You're a woman?" One of them leered at me. "Are you a fuckin' dyke?"

"We don't want any trouble," I said.

"We're gonna teach you what it's like to have a man."

I shook my head slowly.

"I wouldn't advise that."

"I don't give a fuck what you advise," a large man with a bat said.

He swung at my head and I ducked, grasping the bat in my right hand. I swung it over my head with him still hanging on. I tossed him down the street. The others ran off, tails between their legs.

My adrenaline was still pumping as I slid into the car.

"Are you okay?" I said.

"I was getting a little nervous." Her voice shook. "I'm glad you arrived when you did."

"So am I. Are you okay to drive?"

She nodded and started the car.

"Where to?"

"Bourbon Street," I said. "Let's have a couple more drinks and calm our nerves."

"Excellent idea."

I held her hand as we drove toward the French Quarter and could feel her eventually relax a little. She parked the car and I pressed her against it, kissing her hard with a promise of what was to come.

"I'm so sorry that happened," I said. "I'll hunt on my own from now on."

"No, you won't. I'm here for you."

"But when I hunt in less desirable parts of town, you'll stay behind. I can walk. Or run or whatever. The point is, I won't have you experience that level of fear again."

"I appreciate what you're saying, but—"

"But nothing. My mind is made up. I care about you. Deeply. What would have happened if I hadn't shown up when I did? It could have been bad. Awful. And I'd never forgive myself if something happened to you. I don't know how I could go on."

"You say the sweetest things, Alex. And, okay. I'll stay behind on nights you hunt. Now. About those drinks?"

We found a place playing zydeco and got a couple of drinks. We danced, drank, laughed, and overall relaxed. It was a good time. One I'd reflect on for decades to come. The color was back in Shantay's cheeks and her eyes shone with adoration rather than fear. Life was good.

We got home a little after three and I was in an amorous mood. I was ready to show Shantay how much she meant to me. She needed to be reassured that she was the most important thing in my life. The pleasure that would come with it was simply icing on the cake.

Shantay and I kissed, naked, on the bed for what seemed an eternity. I kissed down her cheek and nibbled on her earlobe, loving the feel of her squirming under me.

"Tell me another fantasy," I said. "Anything. Let me make it come true."

"Let me be in charge," she said. "Let me call the shots."

I was a bit taken aback, but if that's what she wanted…

"Okay." I rolled off her and lay on my back. "Do what you want." She got up and went to my dresser.

"May I?" she said.

"Of course."

She took her time looking through my playthings then tossed a dildo on the bed with one hand while she kept her other hand hidden behind her back.

"Anything goes?" she said.

"Anything at all."

There was nothing, absolutely nothing, she could do that I hadn't done before. I'd been around for centuries, after all.

She climbed on top of me, straddling my waist, and kissed me. Hard. I kissed back with equal fervor, my own arousal reaching new heights as I felt her wetness on my stomach. She was as turned on as I, if that was possible.

Shantay scooted lower and took my nipple in her mouth. She pinched, tugged, and twisted the other one. I was bucking on the bed at that point. I loved having my nipples played with.

"Your nipples get so long," she said.

"Mm," was all I could manage.

She finally opened the hand she'd kept clasped and I saw what she had. My hormones raged out of control at the sight. There were two little roach clip looking things and I knew what was coming.

She pinched them open and closed them on my nipples. I moaned in pleasure.

"You like that, do you?" she said.

"God, yes."

She moved between my legs and teased my lips and clit with the head of the dildo.

"You're beautiful down here."

"Thank you?" I didn't want to talk. I wanted, needed, her to fuck me.

She barely placed the tip inside me.

"More," I begged her.

Shantay buried it inside me. All the way inside me. I swear I felt its tip in my throat. She slid it out then shoved it in again. Over and over and over until I lost the ability to think. I could only feel and fuck. I felt good.

"Tell me what you want. What do you need to get off?" she said.

I shook my head, unable to form a coherent thought.

I grabbed her wrist and held the dildo deep inside while I gyrated against it. I opened my eyes and saw her watching my cunt swallow the toy and that was all it took. I slipped from this world into one of pure pleasure and floated there for an eternity before settling back in my body.

CHAPTER SEVENTEEN

Of all the places I'd been in my extensive life, no place, and I mean no place, prepared for Halloween quite like New Orleans. Pumpkins were carved, ghosts and goblins hung in every shop window, and there were no shortages of vampire figurines lining the streets.

I loved it. I reveled in it. It was heaven. Shantay, it turned out, was not a big fan of my favorite holiday.

"It's nonsense," she said. "People don't really believe in creatures of the dark, so why do they celebrate them?"

"Ah, but what about the ones who do?"

"We're in the minority."

"Still, we'll dress up and give out candy when the big day arrives, won't we?"

"You can. I won't."

"Ah, come on," I said. "I'll be Dracula and you'd make a lovely Elvira."

"Surely it's got to bug you. It's like they're making fun of beings like you."

"Actually, I think they're honoring us. And that, my dear, is what I love about it."

"Okay. Well, when you put it that way. I'll try to adjust my attitude."

"Thank you."

It was wonderful getting to know Shantay. Learning about her likes and dislikes and finding out what made her tick. In all those years before we became an item, I'd never thought to sit down and talk to her about her feelings. Now, I couldn't get enough.

We strolled through the Garden District one night checking out the decorations. Cobwebs hung from the old live oaks and mingled with the Spanish moss. Jack-o-lanterns grinned at us, lit by candles. There was a slight chill in the air, but it wasn't really cold. The temperature was in the mid-sixties which was a welcome relief from the heat of the summer.

"So these decorations don't warm your soul?" I said.

"Not really. You know what would warm my soul?"

"What's that?" But I was distracted. We'd come to a house whose large front yard was decorated as a cemetery. There were headstones everywhere, some with skeletons, and some with vampires crawling out of open caskets.

"Earth to Alex?"

"I'm sorry. What were you saying?"

"Never mind. You're obviously in your element here."

I forced myself to turn away from the display and look at her.

"You have my undivided attention."

"Let's go back to the house. Have some champagne in the hot tub and then make love."

"If that's what you want. You know I could never deny you."

We were in the hot tub and the decorations we'd seen were playing through my mind.

"What are you thinking about?" said Shantay.

"Just the decorations. They were so elaborate."

"But they're fake. They're not real. And I feel like they're satirizing you."

"I appreciate that, my dear. But I don't. I feel they're paying homage to me. And I appreciate it."

She turned toward me, pressing her full breasts against me.

"I'll pay homage to you," she whispered.

"Oh, you will, will you?"

"Oh yeah."

She kissed me, a deep, powerful kiss that left me breathless. Her hormones were obviously racing, though why I couldn't be sure. My whole body was alive. The displays we'd seen, the vampires and caskets and everything had me feeling more alive than I had in a very long time. I was more than happy to use that energy to please Shantay.

She nuzzled my neck and whispered in my ear.

"Do you remember when I used the nipple clamps on you?"

I smiled at the memory.

"Uh-huh."

"I saw something else in your drawer. Something I'm very curious about."

"Do tell."

"I think it was some kind of a whip?"

"Ah, yes, my flogger. Don't tell me you're interested?"

"I'm curious," she said.

"How curious?"

"Could you use it and not really hurt me?"

"Of course. I can make you bleed, blister, or not. If you don't wish to feel deep pain, I can do that. Do you think you could enjoy a little pain with your pleasure?"

"I do. Let's pretend I'm a schoolgirl and you're an old-fashioned headmistress who catches me doing something wrong."

I felt the moisture pooling at my center. I loved the way Shantay thought.

"I could do that."

We dried then hurried upstairs to my room. She stood with me as I took out my red-and-black flogger with the hard leather handle. It felt good to be holding it again. I flashed back to the last time I'd used it. It had been forty years ago. I'd accidentally drawn blood, which my partner had loved, but it had been hard for me not to lick up every drop. The experience had been too painful on me. And not in a good way.

"So what did you catch me doing?" Shantay smiled at me.

"I caught you masturbating in your dorm room."

"I love it. That sounds like me."

"And now I'm going to teach you a lesson." I took her wrist and squeezed it. "You'll learn to be a proper lady."

"Yes, ma'am," she said defiantly.

I bent her over the bed face down. I brought the flogger down on her shoulder and dragged it the length of her back, so it just teased her ass. She didn't make a sound. I struck her a little harder, enough for her to feel it, and still she remained silent.

Not knowing whether she was scared or simply disinterested, I decided to really get into my part.

"You filthy little slut," I said. "I'll teach you. Spread your legs wider."

She did so and I was filled with so many ideas. If only I knew her threshold. I didn't want to inflict too much pain and certainly couldn't risk drawing blood. But I had some ideas.

Thwack. I struck her shapely ass with the flogger. *Thwack.* I struck her again.

"I didn't do anything wrong," she finally said. "Just because you're a frigid old bat."

I struck her harder. I saw the evidence of her arousal running down her leg.

"Roll over," I said. She did so, eyes wide. "Spread those nasty legs of yours."

I flogged her belly, watching her eyes for a reaction. The brown pools were darker than I'd ever seen them, and I knew she was enjoying herself. After a few blows on her stomach, I smacked her between her legs. Gently at first, then a little harder.

"Oh, God," she said.

"I'll teach you to touch yourself," I said.

She spread her legs as wide as she could and I whipped her gently, making sure not to catch her with the tips. That would have caused too much pain.

"Okay, Alex," she said. "Enough. Finish me off."

I got on my knees and licked up the copious amounts of juices. I lapped at her tenderly, then with more intensity as my passion raged. I finally turned all my attention to her throbbing clit, and she cried out my name, holding my face in place with her hands.

She finally relaxed her grip and I could breathe again. She collapsed backward on the bed. I climbed up with her.

"Do you like to be whipped?" she said.

"I don't know. I've never trusted anyone enough to whip me."

"Do you trust me?"

I thought long and hard before answering. I did trust Shantay. With my life. Obviously. But did I trust her to know how to mix pleasure and pain in the right parts?

"Of course I trust you," I said finally.

"Then roll over and spread your legs."

She was a natural. She flicked and dragged and whipped my back, causing sharp pain that turned me on no end. I didn't know I'd be into pain of any kind, but I was aroused beyond measure.

She used the flogger between my legs and my sensitive spots swelled at the contact. I was on fire. It burned where she flogged me, and I needed her to soothe me.

"Enough," I said.

"Roll over."

She tenderly kissed where my legs met. She licked and sucked, and finally, I could hold out no longer. I arched off the bed, every muscle in my body tight. White heat coursed through me until it didn't, and I relaxed, falling satiated back on the bed.

We snuggled together for a while. I had very little time left before I'd have to go to sleep.

"We should go somewhere," she said.

"Why? Are you tired of New Orleans?"

"Not at all." She propped herself up on an elbow. "I was just reading about this town in Massachusetts. Apparently, they have a week dedicated to lesbians every October."

"Is that right? That sounds like heaven."

"Right? So, can we go?"

I let out a long breath.

"I'm afraid it's not that simple. How would we get my coffin there? Where would I sleep? How would you explain keeping a casket in your hotel room?"

"That's just it." She sat up. "There are no hotels. It's a little fishing village. We could find a rental. It would be just the two of us and we'd keep your coffin in a room. Or we could find a place with a basement and you could sleep there."

"A fishing village?" I arched an eyebrow at her. "I doubt they'd have basements there."

"True." Her face fell. "Think about it at least. Please?"

"I'll think about it. Now, my dear, I must take my leave. I'll see you tonight."

"Sleep well, babe," she said.

I awoke that night to find Shantay on her computer.

"What's up?" I said.

"I've found places with basements."

"This is really important to you, isn't it?"

"It is. I want to go on vacation with you. I can book a night flight to Boston. We can drive at night to Provincetown and get there in plenty of time for you to get to sleep before the sun comes up."

"I get that you really want to do this. I really do. But, Shantay, I'm going to have to say no. Not this year. Next year, when we've had time to properly plan, I promise I'll take you."

"Do you promise? I mean, really? You give me your word?"

"I do, my dear. I promise."

She closed her laptop, disappointment etched on her face.

"Fine. What do you want to do tonight?"

"Anything you want. Let's make this night all about you."

"I don't know," she said sullenly. "I really want to do something different. We've had a routine the whole time I've known you. I wish we could escape somewhere."

"And I get that. And if you need to, you can. It's a little more complicated for me."

"Oh, Alex. I don't want to go anywhere without you."

That made me feel a little better. I felt like a heel, but traveling was difficult for me. The logistics were insane. And people would question her traveling with a coffin, I was sure. Especially to a small fishing village. It didn't make sense to me to try it.

"Let's go listen to music, have a few drinks, and dance the night away. I know we do that a lot, but it always makes us both feel better."

"You're right," she said. "Let's do it."

The bar had very few patrons so Shantay had her pick of tables while I went to the bar to get our drinks. There was a stack of bright pink flyers on the bar. I picked one up. It was advertising the Voodoo Music and Arts Experience. It mentioned bands, art, and food. I took a flyer with me to the table and showed it to Shantay.

"We should look into this," I said.

"Yeah, we should. This looks amazing. Let's look it up on the computer when we get home to get all the details."

"Sounds good to me."

"Thanks, Alex. I think it'll be just what I need."

I smiled at her.

"That makes me happy."

We danced to the zydeco band, drank our drinks, and snuggled together. I was in heaven. I loved being with Shantay with every ounce of my being. Still, there was a small part of me that hated myself for putting the kibosh on her vacation plans. But at least I'd found something fun to do in New Orleans that would break up the monotony.

With an hour until I had to be in my coffin, we finally went home.

"Let's look at the lineup," she said.

"What?"

"For that voodoo festival. Let's see who'll be there."

"Okay." I laughed. "I have a few minutes."

Her fingers flew over the keyboard, and in no time, she had the festival pulled up.

"Wow," she said. "I've heard of a few of these performers, but not many."

"Does that mean you don't want to go?" I held my breath waiting for her response.

"No! That means I want to go more. I love finding new music to listen to."

"Thank God," I breathed out.

"And look. There will be art on display and tarot cards and lots of original New Orleans and Louisiana cuisine. I am so looking forward to this. And it'll be here in a couple of weeks. I'll buy our tickets now."

"Nonsense. I'll buy. I want a pass for everything. No holds barred. For all three nights. You put your credit card away."

I handed her mine and we got things sorted. She stood and hugged me, and I could tell how excited she was, which pleased me no end. I loved to make Shantay happy. I lived for it. And, at least for that moment, I had succeeded.

"There are going to be so many people there," said Shantay.

"Yes, there are."

"You know what that means, don't you?"

"No. What?"

"You'd better pack that night, if you know what I mean."

"Seriously? At a festival?"

"Not just yeah, but hell yeah."

"Okay." I laughed. "Your wish is my command."

She kissed me, and all thoughts flew from my mind as my crotch throbbed in response. She knew how to kiss, and she was so fucking hot, and I wanted to have her that moment. But I needed to get to sleep. To make love to her then would have been too risky. But she didn't seem like she was going to take no for an answer.

She unzipped her shorts and guided my hand down them. I found her hot, slick, and ready for me. I plunged my fingers deep inside a few times before dragging them over her clit. She closed her legs on my hand and closed her mouth on my shoulder as she screamed.

I withdrew my hand, licked my fingers clean, and felt the burn that let me know I'd been up too long.

"I hate to fuck and run," I said.

"You need to go. Hurry."

She helped me up the stairs where I locked the door behind me and fell into my coffin. I crossed my hands over my chest and, smelling Shantay on my fingers, I fell asleep.

CHAPTER EIGHTEEN

Halloween approached, and the closer it got the more excited I became. I was hoping to wake up in time to see at least some trick-or-treaters. I'd spent a small fortune on decorations for the front yard, including a life-size headless horseman and a life-size vampire. The yard looked great though Shantay insisted it was overdone. No such thing as far as I was concerned.

The weekend before the big day arrived. It was Friday night and we had plans. I dressed quickly and met Shantay downstairs. She looked adorable in khaki capris and a green shirt that matched my eyes. I wanted to take her right then, but could see the excitement in her eyes.

"You ready for a good time?" I said.

"You know it. We're going to have so much fun."

We parked in designated parking and walked to City Park. There were tents all over the place, and the sound of music greeted us. As did the scent of delicious food and the voices of excited people. Shantay squeezed my hand and I looked into her eyes. She was like a little kid at Christmas.

"Where to first?" I said.

"I'm starving. Would you mind if we hit up the food court first?"

"Fine with me. I'll drink while you eat."

The food court was jam-packed with people. We were shoulder to shoulder as we jostled to the front of the line. We took our things away from the crowd and sat on the grass listening to the sounds and watching the people.

"What group do you want to hear first?" I was up for anything. Anything Shantay wanted. She grinned at me, and I could see the excitement in her eyes.

"I can't wait to see Guns 'n' Roses."

"What time are they up?" I looked at my watch. "Do we need to get going?"

"Not so fast, handsome." She stood and offered me her hand, which I declined. "I have plans for you."

"For me?" I stood and she walked off. I followed her to the restrooms. She walked past them, and I wondered what she had in mind.

"Come on," she said. "Hurry up."

We were away from the maddening crowds, yet people still milled around. She found a thick oak tree and walked to the back side of it.

"What are you doing?" I said.

She pulled me to her and kissed me. Our tongues frolicked together, and I lost all reason. I had to have her. I slipped my hand inside her shorts, but she pulled away.

"Please," I begged her.

She turned around, slid down her shorts, and looked at me over her shoulder.

"Did you remember to pack?"

I unzipped my fly and let my dildo loose. I eased it inside her, and she leaned back to take it all in. We were at it for a few minutes and I could feel her whole body tremble. I knew she was close.

All my focus was on getting her off. I had my hands on her breasts, kneading, teasing. I thrust deeper and deeper, forcing my cock as far in as it could go.

And then the hairs on the back of my neck stood up. We were in danger. I looked around as I continued pumping my pelvis. I saw them in the distance. There were three of them, and I knew from instinct what they were. They were a coven.

"Please," Shantay said. "Don't stop."

I had to finish. I owed it to her. But I was scared. Three of them could take me. I hadn't fed in a few days, so I didn't have an enormous amount of strength in reserves. I continued to fuck Shantay until she collapsed back against me.

She raised her arms and ran her fingers through my hair.

"You're my stud," she said.

"Come on," I whispered. "Get yourself together."

She pulled her shorts up and turned to me, eyelids half-mast. Her eyes opened wide.

"Are you okay?" she said.

"We need to go," I said. I took her hand and led her back to the people. We lost ourselves in the crowd.

"What's wrong?" she yelled to be heard.

"Vampires," I whispered in her ear.

She looked around.

"Where? Here?"

"They were back by that live oak. We lost them. I don't sense them anymore."

"How many?"

"Three. I didn't know if they were friend or foe. But I didn't want to find out."

"Do we need to leave?" said Shantay.

"Nonsense. Let's enjoy ourselves."

We found the stage her group was playing on and danced and gyrated and enjoyed ourselves. The music was a little hard for my taste, but I did recognize a couple of songs. Shantay entertained me by singing along with almost every song.

When the concert was finished, I took Shantay's hand and we walked out to the main concourse. I felt a beat beneath my feet. Something was calling to me. It was a deep, mesmerizing rhythm. I liked it. It reminded me of the music I'd heard in Buenos Aires at the women's club on Florida.

"Come on." I pulled Shantay in the direction of the music. There was a fantastic laser show going along with the music. "Who is this?"

"It says Bassnectar."

"I like 'em. Let's get closer."

We got close enough to see that Bassnectar was one person. He was a long-haired DJ who was laying down some amazing tracks. The laser show was the icing on the cake. I was totally engaged in the show. Shantay was jumping up and down and I was watching her, the DJ, and the light show.

"You don't belong here." I heard a voice in my ear.

I hadn't seen them approach. I swallowed hard. How to get out of this predicament without alarming Shantay?

I turned to face three men dressed in black. Their faces were pale. Very pale and I could only assume they hadn't fed recently.

"I don't want trouble," I said. "I'm just here for the music."

"We don't want trouble either. Stay out of our feeding grounds."

"I'm not here to feed. I promise. I won't touch anyone."

"You better not. If we catch you interloping, your days will be over."

"Understood."

And they were gone. It wasn't until after they'd disappeared that I noticed I was trembling. I hoped they hadn't sensed my fear. If they had, I'd signed my own death warrant.

I turned back to Shantay, but she was gone. Panic filled me. Had they taken her, and I hadn't noticed? No. That wasn't possible. I pushed through the crowd toward the stage, my stomach turning to water as I searched without finding her.

And then I saw her. Relief flooded me and I couldn't help but smile as I saw security dragging her off the stage. How the hell had she gotten that close? Security was escorting her out of the concert, and I followed, laughing.

"How the hell did you manage that?" I was still laughing.

"I don't know. The crowd crushed forward, and I went with them. Then climbing on the stage seemed like a really good idea."

"Only you, Shantay."

"Right? Where were you?"

"Good question." Her spirits were high, and I didn't want to bring her down, so I didn't tell her about the vampire and his warning.

"Didn't you see me? I thought for sure you'd be watching."

"I totally lost you in the crowd," I lied. "I was looking all over for you, and then I saw you being helped off the stage."

"That's so funny. Oh, my God. What a rush that was. I want to do it again."

"How about we don't?" But I was still laughing. At least on the outside. She was on top of the world. And it looked good on her.

She gave me a look to let me know she was still in the mood to misbehave. I arched my eyebrows at her, wondering what was next on her agenda. She led me to the oak tree again and I knew what she wanted. But could I focus enough to do my part?

She kissed me, a deep, passionate kiss, and my whole body responded. Fear dissipated, thoughts were gone. Taking Shantay was all that mattered.

She surprised me by unzipping my slacks and running her fingers over my clit. I gritted my teeth and fought not to let go too soon.

"Come for me, baby," she cooed. "Show me that you love me."

I let loose, flooding my boxers with juices of relief. She withdrew her fingers and sucked them clean. I was still aroused. I still needed to take her.

"Let's get home," I said.

"No. Take me here and now."

She unzipped her capris and let them fall to the ground. She stepped out of her thong, and instinctively, I looked around. No one was near. I slid my fingers inside her and thrust as deep as they would go. Spreading my fingers, I slid them out before plunging inside again. I felt her insides quiver and kissed her harder, my tongue's insistence matching my fingers. She dug her fingernails into my back and moaned into my mouth as she found her release.

"I'm hungry again now," she said.

"Okay. Let's get you some food. I could use a drink."

We sat in the middle of the park where we could watch people and hear the music from all the stages. She was rocking side to side to a tune, and I had to know which song had captured her attention.

"I think it's coming from that way." She pointed to a stage to the left of me.

"Finish up and let's go check them out."

The rest of the night was uneventful. She stayed off stages and I avoided any other vampires. When the festival finally closed for the night, we went to Bourbon Street with many of the other revelers. We found a quiet bar and sat enjoying our drinks.

"There's something I should tell you," I said. "I've been debating whether or not to do so, and I've decided to be completely honest with you."

"What's that?" Her face grew serious.

"While you were making your way to the stage? I was approached and threatened by another vampire."

"No shit? Were you scared? What did they say?"

I shook my head.

"It's not really important. Just to stay out of his way and not to hunt in his territory."

"Did he say what his territory was?"

"I understood him to mean the festival."

"Nobody better hunt during the festival," said Shantay. "They'd close it down."

"Right. I don't think he meant the festival per se. Just the park and that area of town."

"Well, you weren't hunting."

"And I told him that."

"So what does all this mean?" she said. "Can we not go back?"

"Of course we'll go back. I just need to pay more attention to who's around me. And I should probably feed before we go. In case I need my strength."

"That makes sense." She took my hand. "I'm so sorry. And I wasn't there for you."

I smiled at her.

"It's best you weren't there. It could have caused trouble. Okay. Enough about that. Let's plan our evening for tomorrow."

"We'll do whatever you want whenever you want. I'd really like to see Brandi Carlisle. She's not on until like nine or so which should give you plenty of time to feed beforehand."

"Sounds great. Am I packing tomorrow night as well?"

She smiled slyly.

"You'd better believe it. And speaking of packing, let's get home and put that harness to good use."

When we were naked on the bed, Shantay got on her knees and licked the length of my cock. She moved in slow motion, dragging her tongue along my length before taking me in her mouth.

My clit twitched as I watched her, and I grew more excited by the second. I finally pulled her away from the dildo and eased her back on the bed. I climbed on top of her and guided myself inside her. She wrapped her legs around my ass, pulling me deeper.

I lowered my head and sucked her swollen, hard nipples. She squeezed her breasts together and I took both nipples in my mouth at once. I was incredibly turned on as I licked and sucked her.

She released her breasts and reached between us. I felt her rubbing her clit and almost exploded at the sheer heat of the action. She cried out, fell back on the bed, and finally released me.

I rolled off of her, panting with my own frustration and need. But I had to let her catch her breath. When she had, she looked at me and smiled.

"Your turn, big boi. Take that harness off, please."

I slipped out of it, fully expecting her to put it on. But she didn't. She removed the dildo and positioned herself between my legs.

"Open up, sweetheart," she said.

And I obeyed. I spread my legs as wide as I could. She pressed the tip into me, into my inner lips, into my clit. I arched my hips, needing her in me.

"Please. Don't tease me."

"You mean like this?"

She slipped just the tip inside me. I reached down, grabbed her wrist, and filled myself with the toy.

"Oh, fuck yeah. That's what I'm talking about," I said.

"Horny much?"

"Yes."

She continued moving in and out of me then lay down and sucked my clit while she fucked me. My insides were tightening. I felt like I was burning up from the inside out. I was teetering on the precipice and needed to fall over. Shantay was the one who could do that. She could send me soaring and I needed her to do that soon.

I felt her tender bite on my clit and that's all it took. I flew into outer space, rocketing out of myself at a record speed. The wave crested and I floated back to myself just in time for her to send me off again.

When she'd had her fun and I began to feel the heat of the approaching dawn, she pulled out of me and cuddled next to me.

"Sleep here tonight, babe. I won't disturb you."

"I'd love that," I said. "But it's not safe."

"Then let me sleep with you. In your coffin."

"No can do, babe. You sleep here where you're safe and I'll sleep in my coffin. I'll see you tonight."

I climbed into my coffin with enough time to play over the events of the night, the good and the bad. The one part that truly stuck out was something Shantay had said to me the second time we'd screwed around behind the tree.

She'd said, "Show me that you love me."

Had she meant that? Did she love me? Did I love her? I fell asleep before I could answer.

Chapter Nineteen

I was up at six thirty that evening, grateful for the longer nights. I quickly dressed, anxious to see my Shantay and talk about our plans for the night. I scrubbed my dildo before placing it in its harness, pulled on my slacks, and hurried downstairs.

Shantay was nowhere to be found. I searched throughout the house, calling her name, but received no answer. I went to the sliding glass door that led to the deck and, through a pouring rain, saw Shantay sitting in the gazebo.

I hurried across the backyard and joined her. She looked sullen and I wondered what had happened.

"Babe?" I said. "Are you okay?"

"Yeah. Just a little bummed."

"Why are you bummed?"

"I really wanted to see Brandi Carlile," said Shantay.

"And what happened? Did she cancel?"

"The whole event is on hold due to this fucking rain."

"Ah." I was bummed, too. It hadn't occurred to me that rain would cancel an event like the Voodoo Festival, but it made sense with all that electrical equipment. "Is the rain supposed to last?"

"I think so."

"I'm sorry, sweetheart. Maybe I'll be able to make it up to you." She snuggled against me.

"Maybe."

I was glad to have her cuddled against me. I was cold. And it wasn't just from the turn in the weather. I needed to feed. I needed to

feed not only for basic needs, but to keep my strength up in case we
went back to the park that night.

"Hey, babe? Would you mind driving me around?"

"Sure. Why?"

"I need to hunt. I'm sorry. But it's necessary."

"I understand," she said. "I need to change my clothes first. I'm
wet and not really dressed for the weather."

"I hear that. I need to put on a sweater as well."

When we were dressed more appropriately, Shantay drove
me through the less desirable neighborhoods, places where I could
potentially find ne'er–do–wells and get a meal. But no one was out.
The wards were quiet, and my stomach began to gnaw at me. I needed
someone but was losing faith.

"Where to now?" Shantay said.

"Jackson Square, please."

She glanced at me sideways.

"Are you sure?"

"Positive. You park on a side street and I'll wander until I find
someone."

"Anything you say Alex. Just please be careful."

"Always, Shantay. I'm always careful."

I wandered through the French Quarter, which was teeming with
people who didn't seem bothered by the rain. I saw no one doing
anything wrong. Everyone was behaving themselves. I walked back to
Jackson Square. The artists weren't out, but people still milled about.
I wandered through the garden, remembering that special night there
with Shantay. I heard a muffled scuffling under one of the bushes and
went to investigate.

A man had a woman held down. She was writhing to get free, but
he seemed strong. I saw him fumbling with the fly on his jeans and
knew I had to act. I picked him up by the back of his neck and looked
down at the frightened woman.

"Run!" I commanded her. And she did. She held her torn dress in
place as she scurried out of the garden.

"Put me down," the man said. "Put me down and fight like a
man."

I set him on his feet and looked him in the eye.

"You think you're a tough guy, don't you?"

"You fucking dyke. I'm going to kill you."

He swung a knife at me, and I grabbed his wrist. I bent his arm toward his neck and made him cut himself in his artery.

"What the…?"

They were the last words he ever spoke. I drank my fill, let him fall to the ground, and hurried off to find Shantay.

"What took you so long?" she said as I slid in the car.

"Sorry. Not much to choose from tonight."

"You must have found someone. Your color is better."

"I did. And the rain has let up. Shall we head toward City Park?"

Her face brightened significantly.

"Yeah. Let's check it out."

The rain had stopped completely by the time we arrived, and the stars shone bright in the night sky. People were scurrying about, setting up equipment and getting everything ready.

"The show must go on, huh?" I said.

"Oh, Alex. This is great. I'm so happy."

"Good. You want some dinner?"

"Yes. I want one of those pretzels I saw last night."

"A pretzel? Will that be enough?"

"Did you see how big they were?"

"No," I said. "I didn't notice."

We made our way to the food court and, with very few people there, got her a pretzel and us each a beer. We found picnic tables away from the festival and sat down to relax and get ready for the evening.

I didn't see them coming. They were sitting at the table before I had a chance to react. Three of them. Dressed in black. Pale faces. Two men and a woman.

"What do you want?" I said.

"She looks delicious," the woman said. "Is she your donor? If not, I claim her."

"Yes," I lied. "She's mine. What do you want?"

"We don't like rogues," one of the men said. "This is our territory and we don't like poachers."

"I'm not poaching. We're here for the festival."

"You'd better not feed on anyone here, asshole," said the second man. "We will find you. We will hunt you down and kill you."

"I'm not here to feed," I repeated myself. "We're only here to have some fun. You have my word."

"We're watching you."

"Understood."

They disappeared as quickly as they'd appeared.

"What's a donor?" Shantay said.

"It's a human who allows us to feed off them. They're considered similar to a pet."

"And you told her I was yours. Why am I not your donor?"

"What? Are you insane? You're my partner. I'd never feed off you."

"You know," she said. "In case of emergency you could. I mean I would let you."

"Thank you. But no. I'll never feed off you. Ever."

"Are you still in the mood for the festival?" she said.

"Sure." I was starting to calm down. "Let's finish up here and go hear some Belinda Carlisle."

Shantay laughed.

"Brandi Carlile," she corrected me. "Who's Belinda Carlisle?"

"She was the lead singer of a group from the eighties." I laughed. "Sorry for the confusion."

"It's all good. We still have some time. Let's look around for a while."

We wandered through the art exhibits, and I paid close attention to the artists Shantay really seemed to like. She had a keen eye for sculptures, and I decided it was time to turn the house into a home. Our home. I'd be shopping accordingly.

After the art, we checked out the interactive haunted house, which I found amusing but which basically terrified Shantay. Or so I thought. I was walking through a blood and guts area when I felt a tug on my hand.

Shantay was pulling me into an alcove where she unbuttoned her jeans and slid my hand inside. It didn't take her long, and her screams were lost among those of the house and its visitors. I was smiling. Shantay never failed to surprise me. Nor did she ever disappoint.

It was finally time for Shantay's main attraction. We got there a little early so we could be close to the stage.

"Are you climbing up again?" I smiled at her.

"Watch and find out."

I watched Shantay as Brandi Carlile took the stage. Her eyes shone and I looked to the stage to see a very attractive woman with a guitar. Her wavy brown hair fell just below her shoulders. I actually felt a tinge of jealousy. Not sure where that came from, I told myself she probably didn't have that much of a voice. My mood was gone. I was jealous and I didn't know how to get around it.

Shantay stood, mesmerized, mouth agape as she stared at this strange woman. I wanted to turn and leave. I wanted to get out of there. I was about to make some excuse when Carlile started to sing. Something shifted inside me. This Brandi Carlile could really belt it out.

Shantay and I danced and twirled to the music, Shantay singing almost every word. I lost track of how long the woman had been singing. She began her introduction for another song and Shantay squealed.

"Oh, my God. It's 'The Story.'"

"The what?" I yelled to be heard over the crowd.

Shantay took my hand and put it on her hip. She did the same with the other. She looped her arms around my neck and pressed into me. We danced like that and I was lost among the crowds. I wouldn't have known what Carlile was singing if Shantay hadn't been singing every word, every single word, into my ear.

"That was our song," she announced as the song ended. And the concert did too. There were hoots and hollers, and Carlile came out for an encore, but then it was really over and Shantay, never having released my hand, guided me through the crowds and toward the center of the park.

"I didn't realize we had a song," I said.

"We didn't. But we do now. Wasn't that song perfect?"

She was right. And I had to admit that.

"It truly was. That, my dear, was a magical experience."

"Are you ready to make some more magic?"

"Back to the oak tree?"

"No. I want to be alone with you. I want us to show each other how we truly feel."

Her words from the previous night came back to me. I decided to push the envelope.

"And how's that exactly? I mean, how do you feel?"

"Let me show you," she answered coyly.

We didn't speak as we drove back to the house. Instead, we listened to Brandi Carlile. All the way home. It was a night I'd never forget. Not even in future centuries, when New Orleans was naught but a distant memory, would I forget that night.

Back home, we held hands as we climbed the stairs to the master bedroom. She undressed me slowly and deliberately, kissing every inch as it was laid bare. I was trembling with need by the time I was naked and struggled as I removed her clothes.

We climbed into bed together, kissing tenderly, sweetly. Each kiss fanned an internal flame that threatened to erupt within me. I kissed her hard as she lay on top of me and she kissed me back.

Her tongue was determined, and I met its every stroke. I rolled over so I was on top of her and began kissing down her body. She grabbed my arm.

"No," she said. "Not yet."

What the hell? What did she mean? I needed to claim her, to possess her. And I needed to do it right then.

"What? Why not?" It came out harsher than I'd intended, but I was frustrated and in need.

"Let's just kiss a little more."

"Are you serious?"

"I am."

I lay next to her and kissed her, hard enough to bruise her lips, but she pulled back and made me kiss slowly, softly.

"What gives?" I managed.

"I just want to take our time. I don't want to rush tonight. We have time. Let's really enjoy each other."

"I tried to enjoy you. You wouldn't let me."

"Do you really care about me, Alex?"

"You know I do. How can I prove that to you if you won't let me?"

She smiled a lazy smile at me.

"It's that important you please me right now?"

"It is."

"Okay then, babe." She rolled over and let her knees fall open. "Have at it."

"Thank you. Oh, dear God, thank you."

When I got between her legs, the strangest thing happened. I was kissing her thighs, her soft, silky thighs, when I was suddenly aware of her throbbing pulse. Her femoral artery called to me, begging me to indulge.

My sheaths pulled back and my fangs were exposed. I licked and licked the spot, fighting the urge to bury them in her. I rolled back and, breathing heavily, waited for my fangs to recede.

"Are you okay?" said Shantay.

"I will be," I growled. "Just give me a minute."

I scooted away from her.

"Alex? What happened? You're scaring me. What's wrong?"

"I'm sorry, babe." I was starting to feel normal again.

"What just happened?"

What to say? How could I explain my behavior? I struggled with myself briefly, then opted for the truth. She deserved that much.

"I'm sorry," I said. And I meant it. "I'm so sorry."

"For what?"

"Your artery...Your femoral artery..."

"Oh, my God. You almost fed off me."

"No. No, no. I didn't. I would never. But it was so tempting."

She moved closer to me and cradled my head against her chest.

"Sh," she said. "It's okay. I understand. It has to be tempting. But why have you never reacted like this before?"

"I don't know. Never before have I heard your pulse so distinctly. Never. And my fangs have never come out before. I was scared. So scared. I didn't know if I could control myself."

"So you moved away. You did the right thing, Alex. And I appreciate it. Maybe from now on you only use your fingers on me."

I shook my head slowly.

"But I love to take you in my mouth. I love to smell you, love to taste you. I can't give that up."

"Then what's our solution?"

"I don't know."

"We don't need to worry about it right now. I think the mood is kind of gone anyway."

"I'm so sorry. I know you wanted this to be a special night."

"And it has been. I'm not upset. But may I ask you something?"

"Sure. Anything."

"What did you mean when you said your fangs came out? I thought those were your fangs?" She tapped on my canine.

"No. Those are part of the sheath. They pull back when my real fangs come out. When I feed, I have very long, very strong, very deadly fangs."

"I see. I have so much to learn about you."

"Ask anything. I'll always answer. And I'll always be honest."

"I appreciate that," she said. "I really do."

"I think I should go to bed. Take some time to ponder what happened. I hope you don't mind."

"No. I get it. I'll curl up here and go to sleep."

"Thank you for being so understanding, Shantay."

"I love you, Alex. I'm going to do everything in my power to make us work."

"I appreciate that. And I love you, too. With every ounce of my being."

I lay in my coffin playing over the events of the night. From the quickie in the haunted house, to the concert, to the near miss in bed. It was indeed a night I'd never forget.

CHAPTER TWENTY

I awoke that night nervous. Shantay had taken the previous night's incident very well. But after having time to think about it, how would she feel now? My stomach was tight as I made my way downstairs.

Shantay was nowhere to be seen. I'd expected her to be at the hall table, dressed and ready to head to the festival. But she wasn't there. A cursory glance toward the gazebo told me she wasn't there either.

Had she left me? Was she gone? If I'd had a heart, it would have sunk. I'd never felt that lousy before. Never. I felt all alone, and I didn't like it. Being a vampire meant a life of solitude. I'd gotten quite used to my own company. But now I was used to Shantay. And her being gone sucked. Big time.

I opened the slider to go sit in the gazebo and contemplate my feelings when I heard my name. I turned to see Shantay soaking in the hot tub. Relief flooded me. I knew I was smiling like I'd just won the lottery, but I didn't care.

"Hey, babe. Why aren't you dressed?"

"I wanted a soak. And I don't really want to go to the festival."

"Why not?"

"For one thing, it ends at nine. For another, a rapper is the closing act and I have no desire to see him."

"Sounds good to me. So what are we doing with our night?"

"Well, for starters," she said, "you're going to get out of those clothes and get in this hot tub with me."

"You don't have to ask me twice."

I stripped and stepped into the churning water. It felt wonderful, though I was bummed she had the bubbles on. I would have loved to have seen her luscious body in all its glory.

She scooted next to me and I placed my arm across her shoulders. I kissed her upturned face, her forehead, her cheeks. I finally closed my mouth over hers and my senses reeled. I had it bad for Shantay. And I needed her to know it.

I also wanted her to know the relief I was feeling. Having her tell me she loved me one minute and fearing her gone the next had really done a number on me.

"You okay?" she said when we finally came up for air.

"Sure. Why do you ask?"

"I don't know. There's something different about you. I can't quite put my finger on it."

"Hm. Perhaps that's my relief you're sensing."

"Your relief? What are you relieved about this evening?"

"I'm so glad you're not gone," I said. "I couldn't find you when I got up and I thought you'd left me."

"What the fuck? Did I not make it clear last night that I'm not going anywhere?"

"Yes." I smiled, feeling like an idiot. "I was just worried."

"Well, that's one thing you'll never have to worry about. I'm here for the duration."

"Thank you."

I kissed her again and dragged my hand along her thigh. The same thigh that had driven me to distraction the night before. It felt soft and harmless to my touch. I inched closer to her center and she spread her legs for me.

She was wet and warm and ready for me. Shantay was always ready for me. I loved that about her. I caressed her lovingly before delving inside. Just a fingertip. Then another.

"You're teasing me," she said.

I laughed.

"I am."

There was no more conversation as our kiss deepened and I plunged my tongue deep in her mouth, just like my fingers now plunging deep inside her. I slowly, deliberately withdrew them and pressed into her hardened clit. Her screams probably woke the neighborhood, and she came for me and me alone.

We sat relaxing in the hot tub for a little while until Shantay expressed her hunger.

"Where would you like to go for dinner?" I said.

"Bourbon Street. I'm in the mood for crowds."

"Always a good choice for me. Let's get ready."

Bourbon Street was teeming with people. Being the Sunday before Halloween, many were in costume. I loved it. I enjoyed the pseudo-vampires mixed in with the witches and naughty nurses.

"Ugh," Shantay groaned. "Just ugh."

"It's wonderful. It's incredible. I love this holiday."

"I know this. I'm trying to improve my attitude, but it hasn't happened yet."

"Keep trying."

We found a restaurant with only a half hour wait so I put my name in, then settled in the bar.

"Seriously," I said. "What is it about Halloween?"

"I don't know." She shrugged. "It's just too weird for me."

"Weirder than being in love with a vampire?"

She laughed.

"Well. When you put it that way…"

"See? Nothing's weird in this world. Everything is beautiful."

"You really believe that, don't you?" said Shantay.

"I really do."

We were shown to our table by an attractive woman with bobbed blond hair who looked to be in her forties. Her name was Eileen and she was a looker. I mean, I would have picked her up and taken her home in my single days.

"You like her." It wasn't a question.

"She's very attractive. I can look, can't I?"

"Of course. We can even bring her home with us. You know I'm game for that."

"We'll see about that. She may not be game. Hell, she may not even play for our team."

"We could recruit her."

I had to laugh. Shantay kept me on my toes. And I loved that about her, too.

Eileen was back a little while later.

"Have y'all had time to look over your menus?"

Damn. That accent. I had to have her. My mind was made up. I smiled warmly at her.

"I think she's still choosing," I said. "I'd love another hurricane though."

I glanced over at Shantay, who was gazing longingly at Eileen as she walked away.

"You really like her?" I said.

"That I do. I think she'd make a wonderful bedmate."

"In that case, we'll make it happen."

I did my best to flirt with Eileen every time she came by our table, which seemed to be quite often.

"Why don't you sit down for a minute and relax?" Shantay said.

"Oh, honey." Eileen laughed. "I wish I could."

She winked at Shantay and backed away from the table. I took her hand.

"Join us for a drink later? What time are you off work?"

"Eleven. And thank you. I'd like that."

Shantay finished dinner and left a note on the table for her to meet us at our favorite watering hole at eleven fifteen. We made our way down the street and settled in for a few drinks while we waited.

Ever responsible, Shantay was drinking iced tea while I continued my consumption of hurricanes. We danced, laughed, and enjoyed ourselves. I'd actually forgotten about Eileen until Shantay waved toward the front door.

I turned and saw Eileen standing there in a short skirt and her white oxford shirt, and my gut tightened. She was hot. I sure hoped she was up for a night of fun with us. That would be outstanding.

She walked toward us on firm, muscular legs. I could feel them clenched against my head and was ready to get out of there and start the games. But I had to be cool. We still didn't know which side of the fence she was on.

She sat down and I went to the bar to order her a drink. I came back to find Eileen and Shantay laughing hysterically about something.

"What's so funny?"

"Eileen was just telling me about some dude who asked her out after we'd left."

"The look on his face when I said I already had a date...with two women, was priceless," Eileen said.

"That's great." I chuckled. "That's really great. So does that make this a date?"

"Oh, honey," she drawled. "This is whatever you want it to be."

That sounded good to me. I glanced over at Shantay who raised her eyebrows at me. We smiled at each other.

"Y'all look like the cat who just swallowed the canary," said Eileen. "What have I gotten myself into?"

"We're harmless," said Shantay. "For the most part."

"Yeah. It's that most part I'm worried about." But there was a twinkle in her eye that said she'd be up for anything. A twinkle I enjoyed seeing. Very much.

"Tell us about yourself," I said.

"I'm boring. I want to know about you two. Your accent is very different, while hers is familiar sort of."

"How rude," I said. "We haven't introduced ourselves. My name is Alex and this is Shantay."

"Nice to meet you. Now where are you from, Alex?"

"I'm originally from Eastern Europe. Romania specifically. But I haven't lived there in years."

She nodded.

"It's faint, the eastern European accent, but it's there. What else am I hearing?"

"I've lived all over the world," I said. "So I'm sure I have a conglomerate of accents."

She arched an eyebrow at me then looked at Shantay.

"Gorgeous and she uses big words. You're a lucky lady."

"Yes, I am." She looked like she wanted to say more, but didn't.

"And, Shantay, where are you from?"

"Originally? Chicago. But I lived in South America for about twenty years before moving to New Orleans."

"Where did you two meet?"

"Buenos Aires," I said.

"Oh, wow. What a beautiful city. I've never been, but it's on my bucket list."

I left them chatting and went to the bar for more drinks. By the time I got back to the table, Eileen was leaning toward Shantay as the chated. She certainly seemed receptive. Interested even.

After her second drink, Eileen stood. I looked at her questioningly.

"I do believe this is where y'all show me your place."

"Is that right?" I said.

"Mm-hm."

Shantay stood.

"Come on, Alex," she said. "We shouldn't keep the lady waiting."

Shantay drove us back to the house. As we pulled into the driveway, Eileen let out a low wolf whistle.

"Nice digs."

"Thanks."

"And all of this just for the two of you?"

"Yes, ma'am," said Shantay.

We made our way up the stairs and into the master bedroom. She looked around.

"Very masculine," she said. "Alex, you must have decorated."

"Yes. It was my room first. Now it's ours."

She moved close to me and dragged a finger down my cheek. I shivered at her touch.

"You intrigue me." She turned to Shantay. "You're beautiful. I want you every bit as much. But Alex here intrigues me."

I shrugged and tried to play cool.

"I don't know why."

"Oh, yes you do. You're mysterious. You're aloof. Yet your eyes betray your passion."

Shantay walked over, and turned Eileen away from me. She kissed her open-mouthed with no pretense of tenderness. Eileen kissed her back as if they'd been kissing each other like that for years. It was hot. Fucking hot.

"So, what are y'all into?" Eileen stepped away from Shantay. "How will my night play out?"

"However you'd like," Shantay said. "You name it, we can make it happen."

"I do like the sound of that."

Shantay unbuttoned Eileen's blouse while I made fast work of her skirt. She took turns kissing us while we undressed her. She wouldn't let us remove her bikinis or bra.

"Oh no," she said. "Y'all strip to your skivvies as well."

We did as we were asked, only I didn't stop at my underwear. I stripped all the way and climbed up on the bed.

"Oh, no, handsome. Not yet," said Eileen.

She took off her underwear and lay on the bed. Shantay and I stood naked at the foot of the bed waiting for our instructions.

"I like to be watched," Eileen said. "Y'all stand there and I'm going to finger fuck myself into oblivion."

Odd request, but I was up for anything. And I could think of a lot worse things than watching a hot blonde touch herself. I glanced at Shantay who swallowed hard, but didn't shift her gaze from between Eileen's legs.

Eileen's lower lips were swollen, and they glistened with the juices of her desire. She licked her fingertips before teasing and twisting her nipples. She massaged her smallish breasts and played with her nipples. I watched as the evidence of her arousal leaked down her thighs.

I wanted to lick those firm thighs. I wanted to devour every drop that escaped her hot pink pussy. But I didn't. I stood still and watched, mesmerized at the show.

Shantay was breathing heavily, and I chanced a glance her direction. She was rubbing her own clit as hard and as fast as I'd ever seen anyone do that. Her gaze was focused on Eileen, though her eyelids were drooping.

I took her by the wrist and brought her fingers to my mouth. I sucked and licked each one clean, her flavor only serving to heighten my arousal.

Meanwhile, Eileen was flat on her back, fingers buried deep, and I knew she'd lost all sense of where she was. Deciding that was as good a time as any to make my move, I motioned Shantay to go around to the other side of the bed and I went to mine.

Shantay kissed Eileen's cheek and neck while I sucked her tight little nipples.

"Watch," she whispered. But it was weak, more like a plea than a command.

"We're watching," Shantay whispered back. "Don't stop now."

"No. Won't stop."

"Good."

I let them have their conversation, such as it was. I knew better than to talk with my mouth full. And it was full. I was used to Shantay's large breasts, but Eileen's were every bit a treat.

Eileen was writhing on the bed, arching her back and thrashing her head as she neared her climax. This would be one for the books. I could tell. I released her nipple and looked between her legs. Her fingers pumped in and out at an incredible rate. I lowered my mouth and took her clit in.

Her free hand held me in place as she thrust her hips forward. Then there was no movement. There was only the ear-splitting scream as Eileen let us know she'd come for us.

"That was hot," Eileen said a moment later. "Thank you."

"You're not through," I said.

"Oh yes, I am. It's my turn to watch now. Show me how Shantay likes it, Alex."

So I did. I made love to Shantay frantically. I was in her, on her, tasting her, fucking her. I lost my head, I was so into pleasing her.

I was between her legs when Eileen entered me. I don't know how many fingers she used. Hell, it might even have been her whole fucking fist. I'd never been so filled before. I rocked against her urging her deeper, begging her with my body not to stop.

Shantay called my name just before I let out my own guttural moan and found a release so intense, I never wanted the ride to end.

Chapter Twenty-one

Halloween finally arrived. And with it, a joyous feeling for me. I could tell Shantay still wasn't into the holiday, but she'd at least decorated the yard for me and bought candy to hand out to trick-or-treaters.

She'd also found me the perfect vampire costume, including a black cape with red lining, and we laughed as I put it on. Something about a vampire dressing up as a vampire was humorous to both of us. We dabbed some fake blood on the corners of my mouth, and I was ready to go. She refused to dress up but sat on the porch with me as I handed out candy.

I was not disappointed. Ghouls and goblins, princesses, and superheroes paraded up our walkway to get their full-sized candy bar. There was no shortage of cute little vampires either. Along with mummies, zombies, and we even saw a young Van Helsing. I almost didn't give him a candy bar.

We ran out of candy a little after nine and had just turned the porch light off when we heard a familiar voice.

"Calling it quits so soon?"

We turned to see Eileen strolling toward us.

"Eileen," said Shantay. "What brings you here?"

"I just thought I'd stop by to see how my favorite couple is doing."

"We're great." I placed my arm around Shantay possessively. I couldn't put my finger on just why, but seeing Eileen at our house again put me way outside my comfort zone.

"You're a vampire?" Eileen made a disgusted face.

"Do you not like vampires? I love them," Shantay said.

"I hate them. I believe they're real, you know? I think they actually exist. I also believe the only good vampire is a dead vampire."

Shantay pulled away from me and stepped toward Eileen, who hadn't come up the steps yet.

"I think you'd better leave," she said.

"Why? Just because she'd dressed like a damned blood sucker doesn't mean she can't strip out of that ridiculous costume so we can all have a little fun."

"Please leave. And don't come back."

"What is your problem?"

I stepped forward and took Shantay's hand.

"Let's just say this isn't a good time," I said.

"You really don't want me to return? You going to tell me you didn't have fun the other night?"

"We did. But that was then, and this is now. Please leave, Eileen."

"Fine. I'll go. Your loss." She picked up a wooden stake from the yard and turned toward me, stake held high. Instinctively, I hid behind Shantay. "I ought to drive this through your thankless heart."

Then she laughed, tossed the stake back into the yard, and wandered off into the night.

I was shaking, trembling all over. That hadn't been funny. Not in the least. She could have killed me.

"You okay?" said Shantay.

"No. Let's get inside."

Shantay carried the empty candy bowl while I walked into the ballroom and collapsed in an overstuffed chair. I couldn't believe Eileen. I hadn't been around a vampire hunter in decades and didn't like the idea that I'd actually bedded one. Brought her here. To our house. She knew where we lived. It terrified me.

Shantay sat in my lap and placed an arm around me.

"I'm sorry," she said.

"So am I."

"I don't even know what to say."

"You don't have to say anything," I said. "There's nothing to say. I'm just shocked. Imagine if she figured out I was truly a vampire? Can you even comprehend what kind of danger I'd be in?"

"I get that. She won't though. There's no reason for her to accept that as anything more than a Halloween costume."

"I hope you're right. I shudder to think we might have to move again."

"We don't. But if you'd feel safer, I'll understand."

"Between the vampires and the vampire hunters, this city may not be safe for me anymore."

She stood.

"So we'll move. We've got to do what's best for you, Alex."

"Not yet. Not right now. We just need to be aware it may come to that."

"And I'll understand. You want to head to Bourbon Street? Have a few drinks? Get out among the living?"

"I don't know," I said.

"Okay. How about a hot tub?"

"I just feel so…betrayed, I guess. I'm sorry. I'll snap out of it. Let's go to the French Quarter. You've got to be starving."

"I really am." She laughed.

I smiled at her. I couldn't imagine anyone else I'd want by my side in this life. And, when she was gone, which wouldn't be for many years, I would remain single. That was a promise I made to myself. No one could replace Shantay.

"Okay. Should I change?"

"Hell no. Everyone will be in costume there. Everyone but me."

"You sure you don't want to dress up?"

"I'm positive."

Bourbon Street was jumpin'. It was curb to curb people. Bars were filled to capacity and people carried their drinks out in the night air. We found a restaurant with only an hour wait, so we put our names in.

I was still struggling to shake my morose mood. Shantay was watching the people parade by and giving me a running commentary on who she saw. I tried to show some interest, but it was hard. My mind kept drifting back to Eileen with the wooden stake. Talk about PTSD.

It wasn't the first time I'd evaded a hunter, but the fact that it was Eileen shook me to my core. Obviously, I knew nothing of the strange women we brought home on occasion. We enjoyed them. They enjoyed us. End of story. But how would I know if one of them could kill me?

"Earth to Alex," said Shantay.

"Sorry. I need to snap out of it. I know this. I apologize for being such lousy company."

"There's got to be more going on in that gorgeous head of yours than simply Eileen being a raging bitch."

"There's so much more. She triggered some flashbacks that were long buried. I wish that wasn't the case, but now I wonder how I'll know who's safe and who's not."

Shantay took my hands in hers.

"Talk to me. Tell me about these flashbacks."

"People used to be so superstitious They believed in all the creatures of the night. And it was back when more of us walked the earth. Before they'd been hunted with stakes or left out to burn. There were lots of us. Anyway. I was living in Africa. In what is now Seychelles. Yes, it was foolish to live in such an isolated area. I've never lived on an island since.

"I thought I'd acclimated very well. Bear in mind I was passing as a man back in those days. I was friendly with pub owners and other townspeople whom I'd met in my nightly excursions. It was a very pleasant place with incredibly kind inhabitants. I'd been living there for about a year when it happened.

"Sundown came, and I made my way into town to go to one of my favorite pubs. When I arrived, no one greeted me. I thought it was odd but still bellied up to the bar. The barkeep poured my beer but did so wordlessly.

"My hackles rose. I sensed danger so I paid for my beer and turned to leave. It was then the townspeople closed in on me. They had pitchforks, which didn't really scare me. Then I saw the wooden stakes and saw strings of garlic cloves. Some people had their swords drawn.

"To this day, I don't know if they planned to decapitate me and stuff me with garlic. Though the way they swung those swords at me I can only believe that was their intent. Men with wooden stakes held high closed in on me. Men held crucifixes high and I shielded my eyes. That was when the first swordsman attacked. He sliced open my side, but didn't do any major damage. It hurt though. It hurt like hell.

"I stumbled back, bent over, and someone hit me over the head with a hard object. I have no idea what it was, but it almost knocked me out. I fell to the ground blinking, fighting to retain consciousness lest I face a certain death.

"Men kicked me, especially in my wounded side. They yelled at me to roll over. They tried to flip me over. I glanced up and saw two men with stakes waiting to finish me off. I was terrified. I felt betrayed, sure, but foremost in my brain I was fearing for my life.

"Gathering all my strength, I shot to my feet, swinging at anybody around me. Bodies went flying. I hurried toward the front door. All I could do was focus on getting out of that pub and getting to safety. That's when I saw movement out of the corner of my eye. I parried, jumping to the left, and heard and felt the blade swish past me. If I hadn't moved, I'd have quite literally lost my head."

"Oh, my God," Shantay said. "How horrible."

I nodded.

"It was pretty bad. No, it was awful. They kept coming at me and I kept flinging them off. I finally made it to the door, pulled it open, and all but flew out of town. I stole a boat and sailed away as quickly as possible. I had to get as far away from there as possible. Eileen just kind of brought it all back to me."

"I'm sure. Well, we'll keep you safe. Whatever that entails."

After dinner, we found a seat in our favorite pub where we sat in the dark, listened to jazz, and sipped our drinks. I had relaxed a bit while Shantay ate and I was in an almost decent mood.

"I don't know that I'll want to bring another woman home. Not for a while," I said.

"That makes sense. I wish there was a way to interview women, you know?"

I laughed.

"Isn't that kind of what flirting is?"

"I suppose so. But how do you flirtatiously ask if someone hates vampires?"

"True. Not exactly a normal topic of conversation."

"Not at all. Oh, well. We can still bring women home. Just not for a while. I understand after tonight."

We drank our drinks, and Shantay finally got me off my ass to dance a few songs. I was feeling better. She was really all I needed anyway. She made my undead life worthwhile. And I appreciated and loved her for that.

"What's up next?" Shantay said at around three. "Where to?"

"Maybe I need to feed. Let's look around."

We wandered along Bourbon Street and I admired anew all the costumes. I especially admired the naughty nuns and nurses we saw but felt a particular fondness for the Elviras.

Soon we were away from the bright lights and sights and sounds. I turned down a side street looking for prey. I saw none. We headed back up Decatur until we reached the back side of Jackson Square.

There I heard muffled cries. Someone was in danger, serious danger.

"Stay here," I told Shantay. "Be vigilant."

I followed the sounds until, a couple of blocks away, I found a man on top of someone who was squirming, obviously trying to get away. I used all my strength to pull the offender off and saw Patricia lying there, clothes ripped, makeup ruined from tears. I threw my cape over her.

"Shantay is waiting two blocks that way." I motioned with my head. "Find her. She'll take care of you."

Patricia nodded her understanding and, holding my cape close, headed off to find Shantay and comfort.

I watched until I saw her get to Shantay, then dragged the ne'er do well into an alley.

"Let me go! Fuckin' dyke."

"Shut up."

"I'm gonna sue your ass. You have no right."

I held him up against the wall. Anger in his eyes quickly gave way to fear as I unsheathed my fangs. I licked them menacingly.

"You've hurt your last woman."

I buried my fangs and drank deeply. I felt warm all over, alive again. Unafraid. It was a heady feeling. I let him crumple to the ground then hurried off to find Shantay and Patricia.

"Are you okay?" I said.

"Where is he?" Patricia's eyes still shone with terror.

"He's gone. He won't hurt you again."

"Are you sure?"

"Positive. The police will take care of him now," I lied.

"Thank you." She hugged me tightly, and I was happy to have helped her. She didn't deserve that. Nobody did.

"Let's head to the house," Shantay suggested. "We will make you some tea and get you some clothes to put on."

"You wouldn't mind?" Patricia said.

"Not at all," I said.

"Good. Because I'm afraid to be alone right now."

"Understood. Believe me, I took care of him, but I get that. Let's walk to the car and we'll settle in at our house."

She nodded and wrapped her arm around my waist. I draped an arm around her shoulder and held her tight as we walked to the car. She was trembling, and no matter how much strength I tried to give her, nothing could stop that.

At the house, Shantay made hot apple cider while I went upstairs to grab some sweats for Patricia. I came down to find them both sitting at the kitchen table. I handed the sweats to Patricia who looked at me sheepishly.

"What is it? There's a bathroom right down the hall," I said.

"Do you have any shorts and an old T-shirt you wouldn't mind getting wet? I feel like I could really use the hot tub."

Back upstairs I went. I came down wearing my board shorts and muscle shirt and carrying another pair of trunks and an old Fleetwood Mac shirt for Patricia.

"Thank you," she said.

Shantay put her suit on and we carried our cider out to the hot tub. Patricia turned on the bubbles and we sat in silence, Shantay against me and Patricia across from us. Patricia's eyes were closed, and she looked relaxed.

"I'm sorry I'm not in the mood to party," she finally said.

"It's okay," Shantay said. "We totally understand. You've been through a lot. I don't think any of us is in much of a mood for extracurriculars tonight."

"Thank you," Patricia said. "I really appreciate this. Y'all are true friends. I'll never forget your kindness. I wish there was some way to repay you. But then again, I hope your lives are never in danger."

"No need to repay us," I said. "Just be careful in the future. I might not always be there to save you."

She shuddered.

"I hate to think what would have happened if you hadn't walked up right then."

"No need to think about that. I was there. That's all that matters."

"I do have one more favor to ask of you two."

"What's that?" said Shantay.

"Can I sleep with you two tonight?"

Shantay sat up straight. I put pressure on her shoulder, letting her know it was all right.

"You and Shantay can head to bed whenever you like. I'll do some work in my study and come to bed later."

"Thank you. No funny business though, right?"

"None whatsoever, Patricia. Nothing like that tonight. Tonight is just to let you know you're safe."

CHAPTER TWENTY-TWO

Patricia was in a much better space when I woke that night. Gone was the terror and trepidation and in its place the fun-loving, sexually charged woman we knew. I went downstairs and found Shantay and Patricia at the kitchen table drinking wine.

"About time you got up, sleepyhead," said Patricia.

"What can I say? I was tired."

"I guess. We missed you last night, didn't we, Shantay?"

"We did," said Shantay. "But then, I'm quite accustomed to you sleeping in your office."

"You're a new couple," Patricia said. "You should never sleep apart."

"Sometimes it happens. I'll be up late on the computer like I was last night and don't want to disturb her by coming to bed. It's all good."

"Okay. Well, now that you're up, let's do something. I'm not ready to go home yet."

"Tell you what," I said. "Let us drive you to the French Quarter and the three of us can barhop as we make our way to your place."

"That sounds good. Are you in, Shantay?"

"Totally."

The first stop on our trip was our favorite bar. Zydeco greeted us as we walked up, and I was afraid I wouldn't want to leave. So much for barhopping. I needn't have worried. Patricia let out a squeal.

"I love zydeco," she said. "Let's just drink here."

"Sounds good to me," I said.

Shantay just smiled and squeezed Patricia's hand as we entered. They found a table and I bought the first round. Hurricanes for everyone.

"So are you two going to tell me there was no hanky-panky last night or maybe this morning?" I knew I would die if they said there had been. I would have felt like that was the ultimate betrayal. I sipped my drink and tried to look calm and cool even as my insides revolted against me.

"Nothing," said Patricia. "We were waiting for you."

Shantay grabbed my hand.

"It wouldn't have been right. And it certainly wouldn't have been the same."

"I appreciate that." Relief flooded over me. I couldn't believe I'd even suspected them.

"Let's dance." Patricia jumped up. "Please?"

Shantay laughed as she stood and led the two of us to the floor. Patricia showed us some new moves. She knew the proper way to dance to zydeco and joyfully instructed us. We laughed at our fumbled attempts, but we soon got the hang of it.

After a half hour of solid dancing, I dragged Shantay back to the table for some much needed refreshments. Patricia was harder to get off the floor, but she eventually joined us.

"I want to do something to pay y'all back for taking such good care of me. And, of course, for saving my life, Alex."

"You don't need to pay us back," Shantay said. "It was our pleasure. Alex didn't even know it was you she was saving. It's all good. Honest."

"I insist. Let me buy y'all dinner. I know a great place just down the street. And the waitresses there are hot."

"I'm not really hungry," I said. "But if you two are ready for dinner, I'll go along for the drinks."

Patricia led us down Bourbon Street and stopped in front of a restaurant Shantay and I were all too familiar with. It was where Eileen worked.

"I don't know," Shantay said. "We've been here before. Let's choose someplace new."

"Nonsense. Best etouffee in New Orleans right here. Come on."

Sure enough, Eileen seated us. I'm sure she looked good, but all I could see was a vampire hater. I didn't feel safe.

"Welcome back to the three of you," Eileen said. "Take a look at your menus and I'll be right back to take your orders."

"Told you there'd be hot women here. And clearly, she remembers you two," Patricia said.

"Clearly." My mood had soured. I wanted them to quickly eat their dinners so we could get back to the bar. I wasn't sure even that could restore my spirits.

Eileen was back and, shockingly enough, had a crucifix hanging from her neck. I quickly looked away.

"Something wrong, Alex?" she cooed.

"Not a thing."

The others ordered their dinner while I simply asked for a hurricane.

"You know," Eileen said. "I've never seen you eat. How do you keep your stamina? Or do I really need to ask?"

"She doesn't like to eat in front of people." Shantay came to my rescue. "It's not a big deal."

"For the record? I don't believe you. I'm coming for you, Alex. I used to suspect, but now I know. And when we get you, you'll be sorry."

"What the hell was that about?"

"She just doesn't like me. Or Shantay, really. That's why we didn't want to come here. Y'all enjoy your dinner." I stood. "I'm going back to the bar."

Listening to the music lifted me somewhat. I even enjoyed sitting alone, though I missed Shantay. I took a deep breath. Shantay and I hadn't made love in a few days, so we were overdue. I hoped to remedy that tonight.

"Where are your cohorts?" I looked up to see a statuesque woman with dark skin and a bright red scarf around her hair.

"They'll be along shortly."

"Will you ask me to dance, please?"

I stood.

"It would be my pleasure."

We danced our way through several songs before she walked back to my table and sat down.

"Would you like a drink?" I said.

"I'd love one. A Sazerac, please."

We sat sipping our drinks.

"I don't recall having seen you before." She was a stunning beauty and I knew I would have noticed her. She laughed.

"I've seen you around. You and your girlfriend. Tonight, I noticed you had a third with you."

"Patricia," I said.

"Yes. Maybe one night you'll consider making me your third."

"Maybe we will. That certainly sounds like a good idea to me. Tell me about yourself. I'm sorry. I don't even know your name."

"My name is Marie. And you're Alex, are you not?" The hair on the back of my neck stood up. How would she know that? She must have seen my expression. "I've asked around. You're quite well known in these parts."

I relaxed a little.

"Is that right? I had no idea."

She smiled.

"Oh, yes. And it's a pleasure to finally meet you."

"I do believe the pleasure is mine, Marie. Is New Orleans your home?"

"Yes, it is. I live by St. John's Bayou. I happen to be a voodoo priestess."

"Is that right?" I didn't know how much stock I put in voodoo.

"It is. And if you need anything from me, anything at all. All you have to do is ask."

She handed me her card just as Shantay and Patricia sat down.

"This is Marie," I said.

They introduced themselves and Marie stood.

"It's been a pleasure finally meeting all of you in person," she said. "I'll be back here another time. Perhaps we can party together then."

"Count on it," I said.

"What happened to interviewing women?" Shantay said.

"Huh?" said Patricia.

"Inside joke." I cast a sideways glance at Shantay who simply rolled her eyes at me.

"Okay. Let's keep the party rolling. Who was that woman, anyway?" Patricia said.

"I'll get you two some drinks and I'll fill you in on what I know."

By the time I got back to the table, Shantay and Patricia were on the dance floor, moving and grooving to the music. I set the drinks down and joined them. After a few songs, we moved back to the table.

"I say we finish our drinks and head back to your place," said Patricia.

"Is that right?" I arched an eyebrow at her. Before she could respond, Shantay spoke up.

"How do you feel about vampires?"

Patricia sat back in her chair.

"Random question. Why do you ask?"

"It's part of our inside joke of interviewing women. We thought we'd ask women the most off-the-wall questions and see how they respond."

Patricia laughed.

"Well, I think they'd be cool. You know, to live forever and only be expected to be out at night? I think they're awesome. How'd I do?"

"You did just fine," I said. "Just fine. Now finish your drinks and let's get going."

I took one long look around the front yard before following them inside the house. I was still upset about Eileen's words, and I couldn't shake the feeling that danger was looming. And not just for me.

Satisfied we were alone, I led Patricia and Shantay upstairs where we quickly undressed and fell into bed. I really enjoyed Patricia. She was a fun, skilled addition to Shantay and me. She latched on to Shantay's nipple, suckling as if her life depended on it. I took her breast in my mouth and ran my tongue over her own hardened nipple.

Soon Shantay's moans distracted me and I climbed between her legs. I devoured her, leaving nothing unlicked or unsucked. She tasted like heaven and soon was crying out her ecstasy.

That left Patricia and me to achieve our releases. Apparently, they'd decided I was next as Patricia sucked my clit and entered me.

Shantay kissed me. Damn, but she could kiss. I was surprised I'd never come just from her kisses. She was that good.

While she kissed me, Shantay pinched and tugged my nipples, twisting them this way and that. I was shaking uncontrollably. I was close. So very close. Every muscle in my body tightened in anticipation.

Patricia continued plunging deeper and deeper as she sucked on my swollen nerve center. I was too far gone to actively participate in kissing so Shantay replaced her fingers with her mouth and that was all it took. I sailed into the ozone and came crashing down before soaring into the atmosphere again. This time, when I came back to myself, I tapped both of them.

"Enough," I said. And then, when my breathing returned to normal, "Your turn, Patricia."

It was then I realized Shantay was nowhere around. I glanced around the room and saw her donning my strap-on. I smiled.

"You driving tonight?"

"You know it."

"Lucky me." Patricia got up on all four.

I watched Shantay enter her and my body quaked anew. It was the hottest thing I'd ever seen. I knelt watching, and without meaning too, I was stroking myself. I was drenched and my clit was rock hard again.

"You enjoying this?" Shantay winked at me.

"Fuck yes."

"I can tell."

Patricia screamed and fell forward, face-first, into the pillow at the same time I brought myself to new heights. Shantay pulled out of Patricia and before I could remove the dildo, Patricia had turned around and taken it in her mouth. She licked and sucked the cock until I couldn't take anymore.

I buried my fingers as deep as they'd go inside Shantay, who gasped then called my name as she came again.

Before I could go down on Patricia, I felt the familiar prickling on my back. I glanced over at the window. Sure enough, the sun was rising. Fuck. How could I explain my disappearance?

Shantay must have noticed my expression.

"Let's get some sleep now," she said. "Come on, Patricia. Lie with us."

Patricia snuggled into bed.

"I need to look at something in my office." It wasn't exactly a lie.

"Hurry back." Patricia sounded like she was already half asleep. I kissed Shantay and hurried to my coffin. The pain was agonizing, and I was weak as I tried to lift the lid. But I got it up and fell into it, asleep as soon as I closed the lid again.

I awoke that evening to find Patricia gone.

"When did she leave?" I said.

"Around three. She wanted to thank you for last night, but I explained you're a professional sleeper and probably wouldn't be up any time soon."

"Thank you for covering for me."

"My pleasure."

We kissed for a few minutes, and I was just about ready to take her upstairs to bed when she spoke.

"So, who was the hottie you were talking to last night?"

I had completely forgotten about Marie.

"I don't know. She knew us, though. She gave me her card." I fished it out of my pocket. "Oh, lookie here. She's a voodoo priestess."

Shantay took the card.

"Interesting. You said she knew us?"

"Yeah. Not sure how. She said we had a reputation or something. She was really excited to meet me."

"I don't know," said Shantay. "That makes me nervous. What if she knows the truth about you?"

"How's that even possible? Besides, she seemed genuinely nice."

"So did Eileen."

"Touché. Let's pay her a visit."

"When?"

"Now. Why not?"

"I don't know," she said again. "I suppose a trip to her business couldn't hurt. But mind you I'm going on record as saying I don't trust her."

"Duly noted."

Shantay drove us to North Broad Street over by Bayou Saint John. We stopped for dinner at a place that boasted comfort food. Shantay made short order of her dinner while I sipped a drink.

We strolled up the street until we came to the address on Marie's card.

"You sure you want to do this?" I said.

"Sure, I'm sure. I want to get to know Marie. She's a looker and I think it's time to interview her."

I laughed as I opened the door and let Shantay enter before me.

"Shantay!" I heard Marie's rich singsong voice. "And there's Alex."

"Hello, Marie," I said. But she was much more interested in Shantay.

"It's such a pleasure to finally have some time with you," Marie said. "Please, sit."

She pointed to a red leather sofa. We sat and I draped my arm across Shantay's shoulders.

"I didn't think you'd come here so soon," Marie continued. "I thought I'd have to make another trip to the Quarter in order to see you two again."

"We thought we'd check out your neck of the woods," Shantay said. "And, as long as we were here, we thought we'd stop in and see how you're doing."

"I'm so glad you did. I'm thrilled, in fact."

"Tell me," I said. "What exactly does a voodoo priestess do?"

"Oh, this and that. Mostly I help people."

"How so?"

"People only seem to come to me in times of need. I help them deal with the crisis. I give advice, sell gris-gris, anything to help them get through."

"Sounds worthy," said Shantay.

Marie smiled.

"I think it is. There's so much sadness and distress in the world today. I'm happy to help minimize that in any way I can."

"How did you learn of us? I doubt we run in the same circles," I said.

"You'd be surprised."

I arched an eyebrow at her, but she didn't seem to want to expand on the statement.

"Are we keeping you from work?" Shantay said.

"I have an appointment in forty-five minutes. So, no. I have nothing to do but get to know the famous couple, Alex and Shantay." She stood. "Where are my manners? May I get you something to drink? Beer? Wine? Sazerac?"

"I think I'd like a beer," I said.

"Turbo Dog? Or Amber Ale?"

"I'll have a Turbo Dog."

"And you, Shantay?"

"I'm fine, thank you."

She disappeared behind some beads and was back a moment later with my beer. It was time for the interview to begin.

CHAPTER TWENTY-THREE

Marie made herself comfortable in a black wingback chair seated next to us. She leaned forward with her elbows on her knees. She looked like she was ready to devour us. Before she could speak, I asked what had been on my mind.

"So, Marie. All coyness aside. How did you hear of us?"

"If you must know, you took a friend of mine home with you. She hasn't quit speaking of the experience yet." She smiled.

"And your friend? Does she have a name?" I held my breath and hoped and prayed she didn't say Eileen.

"Bijou," she said. I breathed a sigh of relief. "Do you remember her?"

"How could I forget her?" I said.

Her front door opened, and the hair on the back of my neck stood up. Three vampires walked in. Shit. Either I'd been set up, she knew I was a vampire, or this was strictly coincidental. I didn't believe in coincidences.

Marie stood and greeted her guests.

"Christian, Sanson, Jehad, what brings you here?"

All three of them stared at me. One finally spoke.

"Just making sure you're okay, Marie. You're not in danger, are you?"

"I'm fine. Oh, my lack of manners is showing again. Gentlemen, meet Alex and Shantay."

"What are you doing here?" The tall, dark one spoke.

"We met Marie last night," Shantay said. "She gave us her card, so we came to visit her."

"You'd better respect her. She's a vital part of this neighborhood. *Our* neighborhood."

"We don't want any trouble," I said.

"Famous last words." To Marie, he said. "We'll be outside if you need us."

"I'm sure I won't, but thank you."

They left and my stomach was in knots. Would they be waiting to jump me when we left? It sure sounded that way to me.

"How do you know them?" I said.

"They roam the neighborhood. They're like our very own neighborhood watch team. They're good guys, but fiercely protective."

"I see."

"Now, where were we?" said Marie.

"I think we'd better get going," I said.

"Nonsense. Tell me all about yourselves. Your accent is so unique, Alex. Where are you from?"

I sat back against the couch again and willed myself to relax.

"I'm originally from Romania, but I moved here from Buenos Aires."

"How exciting." She clapped her hands. "What a journey you've been on. I'm glad your travels brought you here."

"Thank you. And you? Are you New Orleans born and bred?"

"I am. I come from a long line of voodoo priestesses here in New Orleans. Your turn, Shantay. Where are you from?"

"I was born and raised in Chicago. I ran away to Rio de Janeiro when I was fifteen. Eventually made my may to Buenos Aires, which is where I met Alex."

"And how long have you two been together?"

"Since the night I brought Bijou home," I said.

"Is that right? She swore you two were an item already."

Shantay shook her head.

"Nope. We'd never crossed the employer/employee line until that night. So, we're eternally grateful to Bijou."

"Well, I'll be," said Marie. "You do owe her, don't you?"

"That we do," I said.

I'd had two beers and enjoyed my time with Marie, but it was close to time for her appointment and she had to get ready.

"Please don't be strangers," she said. "And I'll make it back to the Quarter soon. I promise."

"Thank you for a lovely time," said Shantay.

"Oh, child. You're most welcome."

We stepped into the front yard and the vampires I'd forgotten about jumped me. I yelled for Shantay to run, but before she could, one of the vampires was off me and holding her.

"What do you want?" I said.

"First, let me take a bite of your human," the one holding Shantay said.

"Don't you fucking dare."

Strength I hadn't known I had came from deep within. I pushed the other two off and faced the one with Shantay.

"Let her go," I growled.

"I see no marks on her," he said. "Which means she's fair game."

"She's mine." I was in his face. "Let. Her. Go."

The other two were standing behind him, leering at me.

"And if I don't?"

"I'll hurt you bad. Then I'll find out where your lair is, and I'll hunt you down and kill you."

He released his hold and shoved her at me. I caught her as she stumbled toward the ground.

"I don't want to see your fucking face around here again. Do you hear me? This is our territory."

"If we want to see Marie, we will. I'm not going to hunt around here. You have my word."

"How do I know your word means shit?" he said.

"You'll have to trust me."

"I'm not big on trust. Now get the fuck out of here before we take her home with us for all kinds of fun."

I felt Shantay shudder in my arms.

"We're leaving. But Marie is our friend. You haven't seen the last of us." We walked the four blocks to our car. "You okay to drive?"

Shantay nodded. She drove to the French Quarter.

"Are we having drinks?" I said.

"We are. I need a strong one."

I pulled her to me and kissed her temple.

"I've got you, babe."

"I know. But what if they'd been serious?"

"I'm no match for three strong vampires. They must not be that old, because I was able to break free. Had they been as old as I am, or older, I never would have been able to save you, I'm afraid. I guess I need to feed before we head back to Marie's. That is, if we ever go back."

"I don't know that I'm going to want to go back," she said. "Maybe I'll change my mind after a bit, but I doubt it."

"Fair enough."

We sat enjoying our drinks, and Shantay's color eventually returned to normal.

"You feeling better?" I said.

"Much. It's so nice to be in our territory, if you will."

"Mm. I agree wholeheartedly."

"Can I ask you a question? About territories?"

"Sure," I said. "Ask away."

"What would you do if you saw another vampire around here? How would you react?"

"I think I'm less territorial in my old age. Plus, I'm not in a coven so I don't have turf to defend."

"So you wouldn't do anything?" said Shantay.

"Not unless they started something. But I haven't seen any around here, so I don't think we need to worry."

She seemed satisfied with my answer and soon had me on the dance floor doing the steps Patricia had taught us. We stayed until three in the morning when my need for Shantay overwhelmed my desire to dance.

Something seemed off to me as we walked up to the front door. I couldn't put my finger on it, but I sensed danger. In a big way. I pulled Shantay behind me and motioned for her to stay quiet.

I looked around the yard, but didn't see anything out of the ordinary. Deciding I was just paranoid after our earlier encounter, I took Shantay's hand.

"You okay?" she said. "What's wrong?"

"I don't know. I sense danger, though I don't know why."

"Maybe this is why?" I turned to see Eileen and several others standing behind us. Eileen had a crossbow while others had guns and knives. I wasn't sure what they thought they were going to do with them, but Eileen had a sharpened wooden stake on her crossbow and that scared the shit out of me. I slowly backed away from the crowd.

"What do you think you're doing?" I tried to sound calmer than I felt.

"We're getting rid of you. We don't like your type down here."

"You don't like lesbians? But I thought you were one."

"You know what I mean. Don't get cute with me."

I shoved Shantay up the steps and heard a gunshot just as the front door closed behind her. Now I was pissed. How dare they? I looked over the crowd until I saw the man with his pistol still aimed at my front door.

"How dare you?" I snarled.

"What do you think you're going to do about it?" Eileen leveled the crossbow at me.

I didn't stick around to see if she meant business. I sped up the steps as fast as I could and let myself in.

"Shit!" I heard Eileen. "Why'd you let her get away?"

"Why didn't you shoot?" someone else said.

"I think you're full of shit, Eileen. They seemed like normal people."

"Yeah. Nice try, Eileen. Spare us from your next hunt."

I leaned with my back against the door, breathing heavily. If Eileen had fired, she could have killed me. Like, killed me dead. I started shaking all over.

Shantay was by my side.

"Come on, babe," she said. "Let's go to the kitchen and get something to calm our nerves."

I watched her make hot chocolate.

"That's going to calm our nerves?"

Then she poured peppermint Schnapps in the cups and I understood.

"Do you think they're gone?" she said.

"I do. It sounded like they were dispersing when you came to get me."

"Are you all right? Seriously?"

"I don't know." I was telling the truth. "I'm scared shitless, to be honest. I don't know how much longer I can stay here, Shantay. We may have to move."

She sat across from me and sipped her hot chocolate.

"Where would we go?"

"I don't know. I hate to do that to you because I know how much you love this city."

"I love you more," she said.

"Thank you." I took her hand. "I'm glad to know that."

We sat in silence for a while. I kept my ears trained on the outside, listening for any hint that there'd be more trouble.

"It's getting early," she said. "You better get to sleep soon."

"You're right. I'll go to my office now. Unfortunately, I've got some research to do."

We walked up the stairs arm in arm. We kissed good night at my office door. I watched until she had disappeared into the master suite before I opened my door and slipped inside, locking all four locks behind me.

I sat at my desk and started googling locations where I might want to live. I only searched the south. Now that I'd gotten a taste of southern weather, I wasn't ever going back to the cold. Ever.

Atlanta seemed to have a large lesbian population, so I put it at the top of my list. It appealed to me, and at the same time made me nervous. Georgia. Sounded rednecky to me. Sounded like a great place for vampire hunters. Still, Atlanta probably wasn't that bad. It stayed on my list.

Austin, Texas, was a college town that was supposedly liberal. I wanted a bigger city though, so it didn't make the list. Memphis surprised me as a possibility. But the more I looked, the more I was drawn to Miami. On the water, left leaning politics, strong latin influence, and most importantly, it was gay friendly. It even had its own Lesbian Chamber of Commerce.

That settled it. We'd move to Miami. And soon. I could feel the sun beating on me and felt the blisters on my back and arms. I fell into my casket and remembered nothing else that night.

"Miami?" Shantay was taking in my thoughts on moving. "When will we go?"

"I'd like to go sooner rather than later. I'm sorry, Shantay. New Orleans has been fun, but it's not safe anymore."

"How can you be so sure vampires and vampire hunters won't bother us there?"

"I can't be, my love. But I know for a fact they're here and they're after us here. I need to get away. I'll need you to find us a place, preferably on the water. According to my research, the neighborhood of Coconut Grove would be perfect. Will you get started on that when you wake up tomorrow?"

"If it's truly what you want, I'll begin my search."

"Thanks, babe."

"You're welcome."

We kissed. It started out chaste enough but soon morphed into something much more. It reminded me it had been far too long since I'd made love to my lady. I pulled away, took her hand, and led her back upstairs.

Our lovemaking was slow and unhurried. We took our time, exploring every inch of each other. She insisted on pleasing me first and she sent me into orbit more times than I could count. I was more satiated than I could ever remember being, yet my hunger for her raged on.

I teased and pleased Shantay in every way I could. I used my fingers, my lips, my tongue. She responded to each. She finally tapped my shoulder.

"No more," she whispered.

I rested my cheek on her inner thigh and inhaled the scent that was all Shantay. It was heavenly. As I lay there, I felt her femoral artery pulsing against my face. My fangs slid out and the different hunger I now felt made my stomach hurt. I needed to feed. And she was right there. One taste. That's all I needed.

I climbed off her and rolled onto my back.

"Damn it."

"What's wrong, Alex?"

"Nothing."

"Don't start lying to me now."

"I'm sorry. Let's take a shower and head out. I'm afraid I need to hunt tonight."

"Ah. So you wanted to take a chunk out of my leg again, huh? What happened to no more going down on me?"

"I can't help it. I love your flavor. And you react so completely to my mouth. You love my tongue on you. You know it."

"I do. I also love my life and hate tempting you so."

"Don't you worry about me," I said. "I'm stronger than you could imagine. Now, would you like to join me in the shower?"

"I'd love to."

We made love again in the shower. Or, rather, Shantay made love to me. She wouldn't allow me to feast on her wetness for fear I'd end up feasting on her thigh. We dried, dressed, and headed to the rundown neighborhoods of the city.

One such neighborhood was teeming with people. I had Shantay drop me off.

"Keep the doors locked. I'll be back," I said.

I wandered the streets looking for a likely meal. I peered down an alley and saw a man holding a knife to another's throat. I didn't know the circumstances, of course, but I sped toward the two. I easily wrestled the knife out of the one man's hand and told the other man to run, which he did.

When he was out of sight, I buried my fangs deep inside the aggressor. He gurgled and fought briefly before I drained him. I let him drop and heard footsteps.

"What the hell do you think you're doing?"

CHAPTER TWENTY-FOUR

I spun and came face-to-face with two vampires. Two menacing looking vampires with their fangs on display. A quick glance at their hands told me they had no weapons, but that didn't mean they couldn't take me. It would depend on how old they were and whether they'd fed recently. Personally, I thought I could take them.

"I don't want any trouble," I said.

"You should have thought about that before you killed our donor."

"Your donor?"

She picked up the dead body. Sure enough, my fang marks were not the only ones there. Shit.

"I'm sorry." I backed away slowly. "I didn't know."

"Who the fuck told you you could hunt here anyway?" the woman said.

"I didn't know this was anybody's territory." I hoped I sounded calmer than I felt.

"Did you bother to check?" the man snarled at me.

"I'll leave now. And never come back."

The woman reached for me, but I dodged her grasp. I ran down the alley as fast as I could. I knew I would be invisible to mortals at that speed, but I could sense the two vampires following me.

I took one corner at breakneck speed. I leaped over one fence and then another, barely missing landing on people. I raced down the main street and turned down a side street. I saw Shantay's car waiting in the distance, and I could no longer sense the vampires. I looked around. They were nowhere to be seen. I slowed my pace and got in the car.

"You okay?" Shantay said.

"Yeah. Bad experience. But it's over. Let's take the scenic route back to the Quarter."

Shantay zigzagged down side streets, and it took us twenty minutes to get to Jackson Square. She parked on a residential street and we walked toward our favorite watering hole.

"You want to tell me what happened?" she finally said.

"I fed on the wrong person this time."

She stopped.

"How so?"

"He was the donor of a couple of vampires."

"How could you have known?"

"I could have," I said. "If I'd checked for marks on his neck. But I didn't, and two vampires tried to take me out for feeding on their donor. But I lost them."

"That's why I had to take the long way around."

"Exactly. I couldn't have them following us."

We arrived at the bar and settled in with our drinks.

"So we should move sooner rather than later," said Shantay.

"Yes, we should."

She let out a long sigh.

"I'll search tomorrow."

"Search for what tomorrow?"

I looked up to see Marie standing there. I stood and pulled out an empty chair.

"Marie. Won't you join us?"

"I'd love to. Thank you."

She sat regally, back straight, hands demurely holding her drink.

"To what do we owe this pleasure?" said Shantay.

"I told you I'd find you two again."

"Fortunate for us," I said. "I just didn't expect to see you so soon."

"Something in the cards told me I'd better hurry," Marie said.

"They did?" Shantay sounded skeptical. I placed my hand on her thigh and gave it a gentle squeeze.

"Are you planning a trip maybe?"

"Maybe. As a matter of fact, we're talking about relocating."

Marie sat back against her chair.

"Say it isn't so. Why, if I may ask?"

I shrugged and tried to look nonchalant.

"I think it's just time for a change."

"How long have you two been here in New Orleans?"

"A couple of years now," Shantay said.

"That's not long enough," said Marie.

I shrugged again.

"Ah, but I think it is. It's time to explore new horizons."

"Like where? Where could you possibly go after New Orleans that would even compare?"

Shantay laughed.

"That's the sixty-four-thousand-dollar question."

Marie smiled warmly. She took Shantay's hand in hers and turned it over to examine her palm.

"Child, you're in danger. Not imminent, but something bad is going to happen to you."

"I thought you were into voodoo," said Shantay.

"I am, but I know my way around a palm as well. Please be careful. I'd say the next six months or so should be critical for you."

Shantay pulled her hand away.

"I'll take that into consideration."

"I'm sorry. I didn't mean to scare you."

"You didn't."

"But I made you uncomfortable. That was not my intention."

"It's all good," said Shantay. "Honest."

"Good." Marie smiled and lit up the whole room. Her straight white teeth shone against her blood red lipstick. Her brown eyes sparkled in the dimly lit bar. "Now, what can I do to put you at ease?"

"How's Bijou?" Shantay said.

"She's well. She misses you two. You should go see her sometime."

"We really should," I said. "It's been too long."

"We should dance," Marie stood. "The three of us."

"You go on ahead," Shantay said. "I'm going to get another drink."

Marie sank back into her chair.

"You don't like me, do you?"

"I like you just fine," said Shantay.

"Please, don't lie to me. Sit. Talk to me."

Shantay sat down.

"Fine. I feel like you set us up last night. We were accosted by your friends when we left your place."

Marie looked genuinely surprised.

"I'm so sorry. I did not know that. I never encourage or condone violence."

"Is that right?" Shantay was clearly in a defensive mood.

"Please believe me, Shantay. I enjoyed our visit very much. I'm sorry those three were less than respectful of you."

"So am I."

"What can I do to make you relax around me?" Marie said.

"Time will tell," said Shantay. "Let's just hang out for a while. We'll see if any more of your so-called friends show up."

"No one will be here but me."

Shantay got up and left the bar. I was just about to go after her when she came back in.

"What's up?" I said.

"She seems to be telling the truth. I don't see any of her bodyguards out there."

"See?" Marie smiled. "I come in peace."

"Let's just relax and have a few drinks," I said.

"Sounds wonderful," said Marie.

"Okay," Shantay said. "I'll try to relax."

The night wore on and Shantay relaxed. She was drinking iced tea and laughing and dancing with Marie and me.

"You two know how to dance," Marie said. "I'm impressed."

"We were taught by a local," Shantay said.

"Really?" Marie's eyebrows shot up. "Who?"

"Patricia," I said. "No idea of her last name."

"Fair enough. Besides, it's not like I know all the locals anymore."

"Have you really lived here all your life?" Shantay said.

"I have. I'm fourth generation New Orleans. And I'm quite proud of that."

"That's really cool," said Shantay. "I wish I could put down roots somewhere."

"Maybe Miami," I said.

"Miami? What could possibly draw you there? Especially when you live here in the Big Easy?"

"Too much danger here," I said. "But I don't want to talk about that. I think we should head back to our place."

"Am I invited?" Marie looked at Shantay, who smiled.

"Of course. Come on."

Shantay parked in the driveway and ordered me to wait in the car.

"What's going on?" Marie said.

"We had an unpleasant experience when we got home last night. She's just making sure they're not back."

"Shouldn't you, as the butch, be checking that out?"

"It's hard to explain," I said.

Shantay gave us a thumbs-up so we got out of the car.

"You two are quite mysterious in some ways," Marie said. "I love it."

"We're just a couple of regular lesbians," said Shantay. "Which apparently isn't everybody's cup of tea."

"I hear that, my dear." Marie hugged Shantay. I could feel the electricity flowing between them. I wanted some of that. And knew I would have some soon.

"Let's get inside," I said.

Upstairs, Marie wandered down the hall to my office. She tried the door. Obviously, it was locked tight.

"What's in here?" she said.

"That's my office."

"And you don't trust your partner with what's in your office?"

"I trust her implicitly. It's other people I don't."

"I'd love to see it."

"I'd rather show you our bedroom," I said.

Shantay took her hand, but Marie didn't budge.

"I'm getting a strange vibe. I can't quite put my finger on it."

"It's called sexual tension," said Shantay.

Marie laughed uneasily.

"I don't think so. I'm afraid I can't join you in bed until you show me what's in this room."

"That's too bad," I said. "Because that room is off limits."

"I'm afraid I'm uncomfortable now. I'm sorry. Clearly, it was a mistake coming home with you two. Shantay, would you be so kind as to drive me back to my car?"

I was disappointed, but if that was how she felt, then so be it.

"Sure," I said.

"Just Shantay, please. I've gotten a strange vibe from you from the beginning that I've tried to overlook. I don't feel safe with you. Shantay, are you ready?"

Shantay and I exchanged a look.

"Go on then," I said. "Just be safe please."

"Always," said Shantay.

Needless to say, my libido had cooled significantly. I had no idea what kind of vibes Marie got from me or my office. All I knew was that I was afraid. Very afraid. What if she figured out I was a vampire? What if I had her and Eileen to worry about now? I'd have to get Shantay to look into Miami sooner rather than later. It was time to pull up stakes and get out of town.

Shantay returned from dropping Marie off.

"What did she say?" I needed to know.

"Not much. She told me she felt you were a danger to me and urged me to leave you."

"Lovely."

"Right? I told her you were anything but a danger to me. I explained that we love each other and there's no way I'm walking away."

"Thanks, babe. Did she mention that I'm a vampire?"

"Nope," said Shantay. "She questioned whether I was in an abusive relationship. She thinks you're too controlling and overbearing. She said it's because you have a dark side you're trying to hide."

"Well, we both know that's not true."

"Yes, we do. Come to the kitchen, Alex. Let me make some hot chocolate."

"With peppermint schnapps?"

"Of course."

We sat at the small kitchen table sipping our drinks.

"I think we should hit the hot tub," she said.

"You do? I think it's too cold."

"I think it'll be just what we need to relax and get you to forget about Marie."

"I don't know…"

"I do. Now, you strip and get in while I make us each another cup."

"Strip? Are you trying to give me pneumonia?"

"Au contraire. I'm trying to heat you up." She winked at me and I felt the familiar lurch in my gut. Maybe tonight wouldn't be a write-off after all. Maybe Shantay and I could salvage something out of the wreckage.

I went to the back deck, uncovered the hot tub, turned the bubbles on, stripped, and got in. The water felt amazing. The jets pummeled tense muscles, slowly unwinding them, and helping me relax.

Shantay showed up with towels and drinks. I watched in admiration as she stripped and stepped in the tub. She was beautiful. Her dark skin glistened in the moonlight and all thoughts of Marie vanished.

I had Shantay. She was all I needed. All I'd ever need. I knew that in my heart of hearts.

"What are you thinking?" said Shantay.

"Just how much I love you."

"Is that right?" She stood and crossed over to sit beside me. "Show me."

I kissed her, full mouthed, tongue demanding entrance to her mouth. She opened her mouth and I tasted her with a coating of chocolate and peppermint. I grabbed her and placed her on my lap so she straddled me. I ran my hands up and down her thighs, and dug my thumbs into her.

She took my hand and placed it on her slick pussy. I entered her, sighing in ecstasy as she grabbed my fingers and pulled me deep. She felt amazing. She was hot, wet, tight, everything I could have wanted.

Shantay kissed me harder and pressed her full breasts into mine. I was on fire. I needed to own her, to claim her, to make sure she knew she was mine and only mine. She bucked against my hand as I fucked her, urging me onward.

I moved my free hand between her legs and gently circled her clit. She moaned into my mouth, but soon lost patience with me. She placed her hand on top of mine and forced me to rub harder and faster. Together, we got her off and I was rewarded with her pussy clamping on my fingers, squeezing them as she came.

She snuggled against me, her head under my chin, and her arms around me.

"I love you, Alex," she said.

"And I love you."

"I'm not going anywhere. I just want you to know that. You don't scare me."

"I should hope not. I should never scare you. I've been honest with you for years now and I'll continue to be honest with you."

"Thank you. I know who you are. I know what you are. And I still dedicate my life to you."

I kissed her again. A soft, chaste kiss that soon grew in its passion. Shantay pulled away then and kissed down my neck and chest and took a nipple in her mouth. I arched into her, letting her know how good she made me feel.

I felt her hand skim up my inner thigh, stopping to tease my lower lips. I spread my legs as wide as I could, and she chuckled.

"Someone want something?" she said.

"Take me, Shantay. Now."

She entered me. She filled me completely. I was lost in the feelings she was creating as I slipped away from my body and watched her plunging deep inside me. I slammed back into my body when I felt her thumb brush my swollen clit. One, two, three swipes, and I was catapulted out of this world for a few seconds. I floated gratefully in the oblivion before I gently made my way back to my body.

"Thank you, my love." I finally found my voice.

"My pleasure. I told you the hot tub was a good idea."

"You were right. As always."

She was silent for a few moments.

"Alex?"

"Hm?"

"How do you feel about marriage?"

"You mean like us? Like you and me getting married?"

I wasn't sure how I felt. I loved her. Of that there was no doubt. But marriage? She would grow old and I would stay young. That was hard enough to take. But did I want to marry her?

"Yeah," she said. "I think we should get married."

"I think it's definitely something to think about. Give me some time to process it, okay?"

"Take all the time you need, my love. As I said, I'm not going anywhere."

CHAPTER TWENTY-FIVE

December brought cooler temperatures, colored lights, and decorations everywhere. It turned out Christmas was Shantay's favorite holiday, and the house had never looked better. There were garlands everywhere, including wrapped around the wrought iron stair railing. We had a huge Christmas tree in the ballroom, another nice sized one in the living room, a smaller one in the hall, and a tabletop tree on the kitchen table.

Every night when I awoke, I'd find more decorations. It was wonderful. I loved the season and was thrilled to share that joy with Shantay.

"Do you go to services?" I asked her one night as we decorated the tree in the hall.

"What do you mean?"

"On Christmas."

"No. At least I haven't in years. I'm not very religious."

"Nor am I," I said. "But I do so enjoy the pageantry of Midnight Mass."

"You do?" She stopped what she was doing and stared at me.

"I love it. I will want to go this year, as well. I'm sure St. Louis Cathedral puts on a beautiful Midnight Mass."

"But the crucifix?" she said.

"I simply don't look at them."

"But there's a huge one right above the altar." She was still staring at me in disbelief.

"I'm serious. I can watch the service and not look at the crucifix. And even if I did happen to catch a glimpse, I'll sit far enough away from it. That's a big cathedral and I can sit in the back row."

"I'll go with you then. I mean, if it's important to you."

"It is important. Very."

Someone rang our doorbell. My heart stopped. Would it be Eileen and her friends again? Or perhaps Marie was back with her vampire friends. Shantay moved toward the door. I grabbed her arm and shook my head.

"Let me at least take a look."

I released her arm and watched as she looked through the peephole and then opened the door. Slowly, deliberately, I walked toward the open door. All my senses were on alert. I readied myself to do battle.

And then I heard the singing. A group of carolers, maybe ten of them, stood on our porch singing in perfect harmony. I felt my tension melt away. They finished their song and turned to leave.

"Please," I said. "Sing another song."

"Wait," said Shantay. "May I bring you each a glass of wine for your troubles?"

"Thank you," said a tall, husky man. "That would be wonderful."

Shantay disappeared and I visited with the carolers while we waited for her return. They were from the Garden District and had been caroling every Christmas season for twelve years. I made myself comfortable at the small table on the porch and gladly accepted a glass of wine from Shantay as well.

We sat listening as they sang carol after carol. Finally, a woman stepped forward, set her empty glass on the table, and began "O Holy Night." I got goose bumps. It was the most beautiful rendition I had ever heard.

We said our good nights and they left. I was in a very festive mood, but didn't want to decorate any more at the moment.

"Let's go dancing," I said.

"That sounds wonderful."

We drove to Jackson Square, then walked through the French Quarter, marveling at the colored lights, tinsel, trees, snowmen, angels, and Santa Clauses. If it was a Christmas decoration, it was lining Bourbon Street.

Shantay gasped as we entered out favorite bar. The lights on the tables were all red and green and garlands hung from the ceiling. It was breathtaking. Even the stuffed alligator in the corner had on a Santa hat.

The zydeco didn't really jibe with the decorations, but we enjoyed it as we sipped our drinks. We danced to several songs, tapped our toes to others, and just relaxed the night away.

"Fancy meeting you here." I recognized the voice but couldn't put my finger on it. I turned to see Patricia standing there.

Shantay jumped up and hugged her.

"Patricia," she squealed. "How have you been?"

"I've been good," she said. "Really good. How about you two?"

"Living the dream," I said.

She laughed.

"That's what I like to hear. I don't want to intrude. I just stopped to say hi."

"Please join us," said Shantay. "Please?"

Patricia looked from Shantay to me and back again.

"If you're sure you don't mind?"

"Not at all," I said. "I'd love it."

"Let me get a drink and I'll be right back," said Patricia.

"Nonsense," I said. "You sit and I'll buy. What are you drinking?"

"Eggnog."

"Coming right up."

We stayed until just past three when I'd had enough titillation and was ready for action.

"Y'all ready to head back to the house?" I stood.

"Am I really invited?" said Patricia.

"Of course," said Shantay. "Please say you'll join us?"

"I could never turn you two down."

It was too cold for the hot tub in my opinion, though they both argued that it wasn't. I slipped into my sweats and wrapped a blanket around me so I could sit on the deck and watch them.

Two naked beauties right in front of me and I couldn't touch them. Not yet. They teased and kissed and looked pleadingly at me, but I stayed strong. I was cold. I didn't do well when the temperature dipped below fifty. Maybe if I'd fed earlier. But I didn't, so I watched them and had to rearrange my sweats several times the wetter I grew.

"Come on. Let's get inside," I said. They got out and wrapped towels around each other. I watched them shiver. "Now tell me. Was it worth it?"

"Yes." Though their teeth chattered as they spoke.

I laughed at them and followed them into the blessedly heated house. They rushed up the stairs and were in bed when I got there.

"You got the bed wet." But they knew I wasn't serious.

"Isn't that the idea?" said Patricia.

We all laughed, and I made short order of my sweats and climbed in with them. They were ice-cold to the touch, and I threatened not to touch them until they warmed up.

"Fine," said Shantay. "We'll warm each other."

Before I could respond, I was treated to the sight of a full mouth kiss between them. I knew tongues were rolling over each other as their hands roamed the length of one another. Shantay's hand was on Patricia's breast while Patricia kneaded Shantay's ass.

"I think you're probably warm enough now," I said but received no response. So I reminded them of my presence by running my fingers between Patricia's legs and burying my tongue inside Shantay.

"Don't you fucking tease me." Patricia laughed. "Do me right already."

I slid my fingers inside her and she ground down against them. In no time she was crying out. I moved my mouth to Shantay's clit, and she screamed my name into the night.

It was my turn, but I'd have to wait. Shantay was still catching her breath, and Patricia had climbed out of bed.

"Where are you going?" I said.

She didn't answer but rummaged through my top dresser drawer.

"What are you doing?" said Shantay.

"Looking for toys. And, damn! Do you two have a lot. Whose is this?" She turned with the long forgotten butt plug Shantay had insisted we buy all those months ago.

"Mine," Shantay said sheepishly.

"It doesn't look like it's ever been used."

"It hasn't," I said. "Shall I use it on you?"

"No," Patricia said, "You should use it on Shantay. Right now."

I glanced at Shantay, whose eyes were wide.

"What do you say?" I said.

"I don't know…"

"Come on," said Patricia. "I want to see that."

"Grab my strap-on and some lube," I said.

Patricia climbed back into bed after securing me in my harness. She got on her knees and deep throated me. She ran her tongue over every inch of my cock. It was nice and wet. And ready.

"Come here, babe," I said to Shantay. "Get on all fours for me."

"Are you going to use that butt plug on me?"

"Only if you want it. You know I'll never do anything you don't want."

She nodded and got on her hands and knees. I slid the dildo between her legs, running its hard length against her.

"Please," she said.

I buried the tip inside and slowly slid it out again.

"You're teasing me. Give it to me," she said.

I thrust forward and filled her. She rocked back against me and urged me onward. I continued to move in and out of her until she was moaning and muttering incoherently.

"Do you want me in your ass?" I said, my own excitement cresting again.

"Yes. Oh God, yes. Fill me, Alex."

"I got this," said Patricia. She slathered lube on the plug then barely entered Shantay. "How's this?"

"God that feels good. More," Shantay said.

Patricia looked at me questioningly, and I nodded. I wanted to see Shantay completely filled in both holes. Patricia slid it in a little farther.

"Still okay?"

"Yes."

She buried the toy to its base inside Shantay's ass, and the sight was almost too much for me. I was quivering with carnal lust and hoped Shantay would finish soon so I could finally come.

Shantay screamed a bloodcurdling scream and collapsed into a pillow.

"You like?" Patricia said.

"Hell yeah."

"Good."

Patricia and I each withdrew, and I took off my harness and lay on my back. I was so swollen and throbbing so hard and I was half tempted to take matters into my own hands when Patricia took the cock out of my harness and slammed it into me.

"I probably should have made sure you were ready," she said.

"I'm fucking beyond ready."

She plunged it in and slowly dragged it out. Over and over, she fucked me with it until I was teetering on the edge. Shantay took my clit between her lips and flicked her tongue over it. My insides were mush. I was writhing on the bed, close, so very close, but still not able to let go.

I felt the ball of heat coalesce in my very center. It was so very tight. Until it wasn't. There I soared, into space, missiles of heat shooting over every inch of me. I floated back, but before I could relax, those two catapulted me back into orbit. I came back to reality feeling like a wet noodle.

"Well," said Patricia. "That was fun."

"No doubt," said Shantay.

"Indeed." But I couldn't say anything more. Blisters were starting to form on my arms and chest. The sun was up. Too far up for me. I jumped out of bed.

"Where are you going, hot stuff?" said Patricia.

"I need to take care of something." I dressed as quickly as I could lest she see what was happening. "Y'all snuggle in and I'll join you in a bit."

I went to kiss Shantay, but she was out cold. I hurried down the hall and fumbled with the keys to the office. I was shaking uncontrollably, and the searing pain was like none I'd experienced before.

It took every muscle I had to get my coffin lid open. I fell into it, pulled it closed, and that was all she wrote.

When I woke that evening, I found that I had forgotten to lock the office door behind me. That was a bonehead move that could cost me my eternal life. I wouldn't do it again. I promised myself that. I also vowed never to stay up that late again, no matter how much my libido complained.

"Merry Christmas Eve," said Shantay as I came downstairs.

"Mm." I kissed her. "Merry Christmas Eve to you, too."

"I've made us some eggnog. How does that sound?"

"Delicious."

We sat at the kitchen table and I was happier than I'd ever been at Christmas. I'd finally found my soul mate. Why did she have to be mortal?

"I also made reservations for dinner," she went on.

"Really? Where?"

"Commander's Palace."

"I hope you're hungry."

"I'm famished. I got the last reservation."

"What time is dinner?"

"Nine thirty."

"Sounds good," I said. "What shall we do until then?"

"I thought we could hot tub. Maybe go back to bed?" She wiggled her eyebrows.

"I think we could do both those things. Not necessarily in that order."

We headed back upstairs, drinks forgotten. I slowly, methodically, took every piece of clothing off her. When she stood naked before me, I was at a loss. Her beauty astounded me.

"You take my breath away," I said.

"You're so sweet."

"I'm honest."

"Get naked," she said.

I stripped and we lay together, legs entwined, arms embracing. I kissed her full on her mouth and tasted the eggnog on her tongue. She was delicious and gorgeous and mine. Her nipples were puckered peaks, and I kissed my way down so I could take one in my mouth and run my tongue over it. She arched into me and held my head in place.

Her skin was like satin under my fingertips as I glided my hand all over her body. I finally came to rest between her legs, where I dragged my fingers along her outer lips before spreading her inner ones.

"Please," she said. "Please make love to me."

And that's what I did. I took my time and gave every inch the attention she deserved and so clearly desired. I entered her slowly with two fingers. Then three. I pressed my palm into her clit and felt how slick and swollen she was. Just for me.

Shantay reached the pinnacle of ecstasy as she came three times for me. I was honored to be able to do that for her. My heart was full of love, pride, and my own need.

"That was something else," she said. "I love it when you take me gently."

"I love taking you gently. I love taking you fast and furious. I just love making love to you."

Shantay returned the favor, loving me tenderly yet fiercely. The feel of her tongue on me and in me had me seeing stars. She knew just what I needed and when I needed it. She pleased me continuously and deliberately until I could hold off no longer. One final swipe of her tongue on my nerve center sent me shooting into the galaxy where I remained for a few precious seconds before finding my way back to myself.

CHAPTER TWENTY-SIX

A fter dinner, we walked along Bourbon Street listening to carolers and enjoying the decorations. The air had a buzz in it. Everyone seemed festive and it was contagious. I sang along with the carolers but not as loudly as Shantay, whose beautiful voice outshone them all.

I smiled with pride at her as she poured her heart and soul into every song. She was amazing. She was talented. She was perfect. And she was mine.

We stopped several times to enjoy eggnog and all the sights and sounds. It was after eleven when I finally decided it was time to make our way to the cathedral.

"We want to be early so we can get a seat," I said.

"I still don't get your obsession with Midnight Mass, but I'm ready to go now."

"Thank you. It reminds me of Christmases of my youth. Midnight Mass in the old country was an exciting and elegant celebration full of pomp and extravagance. And after, we'd go home and eat a delicious pork dinner Mother had made. We kept pigs and Father would slaughter one on the twentieth, as was tradition. Then Mother would cook all evening on Christmas Eve, and we would sit down to a fantastic meal."

"Sounds lovely." Shantay wrinkled her nose. I laughed.

"It was."

We entered the cathedral and I escorted Shantay to a back pew. It was almost standing room only already and I was happy to have found a seat far enough back that the large crucifix behind the altar wouldn't disturb me.

Mass was wonderful. At once, it made me homesick yet happy to be with Shantay. I gave thanks to the powers that be that I could spend part of my immortality with her. I hoped she'd live many years so we could be together. I knew I'd be crushed when she was gone, and I hoped that wouldn't happen for a very long time.

The service lasted an hour and a half, and after, I was at peace and ready to deal with mortals for another year. Shantay seemed to have enjoyed herself. She sang along with all the hymns and didn't fall asleep during the sermon. I considered that a win.

"What did you think?" I said as we wandered back toward Bourbon Street.

"I get what you said about the pageantry. It really was steeped in tradition, wasn't it?"

"Indeed, it was." I draped my arm over her shoulders and held her tight.

"I still don't get your obsession, but I'll admit, I didn't hate it."

I laughed.

"Well, that's something anyway."

We drank more eggnog and listened to carolers until group by group, they started to disappear.

"I suppose it's time to get home," I said.

Shantay's face lit up.

"And open presents."

I laughed again.

"And open presents," I said.

The amount of presents around the tree in the living room was absolutely obscene. We had obviously spoiled each other, and I couldn't help but comment.

"There are hungry people in the world, in this city. We could have done better with our money."

"Don't be a Scrooge. We love each other and wanted to lavish presents on each other. Don't bring me down. Just start opening presents."

"Which one should I open first?"

Shantay had bought me lots and lots of clothes. Jeans, hoodies, tennis shoes, and socks.

"What is with all these clothes?" I finally said after opening my third pair of Levi's.

"You need to be more modern. Come into the twenty-first century. You always look nice. Don't get me wrong. But I think you'll be more comfortable in these clothes. Now, go try them on."

"Not until you open your presents."

"I've already opened so many. I love the negligees, and the jewelry is perfect. I don't think I can open one more gift."

But there were still four huge boxes just outside the ring of discarded wrapping paper.

"There are more. I must insist," I said.

She got up and walked over to the first large gift.

"What in the world?" she said. She unwrapped it and stared at the box, which really didn't give anything away.

"Open the box." I was trying not to be impatient, but I was so excited, I was beside myself.

She finally did as I'd requested and she backed away, hands over her mouth.

"Oh, Alex, you didn't!" I crossed the room and wrapped my arms around her. Each box contained a sculpture by an artist she had admired at the Voodoo Festival.

"Thank you so much."

"You're so welcome," I said. "Now you need to decide where they go. And we can get rid of anything in the house to make room for them."

She hugged me again, then looked into my eyes.

"Should we keep them boxed up until we move?"

I shrugged.

"That's up to you. They're yours, my love. Do with them as you see fit."

"I'm sorry I haven't found a place for us yet in Miami." She grew serious. "There just aren't any waterfront properties for sale or even for rent yet."

"And that's fine. When one comes available, we'll jump on it. Until then, we'll stay here. It's not like living in New Orleans is a hardship."

"True." She smiled. "Would you like a drink?"

"I'm about eggnogged out."

"How about a glass of wine then?"

"Sure."

"Okay. Climb into the hot tub. I'll bring the wine out."

"Hot tub?" I said.

"Hot tub. And here. Don't forget your new fluffy robe to wrap up in when you get out."

I took the kelly green robe and went out to the deck. I was soaking comfortably when Shantay arrived, bearing a bottle of Pinot Noir and two glasses. She drove me crazy as she slowly stripped and carefully stepped into the bubbling water.

The bubbles obscured all her good parts, but that was okay. I enjoyed looking at her, her face. Her chocolate eyes stared back at me full of love and admiration. I knew my own eyes reflected those sentiments tenfold.

She came over and snuggled next to me. Her soft skin pressed into mine was the ultimate aphrodisiac. Never had I longed to be with a woman like I did with Shantay. In all my hundreds of years with thousands of women, none had begun to affect me like she did.

"Were you serious?" I said.

"When?"

"When you were talking about marriage?"

She looked into my eyes.

"Yes. Why?"

"I think we should do it. I think we should get married."

"Really?" Her whole face lit up. "When?"

"I don't know. How would you feel about being a June bride?"

"I'd cherish it," she said. "You're making me the happiest woman on earth. I'll start looking for wedding venues tomorrow."

"That's how you're going to spend your Christmas? I don't think so."

"I can look. Oh, Alex. I do so love you."

"And I love you. A reminder. You'd better look for venues in Miami, too. I really hope we'll be living there by then."

"You're so right. You think of everything."

"I try," I said. "We'll have to get you a ring."

"Let's go look at them now." She stood.

"No place is open."

"The internet is."

She was out and wrapped in a towel before I could respond. Laughing, I got out, dried off, and put on the warm, fluffy robe she'd given me. I gathered the wine and dutifully followed her into the living room where she sat on the brown leather couch and opened her laptop.

I sat next to her, knowing this was all about her and that my opinion really wouldn't be needed. I poured wine for us and sipped mine while she tapped frantically on the keyboard.

"What are you looking up? Like just engagement rings?"

She turned the laptop so I could see she was looking at Tiffany's on Canal Street. I didn't complain. Nothing but the best for my baby, and if she wanted Tiffany's then Tiffany's she would have.

"Do you see any you like?" I said.

"I'm designing one now."

"May I watch?"

"Of course."

She sat back so I could follow along with her. Princess cut. Solid gold band. It was simple yet beautiful. Just like her.

"Are you sure?" I said. "We can get something fancier."

"I like this. I think it's elegant. And don't you worry. My wedding ring will be plenty fancy."

"Fair enough." I nodded. "Shall we shop for that now, as well?"

"Sure." Her face lit up. She studied ring after ring until she gasped, "This is the one."

I leaned over to see which one she had chosen. It was a wide ring in eighteen-karat gold with pavé diamonds. It was stunning.

"That's gorgeous," I said. "Stunning even."

"Now let's choose yours."

She tilted the computer again so we could both see and started scrolling again.

"Babe? Let's look at men's rings."

"Oh, yeah. Sorry. I was thinking we could get the same rings maybe?"

"Nope. I want a man's ring, Shantay. I would feel ridiculous wearing something like that."

She switched to the men's category and stopped at every ring to look at me for my opinion. I shook my head time after time.

"There," I finally said. "That's the one."

It was a wide platinum ring with a baguette diamond in it.

"Oh, baby! That's perfect for you."

"Right?"

"Right."

She kissed me, her laptop forgotten. I pulled away after a while.

"Let's get those ordered," I said.

"It doesn't work that way."

"Why not?"

"We need to go to the store to try them on and get them fitted."

"I need to go to a jewelry store? That's going to be rather difficult for me, my love."

"We'll go right before they close. Right after you wake up. Okay?"

"Okay."

Her whole face glowed. Never had I seen her so happy. And I promised myself then and there to make her face glow like that every day for the rest of her life.

She closed the laptop and set it on the coffee table. I leaned back against the couch, and she snuggled up against me.

"Are you happy, sweetheart?" I said.

"Beyond. Do we have any champagne?"

"You would know that better than I."

"True." She laughed. "I think we do. And we're celebrating being engaged."

She disappeared into the kitchen and I opened her laptop to look at the rings one more time. I was still shocked that I was actually getting married. Never in my wildest dreams had I thought I'd do that. For one thing, it hadn't been legal the first five hundred plus years of my existence. So there was that. And I'd made a point never to get close to anyone. Now, I was engaged to the most wonderful woman who had ever walked the earth.

Shantay returned with champagne in a bucket and two flutes. She handed me the bottle.

"Would you do the honors?" I filled the glasses and she raised hers. "To us."

"Indeed. To us forever."

I took a sip of the champagne. It was nice. Very smooth. I looked at the label. Armand de Brignac. My all-time favorite. Sure, Dom Perignon cost a little more, but it didn't please my palate like Armand.

When I set the bottle back in the ice, I noticed Shantay had a weird expression on her face.

"What's up?" I said.

"You said forever."

"You know what I mean."

She nodded but didn't look assuaged.

"What does that even mean? Forever? You'll go on after I die. What will you do then?"

"Mourn you for all eternity."

"Alex, I'm serious," she said.

"As am I."

"You'll have to go on. It's what you do."

"And I will. But I'll never love again."

"Don't say that."

"Shantay," I said, "I've spent almost six hundred years on the earth. Never once did I look at another woman for anything more than a good time. I've never been in love before and I'll never be in love again. For as long as I wander. I promise you that."

"I don't want that promise."

"Why not?"

"I can't bear to think of you alone for eternity."

"It's what I do. It's how I live. This? What we have? It's an anomaly."

"Promise me when I'm gone, you'll find someone else," said Shantay.

"I can't promise you that."

"Please?"

"Why?" I said.

"Because it's important to me. I want to look down from wherever I am and see you happy."

"It's that important to you? Really?"

"Yes." She nodded solemnly.

"I promise. I'll try to fall in love again. It won't be the same, though. It won't be what we have."

"I can accept that. And I appreciate that. I just don't want you to be alone."

"You'll always be with me, you know."

"I know this. But it's not the same."

"Okay. I've promised. Now can we relax and enjoy the champagne?"

"Of course. In the hot tub."

Before I could object, she'd picked up the bucket and her glass and crossed the living room to the dining room. I stood and followed her out the sliding glass door onto the deck. It was cold out there. Hell, it was December after all. And I hadn't fed in a few nights, so I had no internal warmth.

I stepped out of my robe into the bubbling water and immediately felt better. The warmth engulfed me as I sipped my champagne and looked across the tub at Shantay sipping hers.

"Happy?" I said.

"Never happier."

Chapter Twenty-seven

The days were getting longer again, but the sun was still setting right around six, so Shantay and I had plenty of time together. We spent much of our time making love, soaking in the hot tub, hanging out at our bar, or searching for places to live in Miami. We hadn't had any incidents in several months, but I still didn't feel safe and, although Shantay hated the idea of leaving New Orleans, she understood my trepidation.

I rose that night full of excitement. It was another one of my favorite days, Mardi Gras. Shantay was sitting in a chair right outside my office, and when I opened the door, she threw her arms around me and hugged me tight.

"Happy Mardi Gras," she exclaimed.

I laughed.

"Happy Mardi Gras to you, too." I stepped back and admired her outfit. She was wearing loose flowing gold pants and a tight purple T-shirt. "You certainly look ready."

"I am."

"Great. Let me change my clothes into something more festive, then we'll go brave the crowds."

I put on black skinny jeans with a green and yellow T-shirt. I was ready for the party of the year. We had to park five blocks away from Jackson Square due to the sheer volume of people who were at the French Quarter.

The crowd greeted us at St. Louis Cathedral, and it took us a half hour to press through the throngs to get to our favorite bar. It was already standing room only there, but we each ordered a hurricane, then found a spot along the wall to stand and watch the crowd.

"We may as well head outside again," Shantay yelled to be heard.

I nodded and we made our way out to Bourbon Street where we were instantly separated among the millions of revelers. I fought through people and found Shantay laughing at the antics of a man on stilts trying to make his way down the street.

"Shantay," I called. She didn't appear to hear me but saw me as I got closer. "Give me your hand."

We held hands and pushed our way to the middle of the street where we let the crowd force us onward. Shantay pulled me out of the wave of people and to the sidewalk. She looked up and I saw people with beads on the balcony. Shantay lifted her shirt and was rewarded with a slew of beads. She caught most of them and placed them around her neck. She looked at me like an excited child who just discovered the ice cream truck.

If I'd had a heart, it would have soared. Not only did the sight of her breasts thrill me anew, but her childlike enthusiasm was contagious. She stopped at the next balcony and the next. She had so many beads, she started looping some around my neck as well.

We wandered farther down Bourbon, watching the people on the balconies as well as those in the street. Above the din, I swear I heard my name. I looked around and saw no one, but the hairs on the back of my neck stood up. Who knew we were there?

I heard Shantay's name called, but she seemed oblivious. I heard my name again along with an, "Up here."

Looking up to the balcony, I made eye contact with Patricia. She smiled broadly and motioned us up to join her. I pulled Shantay, who was staring lasciviously at a woman with her shirt up. She reluctantly tore her gaze away and followed me.

"Where are we going?" she called.

"You'll see."

"Is this Patricia's place?" she said.

"It is indeed."

We climbed the steps in the back and Patricia flung the door open and took us in her arms.

"Happy Mardi Gras," she said.

"Right back atcha," I said.

With no warning, Patricia planted a kiss on Shantay, who seemed more than happy to return it. My libido sped up as I looked on, the combination of breasts and this kiss almost too much for my hormones to handle.

Patricia stepped away from Shantay and kissed me. It was a much more chaste kiss, but that was okay. Anything more and I probably would have unceremoniously ripped her clothes off her.

"Come on out to the balcony," she said. "I've got a shitload of beads, and women are flashing me right and left."

"Sounds wonderful," said Shantay.

We carried two chairs out to the balcony and sat with Patricia. Shantay handed me some beads before taking an armful for herself. She and Patricia sat close to each other, and I pondered what a good thing it was that I wasn't the jealous type. The more worked up they got each other, the more likely I'd get to provide them both with much needed relief.

Shantay and Patricia didn't sit long, though. They stood at the railing, Shantay squealing as she tossed string after string of beads to women of all shapes and sizes. Laughing, I stood and joined them, tossing my own beads down to beauties who bared their breasts.

Patricia disappeared inside and came back with three hurricanes.

"Yum. Thank you," said Shantay.

"You're quite welcome. Drink up."

I tasted my hurricane. I supposed there was some passion fruit syrup in there somewhere, but it tasted mostly of rum. Good thing I liked rum. Shantay took a huge swig of hers, and I had to remind her she was driving.

"You're not going anywhere," said Patricia. "We'll be here all night. And after, my bed will be perfect for us."

"See?" Shantay said.

I didn't want to spoil her good time by reminding her I would not be able to sleep there. I figured we'd cross that bridge when we came to it.

So we stood on the balcony tossing down beads for hours. Finally, I'd seen so many large and small areolas, long and short nipples, tiny and voluptuous breasts, that I needed to do something to soothe my racing hormones.

"Let's go to bed," I yelled.

"But the night is young," said Patricia.

"We can come back out in a bit. Let's go fuck."

"Now you're speaking my language."

Shantay didn't say a word. She just dumped her beads in the bucket and went inside. We followed her through the beads and into Patricia's bedroom. Patricia spun and kissed me hard on the mouth. Her tongue was demanding, and I welcomed her in to frolic with my tongue. She tasted good, like rum, and I found myself longing to bury my tongue in other wonderful tasting places on her body.

Patricia turned away from me and kissed Shantay, placing a hand on Shantay's full breast. I watched her tease Shantay until her nipple poked to attention under her tight shirt. I needed them, both of them, and I didn't want to wait.

I stripped and lay in bed with my legs spread, as if begging someone to eat me. This got Patricia's attention as she pulled away from Shantay and got naked herself. Shantay disrobed quickly, and together they lay on the bed, Patricia on my right and Shantay between my legs.

Patricia sucked and tugged on my nipple, leaving me breathless with need. I arched into her mouth while I bucked my hips, urging Shantay to finish me off. But Shantay didn't seem in any hurry. She dragged her tongue all over me, from one end to the other, lazily taking her time as if I wasn't in desperate need to come.

I placed my hand on the back of Shantay's head and held her in place.

"Finish me," I begged her.

She licked deep inside me, her strong tongue probing all my sensitive spots. I held her against me, but she finally broke free so she could move her mouth to my throbbing nerve center. I felt her lips holding it while her tongue swiped over it. Once, twice. I lost count as I blanked out and simply felt. I couldn't think. It wasn't possible. My brain was mush. My whole body tightened, every inch of it.

I focused every ounce of my energy on what Shantay was doing to my clit and soon was rewarded when I arched off the bed and out of my being. I soared high for seconds on end before finally floating softly back to my body.

"Fuck yeah," I said when I finally found my voice. "Happy Mardi Gras to me."

"My turn," Patricia said.

"Okay," said Shantay.

But before we could take Patricia, she was out of bed and leaving her room.

"Where are you going?" I called.

She was back with a dildo that looked like it would split her in two. It was over a foot long and almost as wide as my fist.

"I've been waiting for a special occasion." She grinned.

Patricia handed the toy to me and got on her hands and knees.

"Do you have any lube?" I said.

"I won't need it."

I wasn't convinced, but figured she knew her own body better than I. Shantay lay under her, sucking her tits and rubbing her clit while I pushed the tip inside Patricia.

"More," she said.

I slid more inside her, twisted it around, and pulled it back out.

"You have no idea how good that feels," said Patricia. "Give it all to me. Please."

I carefully filled her with the dildo, worried that I was going to hurt her. I spun it around inside and withdrew it. Her response, leaning back against me and taking it all in, told me she was fine, so I plunged it in again. Deep. Hard. Over and over until Patricia screamed like a banshee then collapsed on the bed.

She still had a firm grip on the toy, so I couldn't pull it out. Seeing it buried deep inside her had me throbbing all over again. It was so fucking hot. I could hardly contain myself. I wanted to reach down and rub my clit until I exploded again.

I finally got the dildo out of her and Shantay climbed up on all fours.

"My turn."

"Baby, this will hurt you. You're too tight."

"Please?"

I couldn't say no to Shantay. So I eased the tip inside her. She jumped and pulled away.

"No. I can't take that."

I tossed the dildo to the floor and buried my face in her pussy. She was drenched, absolutely drenched, and tasted divine. I sucked her lips then plunged my tongue as deep as I could go. She rubbed herself all over my face and I was beside myself as I finally licked my way to her clit.

As I took her in my mouth, I felt Patricia close around my own clit and braced for what I knew would be another powerfully intense orgasm. But Shantay first. I licked and sucked and licked some more until she called out my name and shuddered, then fell face-first into the pillow.

Patricia made short order of me and soon the three of us lay together, satiated. I could easily have dozed, and Patricia's eyes were closed, so I figured she was ready to sleep, as well.

But Shantay jumped up and got dressed.

"Where are you going?" I asked drowsily.

"Come on," she said. "Let's give out more beads."

I checked my watch. It was four. I still had a couple of hours before the sun came up.

"Okay, okay," I said. "Give me a minute."

"I'll meet you out there," said Shantay and she was gone.

Patricia laughed.

"Well, I suppose we'd better get up. Unless you want to go again?" Her eyes were dark with passion. I wondered what the rules were. Was I allowed to take Patricia again? I wanted to and clearly, she wanted me to.

No. I was engaged to Shantay. If Shantay was with us, it would be one thing. But I couldn't fuck Patricia one-on-one. It wouldn't be right.

"Nice try," I said. "If Shantay wants to throw beads, then that's what we shall do."

"Fine. I'm getting dressed, too."

We walked out to see Shantay leaning far over the balcony dropping beads on someone. As we got closer, I saw a woman with her shirt off, huge breasts on display. Shantay obviously approved as she was about to fall off the balcony in her attempt to get a better view.

I pulled her back, laughing.

"Don't fall, babe. That wouldn't be good."

The woman with the large breasts was still there, shirt in her hand.

"Let's see yours now," she called.

Shantay surprised me by lifting her shirt and shaking her breasts for the woman's pleasure.

"Woot," the woman said and put her shirt back on as a mounted police unit approached. She blew Shantay a kiss and was swept away by the crowd.

"Are you having fun?" I said.

"Tons."

"Good."

"Is that Bijou?" Shantay pointed to the crowd. I searched, and then I sensed danger. Something was wrong. I quit looking for Bijou and started scanning for unwelcome visitors. I didn't see anyone and almost missed Shantay saying, "It is Bijou. Right there."

I followed her outstretched finger and saw Bijou and Marie in the center of the crowd.

"Come on," I said. "Let's get inside for a minute."

"What?"

"Hey!" Marie had spotted us. "You're evil!" I stood transfixed as she hurled insults at me. "You're the devil incarnate. Satan's spawn."

It only lasted a minute or so as they were whisked away by the crowd.

"What the hell was that?" said Patricia.

"A woman scorned," I said.

"I guess. Evil? You? Nothing could be further from the truth."

"Right you are," said Shantay. "Alex is a sweetheart."

"Yes, she is."

"Thank you. Both of you." But I couldn't shake the gnawing feeling in my gut that maybe Marie knew what I was. I really couldn't stay in New Orleans any longer. My life depended on us leaving. And soon.

I checked my watch. It was after five. We'd have to fight our way against the crowds to get back to the car and I couldn't risk being awake much longer. "I think it's time for us to go."

"Do we have to?" Shantay said. "I don't want to."

"I'm afraid it's time, my sweet. We need to get back to the car and I need to be asleep soon."

Reality seemed to dawn on her.

"Oh, shit. Yeah. Sorry. Patricia? Will we see you again?"

"Count on it."

"Great."

We said our good-byes and fought through the mass of people. We finally got to our car around five thirty and Shantay had us home by five forty-five.

"Did you enjoy Mardi Gras?" I said.

"It was the best."

"Good. That makes me happy. Now, I need to get to sleep."

"Mm. Me, too. I'll see you tonight."

"Yes, you will, my love."

I climbed into my coffin feeling happy and loved. Until I thought of Marie. What did she know about me? Had her vampire friends told her what I was? I hoped not. I resolved then and there to move to Miami even if we couldn't have beachfront property right way. I needed to go, needed to put New Orleans in my rearview mirror. It was time.

CHAPTER TWENTY-EIGHT

Y ou're lucky you're immortal," Shantay looked up from her computer.

"Why's that?"

"You won't get sick from this coronavirus thing."

"You don't need to worry about it either, do you?"

"I don't know. They're saying cases have escalated because of Mardi Gras."

"Then it's a really good thing we hung out with Patricia rather than stay in those crowds."

"You are so totally right," she said. "As usual. But they're shutting things down and quarantining people."

"Are you serious?"

"Yeah. Like the bars on Bourbon Street are closed."

"No. Today's St. Patrick's Day. I want to celebrate."

"Sorry, Alex. No can do. I'll make you an Irish coffee if you'd like. Or we have Guinness."

"I'll go grab each of us a Guinness," I said.

When I got back from the kitchen with the beers, there was a knock on the front door. I froze. Who the hell could it be? Eileen? Marie? A whole slew of vampire hunters? Whoever it was knocked again.

"Are you going to answer that?" said Shantay.

"Sure."

I looked through the peephole and what a sight for sore eyes. Patricia stood there, looking delectable in skinny jeans and a Saints hoodie. I opened the door.

"Patricia. Welcome. Come on in."

"Thanks." She coughed.

"Are you okay?" I said.

"Yeah. Allergies."

She and I walked into the living room. Shantay put her laptop on the coffee table and stood.

"Isn't this a pleasant surprise?" she said. "What brings you here?"

"Honest?"

"Please," I said.

"It's St. Patrick's Day. All the bars are closed. People are all terrified of this COVID-19. But I figured you two would be celebrating." She motioned to the beers on the table. "And I wanted to party, so I thought I'd come over. I hope you don't mind."

"Not at all," said Shantay. "I'll go get you a Guinness."

We sipped our Guinness and talked of the world's issues.

"Is your store closed?" I asked Patricia.

"It is. I'm telling you. This is all overblown. People are going to feel stupid about overreacting in no time."

"Do you really think they're overreacting?" said Shantay. "It seems like this coronavirus is pretty serious. And they're saying the numbers are spiking after Mardi Gras."

Patricia looked like she was about to answer, but then succumbed to a coughing fit that lasted a couple of minutes.

"I don't believe them," she finally said. "I don't think this supposed virus is deadly. I'm not even sure it's real."

"But it's killed people all over the world," Shantay said.

"It's just like the flu. No biggie. We don't close businesses during flu season every year, do we?"

She took a deep breath then coughed again. She took a long pull off her Guinness.

"That cough doesn't sound good," Shantay said.

"It's allergies. Cough and sore throat. Happens every year."

"You want some allergy medicine?"

"I'd love it if you have some," said Patricia.

Shantay went back to the kitchen and returned with an allergy pill for Patricia, who took it with a sip of beer.

"We should hit the hot tub and forget about this virus," I said. I figured as long as Patricia was there, we should take advantage of the situation.

"Now you're talking," said Patricia.

"I'll make Irish coffees to drink out there," Shantay said. "Since we finished our beers already."

"Yum. Can I help?"

"No, thanks. You and Alex get in the water. I'll be right out."

She didn't have to ask me twice. I stepped onto the deck and stripped. As I was getting in the water, I noticed Patricia trembling.

"Are you okay?" I said.

"Yeah. It's just cold, you know?"

It was actually in the low sixties, so it was chilly, but not that cold.

"Get in the water, okay? You'll warm right up."

She stepped in and snuggled against me.

"This is much better."

"See?"

Shantay came out with our drinks. I took one sip and closed my eyes. The taste carried me back to the years I'd spent in Limerick, Ireland, where the drink had originated. It was during the fifties when I'd been there and some of the happiest times of my long life were spent in Ireland.

"You with us, Alex?" said Shantay.

"I am. I was just enjoying the drink. It's delicious."

"Thank you. Believe it or not, I found the original recipe and followed it."

"I do believe you." I winked at her.

"How're you feeling, Patricia?" Shantay said.

"I'm fine. I feel fine. Just can't catch my breath and this damned cough is driving me batty."

"That's too bad. You sure it's just allergies?"

"Positive."

Shantay got in the water and sidled up to the other side of me. I had my arms out, one around each of them. I thought to myself how lucky I was.

"So, you two scoundrels," Patricia said. "I noticed a diamond ring on Shantay's finger during Mardi Gras but didn't comment. Does it mean what I think it means?"

"It most certainly does." Shantay held out her hand and Patricia fawned over the rock.

"It's beautiful. And congratulations."

"Thanks," I said. "We're getting married in June, and of course you're invited."

"I am? Excellent. I wouldn't miss it."

"Great. It should be a party," said Shantay.

"I would expect nothing less," Patricia said.

I felt Patricia shudder.

"You sure you're okay?" I said.

"I don't know. I'm starting to feel like shit. Sorry to break up the party, but I think I'd better get going."

"That's a shame," I said.

"Yeah, but I need to go. Thanks for the hospitality. I'll be back when I'm feeling better."

"Sounds good." Shantay got a towel and wrapped it around Patricia. "You feel better soon so you can come over for some real fun."

"Oh, don't worry. I will."

Shantay came back from walking Patricia to the door and climbed back in the tub.

"Too bad she had to leave," she said. "But I don't mind a night just the two of us."

"I don't mind either." I pulled her close.

A few nights later, I woke to find Shantay still in bed.

"What's going on?" I said.

"I don't feel good. I ache all over and I'm running a fever."

"What can I get you? Soup? Juice? Aspirin?"

"I've already taken ibuprofen. But I'd love some orange juice. If I OD on vitamin C I'm sure I'll feel better in no time."

I brought her a glass and a pitcher of orange juice. She drank a swig then made a horrible face.

"What's wrong?" I sat on the bed next to her, concern flooding me.

"Nothing," she said. "It just hurts to swallow."

"Maybe we should get you to a doctor."

"No. I'm sure Patricia just shared her bug with me. I'll be better in a day or two."

But she didn't get better. In two days' time she was markedly worse. Her breathing was labored.

"You ready to get checked out?" I said.

"I can't go anywhere."

"Why not?"

"Because the elephant on my chest won't let me."

"What?" I didn't know what she was talking about.

"Damn, Alex. I really don't feel good."

"We're going to the hospital."

"How? You can't drive and I can't…"

That was it. She passed out and I panicked. I suppose I could drive if I had to, but it had been years since I'd been behind the wheel.

"Shantay?" I shook her. She didn't respond.

I called 9-1-1 and begged them to hurry. The paramedics arrived wearing masks.

"Why do you have masks on?" I said.

"There's a pandemic?" one of them said.

I nodded and they hurried past me, up the stairs.

"First door on your left," I called after them.

By the time I got back to the room, they had an oxygen mask on Shantay and were working busily all around her.

"What is it?" I said. "What's wrong with her?"

"Looks like COVID."

"But that's deadly!"

The paramedic nodded solemnly.

"She's in good hands now."

"Can I ride with you? In the ambulance?" I was panicked. I couldn't lose Shantay. My mind was racing. I needed to think of a way to cure her. But I was helpless. I hated that feeling.

"You won't be allowed inside the hospital. No one is allowed except patients and staff right now. It's best if you stay here and pray for her."

Pray? To whom? There was no one to pray to. I knew that but couldn't tell her that.

"I have to be with her." I could feel my anger rising. I told myself to stay calm. I could do some serious damage to this mere mortal, but wouldn't. Shantay needed her and the rest of the crew to help her.

"That's not possible."

But that was the last thing she said to me as they wheeled Shantay down the stairs and out to the waiting ambulance.

"Where are you taking her?" I called just as they were about to drive off.

"Touro."

And then they were gone. And so was the love of my life. She was clinging to her own life and there was nothing I could do about it. Never had I felt so impotent. I needed to do something, anything. I couldn't just sit at home waiting for a phone call.

I decided to go for a walk. I walked around the neighborhood, but it didn't dispel the energy churning inside. I needed more. Had to do more. I picked up my pace and jogged around a couple of blocks. Still, the need burned.

Switching to preternatural speed, I rushed down Prytania Street, past Louisiana Avenue, and on to Aline until I found myself at Touro. Once there, I had no idea how to proceed. I needed to get inside. That much was obvious. But, how?

I sat on a bench in front of the hospital and willed myself not to cry. I hadn't even realized my tear ducts still worked, but my eyes were welling with unshed tears as I sat contemplating my helplessness.

Shantay needed me. That was the issue I had to focus on. She needed me and I needed to be there for her. I wiped my eyes and took a deep breath. I had to quit feeling sorry for myself and come up with a plan.

The emergency room doors were right there. I could walk in, find Shantay, make sure she was okay, then I'd leave. I just needed to be sure she was getting help and that she was all right.

Mind made up, I sauntered as casually as I could through the large doors.

"You can't be here." A bulky security guard rose to block my path.

"But—"

"No buts." He was standing in my space and I trembled with rage, fighting the urge to take him out. "No one but personnel and patients in here."

"But my fiancée…"

"Sorry. I'm going to have to ask you to leave."

Dejected, I left. I needed another plan. Obviously. Another ambulance arrived and I saw my opportunity. As they wheeled a bloody patient through the doors, I entered at my highest speed so that pesky guard wouldn't see me.

I ran from bed to bed in the ER but there was no sign of Shantay. Where was she? Had she died? No. They would have called me. Where had they taken her? I ran again, before I could be seen.

First floor covered. No Shantay. Up the stairs. Floor after floor. Still no sign of the love of my life. The third floor housed what appeared to be an intensive care unit. Shantay wasn't there and I breathed a sigh of relief.

I continued up until I reached the sixth floor. There was another ICU. There lay Shantay hooked up to all kinds of machines. She appeared to be sleeping peacefully. I almost left. I should have left, but I couldn't.

She looked so small and helpless lying there. I stopped and took her hand.

"Shantay? Can you hear me?"

There was no response. Her machines kept beeping. I wanted to kiss her, to tell her I loved her, but she had a tube down her throat. Still, I kissed her cheek. Her machines continued to beep as normal. There was no sign she knew I was there.

As I stood there, her machines started beeping louder. The cacophony hurt my head and made my body tremble. I knew it wasn't good. Whatever was happening. And I knew I needed to get away.

Footsteps approached and I moved to crouch behind another bed, with my head up just enough to see what was happening. But I couldn't see anything. Shantay's bed was surrounded with nurses calling out instructions and numbers to one another.

It took an eternity for them to get Shantay stabilized, but finally, her machines were beeping rhythmically again.

"She's not going to make it." I heard a nurse say as she walked away. "This damned disease doesn't discriminate."

If I'd had a heart, it would have sunk. I fought to keep my stomach from emptying its contents. Shantay wasn't going to make it. I couldn't lose her. I needed another sixty years with her. She should die of old age after spending her life with me. As my wife. I wasn't ready to let her go.

Damn. If only I knew more about this COVID. Maybe I could do something to offset it. But I didn't. This was new. We'd had deadly diseases many times throughout my life, and people I'd known had died.

But they weren't Shantay. They weren't people I'd loved, planned to marry. No, they had been mere acquaintances. Shantay was anything but.

When the coast was clear, I went back to her bed.

"Baby?" I said. "Shantay? You've got to come out of this. I can't lose you."

It might have been my imagination, but I swore she squeezed my hand.

"Can you hear me? Squeeze twice if yes."

She squeezed my hand twice. They were faint squeezes, but I felt them.

"Are you scared?" Two more squeezes. "I'm here now. I'll think of something. Should I take you away? Out of the hospital?"

She only squeezed once, and I realized she was right. She was where she needed to be. She would die for sure if she left there. But was she going to die anyway?

"I wish I could help," I said.

Her eyes fluttered, then opened. Barely. But enough to meet mine. There was a pleading in them, and I wished I could die with her. I couldn't imagine going on without her.

She mumbled something but I couldn't make it out.

"What?" I shook my head. "I can't understand you."

"Save me," she whispered hoarsely.

"I'm trying. I don't know how."

She nodded and I thought she understood. But her eyes still begged me. For what? How could I save her life?

"...me."

"What?"

She said something that I didn't understand. She kept repeating it, but I just couldn't make it out. Finally, she looked at the bedside table and nodded. I saw a paper and pen. I held it up.

"This?"

She nodded and I handed them to her. I braced myself for a good-bye note. We both knew the end was near. I wasn't sure what I would do when that time came, but I had to be strong and be prepared to guide Shantay to the other side.

She handed me her note.

"Turn me."

EPILOGUE

The waters on the Mediterranean were the bluest of blue. Even in the moonlight. We sat on our back deck sipping our cocktails and enjoying the warm breeze off the water. It was June, and the daytime temperatures had climbed to an almost uncomfortable high, but we slept through them and then nights were pure heaven.

The year was 2120. It had been one hundred years since that fateful night I'd made Shantay one of my kind. We'd argued that night. I'd been adamant, but so had she. I still remember hearing her machines start to beep again and knowing I was about to lose her for good.

So I'd done the unthinkable. I'd turned her. I made her a vampire and condemned her to walk the earth for eternity. I felt horrible about doing it, but in the end, I'd had no choice. I could lose her or keep her with me forever.

I'd opted for the latter, obviously. And, so far, we'd spent our time together in bliss. Once she was a vampire, she understood my need to leave New Orleans, and was excited to move to Miami to start over.

Miami was a hotbed of unrest after fifty years though. The ultra-rightwing government had remained in power for all those years. There were riots everywhere, but the military presence was everywhere in the States, and eventually, people stopped protesting and accepted the way things were.

Most of Florida was fine with the way things were, but Miami was not. And, after fifty years, they began rioting again. Many cities across the country followed suit and a civil war ended up breaking out.

We didn't feel safe, so we escaped to Nice, a lovely community on the French Riviera. We only stayed a few years though, as Shantay was still a young vampire and needed to feed more often than I. There were usually tourists to nourish her, but soon the police noticed the trend and started investigating.

We contemplated moving to Greece, to the Isle of Lesbos, but the same problem presented itself. Shantay would need to feed and we'd soon be caught. That couldn't happen. One evening, soon after waking, Shantay made a suggestion.

"We could move to Ibiza," she said.

"That's like party central," I said. "That could be fun."

"That was last century," she said. "It's been turned into a women's island. It would be the perfect place for us."

"But it's small. And it's an island. We'd run into the same issue we're having here."

"Au contraire. It's ninety-three miles from Valencia, Spain, which has its slums. I could feed the way you used to. Please, Alex. Please say we can move there."

I laughed. I still had a hard time denying Shantay anything she desired.

"Okay. We'll try it. But if it's not safe, we're not moving."

But it was safe. Valencia proved a worthy feeding ground, and Ibiza was heaven. It was still a thriving music hotspot, so the nightclubs were always jumping and always fun. We frequented several of them, but some nights we stayed home. We sat on our deck overlooking the water, sipped our cocktails, and enjoyed the quiet.

That night, we were reminiscing about New Orleans.

"Do you think Patricia had COVID?" Shantay said.

"I do. I think she gave it to you."

"I wonder if she survived."

"Hard telling."

"I miss her," she said.

I smiled at her.

"I miss a lot of things about New Orleans. But I'm very happy here."

"As am I."

Our doorbell rang and we looked at each other. I recognized the fear in Shantay's eyes and knew it was reflected in my own.

"I'll get it," I said.

Our neighbors were on our porch, so I opened the door and invited them in.

"We're drinking margaritas," Anna said with her strong Spanish accent. She held up a blender while her partner, a quiet butch named Ora held up a gallon bottle of tequila in one hand and a bottle of mix in the other. "And you're invited to join us."

"Why thank you," I said. "This should be fun. Let me go grab Shantay."

As I cut through the villa to get Shantay, I pondered again how fun it would be to get those two hot-blooded Spaniards into our bed. We had discussed it often and, while Anna had seemed like an easy target, Ora was a bit more challenging. Neither of us could imagine her letting her guard down enough to climb into bed with us.

We drank margaritas that night. We set up the blender in the courtyard, and Ora selected music for the stereo. We danced, we laughed, we had a blast. After three hours or so, Shantay took over the music. She played music from the eighties. The nineteen eighties, and she and I danced like fools while Anna and Ora stared at us.

"This music is different," said Anna. "What is it?"

"It's old music. But we love it," I said.

"I like it a lot." Ora grabbed Anna and danced with us.

We listened to the Go-Go's, the Police, Survivor, the Tubes, and many others. It was a night to remember. Finally, it was getting late and I was horny.

"Tell me," I said, "Do you two swing?"

"Do we what?" said Anna.

"Never mind," Shantay said. "Alex is talking crazy."

Anna smiled.

"I like Alex. She can talk any way she wants to."

I glanced at Ora who winked at me. What the hell was going on? Was my fantasy about these two about to come true?

"Are you two monogamous? I think that's the word," said Ora.

"We are, why?"

"Too bad. At the risk of ruining our friendship, Anna has often spoke of joining you two in bed."

"What about you?" Shantay sidled up to Ora. "Will you join us as well?"

Ora shook her head.

"I watch."

"Fair enough," said Shantay. She took Anna's hand. "Come on. Let's get this party started."

"Should I watch, too?" I asked Ora.

"Oh, no. You should please Anna. She'd like that. And Shantay."

"Okay."

I headed down the hall with Ora right behind me. I felt like I was about to be graded but didn't care. It was an exam I knew I could ace.

When we got to the bedroom, Shantay and Anna were already naked and making out like teenagers. Anna pulled away from Shantay as I began to undress.

"This I've got to see," she said. "I've waited for this for so long."

When I was naked, they made room for me on the bed. Anna kissed me long and hard until I was flat on my back. She climbed on top of me, and my belly was wet from her rubbing on me.

My head was spinning as my libido ratcheted up a notch. I was ready to take Anna to places Ora never could. I turned over until she was under me. I kissed down her belly as Shantay took an ample breast in her hands and bent to suck her nipple.

I heard Anna mewl and knew she was ripe for the taking. I made myself comfortable between her legs and buried my tongue deep inside. She tasted divine, musky and slightly spicy. It was a unique flavor and I was loving it.

My fingers replaced my tongue and she moaned as she arched to take me deeper. I fucked her with fervor, in and out, in and out, each thrust harder and deeper. I took her clit between my lips and licked it until she arched against me, making it impossible to breathe. I didn't care. What a way to go.

She cried out my name over and over until she relaxed against the mattress. I glanced up and saw need in Shantay's eyes. I kissed her hard then kissed her breast. Her nipple extended in my mouth, and I knew she was ready for anything.

I moved my hand between her legs and felt the back of Anna's head. Smiling to myself, I focused my attention on one nipple and then the other. I heard Anna enter her. I heard Shantay's hot, wet pussy sucking on Anna's fingers. The sound was music to my ears.

Shantay was writhing on the bed, and I knew she was close. I sucked one nipple and twisted and tugged on the other. In another minute, she let out the loudest, most guttural moan I'd ever heard from her. She collapsed against me.

"You good, babe?" I said.

"Mm-hm."

"Good."

Before I could say another word, Anna was licking and sucking my lower lips and I lost the power to think. She had me feeling so good. Her tongue dove deep inside me, lapping at my walls and sending me into a frenzy.

Shantay joined her and licked and sucked my clit until I couldn't take any more. Their talented tongues sent me reeling. I lost touch with reality while my body shook with the force of the orgasm.

When I came to, I had two naked beauties in bed with me. I reached for Anna and kissed her just before Ora spoke.

"Enough," she said. "That was good, but enough for now. Anna, get dressed. We should get going."

"Are you sure?" Shantay sat up. "We'd hate to see you go."

"We'll be back," said Ora. "Another time. It's late though. We should get home."

I got dressed and, on shaky legs, walked them to the door.

"Thanks for everything," I said. "It's been fun."

"Thank you," said Anna. "Take care and we'll be back soon."

"Sounds good."

I watched until they were inside their house. Then I went back to the bedroom, but it was empty. I followed the sound of seventies rock to the courtyard where I found Shantay with a margarita in hand.

"What are you doing?" I laughed.

"Just enjoying life," she said. "Or death, or whatever this is."

"This, my love, is the best of both worlds."

"That it is."

"And I'm thrilled to be spending it with you," I said.

"Me, too."

I took her margarita and set it on the table. I took her hand and led her back to the bedroom where I proved to her time and again how happy I was that she was mine.

About the Author

MJ Williamz was raised on California's central coast, which she left at age seventeen to pursue an education. She graduated from Chico State and it was in Chico that she rediscovered her love of writing. It wasn't until she moved to Portland, however, that her writing really took off, with the publication of her first short story in 2003.

MJ is the author of twenty books, including three Goldie Award winners. She has also had over thirty-five short stories published, most of them erotica with a few romances and a few horrors thrown in for good measure. She lives in Houston with her wife, fellow author Laydin Michaels, and their fur babies. You can find her on Facebook or reach her at mjwilliamz@aol.com.

Books Available from Bold Strokes Books

A Turn of Fate by Ronica Black. Will Nev and Kinsley finally face their painful past and relent to their powerful, forbidden attraction? Or will facing their past be too much to fight through? (978-1-63555-930-9)

Desires After Dark by MJ Williamz. When her human lover falls deathly ill, Alex, a vampire, must decide which is worse, letting her go or condemning her to everlasting life. (978-1-63555-940-8)

Her Consigliere by Carsen Taite. FBI agent Royal Scott swore an oath to uphold the law, and criminal defense attorney Siobhan Collins pledged her loyalty to the only family she's ever known, but will their love be stronger than the bonds they've vowed to others, or will their competing allegiances tear them apart? (978-1-63555-924-8)

In Our Words: Queer Stories from Black, Indigenous, and People of Color Writers. Stories Selected by Anne Shade and Edited by Victoria Villaseñor. Comprising both the renowned and emerging voices of Black, Indigenous, and People of Color authors, this thoughtfully curated collection of short stories explores the intersection of racial and queer identity. (978-1-63555-936-1)

Measure of Devotion by CF Frizzell. Disguised as her late twin brother, Catherine Samson enters the Civil War to defend the Constitution as a Union soldier, never expecting her life to be altered by a Gettysburg farmer's daughter. (978-1-63555-951-4)

Not Guilty by Brit Ryder. Claire Weaver and Emery Pearson's day jobs clash, even as their desire for each other burns, and a discreet sex-only arrangement is the only option. (978-1-63555-896-8)

Opposites Attract: Butch/Femme Romances by Meghan O'Brien, Aurora Rey, Angie Williams. Sometimes opposites really do attract. Fall in love with these butch/femme romance novellas. (978-1-63555-784-8)

Swift Vengeance by Jean Copeland, Jackie D, Erin Zak. A journalist becomes the subject of her own investigation when sudden strange, violent visions summon her to a summer retreat and into the arms of a killer's possible next victim. (978-1-63555-880-7)

Under Her Influence by Amanda Radley. On their path to #truelove, will Beth and Jemma discover that reality is even better than illusion? (978-1-63555-963-7)

Wasteland by Kristin Keppler & Allisa Bahney. Danielle Clark is fighting against the National Armed Forces and finds peace as a scavenger, until the NAF general's daughter, Katelyn Turner, shows up on her doorstep and brings the fight right back to her. (978-1-63555-935-4)

When in Doubt by VK Powell. Police officer Jeri Wylder thinks she committed a crime in the line of duty but can't remember, until details emerge pointing to a cover-up by those close to her. (978-1-63555-955-2)

A Woman to Treasure by Ali Vali. An ancient scroll isn't the only treasure Levi Montbard finds as she starts her hunt for the truth—all she has to do is prove to Yasmine Hassani that there's more to her than an adventurous soul. (978-1-63555-890-6)

Before. After. Always. by Morgan Lee Miller. Still reeling from her tragic past, Eliza Walsh has sworn off taking risks, until Blake Navarro turns her world right-side up, making her question if falling in love again is worth it. (978-1-63555-845-6)

Bet the Farm by Fiona Riley. Lauren Calloway's luxury real estate sale of the century comes to a screeching halt when dairy farm heiress, and one-night stand, Thea Boudreaux calls her bluff. (978-1-63555-731-2)

Cowgirl by Nance Sparks. The last thing Aren expects is to fall for Carol. Sharing her home is one thing, but sharing her heart means sharing the demons in her past and risking everything to keep Carol safe. (978-1-63555-877-7)

Give In to Me by Elle Spencer. Gabriela Talbot never expected to sleep with her favorite author—certainly not after the scathing review she'd given Whitney Ainsworth's latest book. (978-1-63555-910-1)

Hidden Dreams by Shelley Thrasher. A lethal virus and its resulting vision send Texan Barbara Allan and her lovely guide, Dara, on a journey up Cambodia's Mekong River in search of Barbara's mother's mystifying past. (978-1-63555-856-2)

In the Spotlight by Lesley Davis. For actresses Cole Calder and Eris Whyte, their chance at love runs out fast when a fan's adoration turns to obsession. (978-1-63555-926-2)

Origins by Jen Jensen. Jamis Bachman is pulled into a dangerous mystery that becomes personal when she learns the truth of her origins as a ghost hunter. (978-1-63555-837-1)

Pursuit: A Victorian Entertainment by Felice Picano. An intelligent, handsome, ruthlessly ambitious young man who rose from the slums to become the right-hand man of the Lord Exchequer of England will stop at nothing as he pursues his Lord's vanished wife across Continental Europe. (978-1-63555-870-8)

Unrivaled by Radclyffe. Zoey Cohen will never accept second place in matters of the heart, even when her rival is a career, and Declan Black has nothing left to give of herself or her heart. (978-1-63679-013-8)

A Fae Tale by Genevieve McCluer. Dovana comes to terms with her changing feelings for her lifelong best friend and fae, Roze. (978-1-63555-918-7)

Accidental Desperados by Lee Lynch. Life is clobbering Berry, Jaudon, and their long romance. The arrival of directionless baby dyke MJ doesn't help. Can they find their passion again—and keep it? (978-1-63555-482-3)

Always Believe by Aimée. Greyson Walsden is pursuing ordination as an Anglican priest. Angela Arlingham doesn't believe in God. Do they follow their vocation or their hearts? (978-1-63555-912-5)

Best of the Wrong Reasons by Sander Santiago. For Fin Ness and Orion Starr, it takes a funeral to remind them that love is worth living for. (978-1-63555-867-8)

Courage by Jesse J. Thoma. No matter how often Natasha Parsons and Tommy Finch clash on the job, an undeniable attraction simmers just beneath the surface. Can they find the courage to change so love has room to grow? (978-1-63555-802-9)

I Am Chris by R Kent. There's one saving grace to losing everything and moving away. Nobody knows her as Chrissy Taylor. Now Chris can live who he truly is. (978-1-63555-904-0)

The Princess and the Odium by Sam Ledel. Jastyn and Princess Aurelia return to Venostes and join their families in a battle against the dark force to take back their homeland for a chance at a better tomorrow. (978-1-63555-894-4)

The Queen Has a Cold by Jane Kolven. What happens when the heir to the throne isn't a prince or a princess? (978-1-63555-878-4)

The Secret Poet by Georgia Beers. Agreeing to help her brother woo Zoe Blake seemed like a good idea to Morgan Thompson at first...until she realizes she's actually wooing Zoe for herself... (978-1-63555-858-6)

You Again by Aurora Rey. For high school sweethearts Kate Cormier and Sutton Guidry, the second chance might be the only one that matters. (978-1-63555-791-6)

Coming to Life on South High by Lee Patton. Twenty-one-year-old gay virgin Gabe Rafferty's first adult decade unfolds as an unpredictable journey into sex, love, and livelihood. (978-1-63555-906-4)

Love's Falling Star by B.D. Grayson. For country music megastar Lochlan Paige, can love conquer her fear of losing the one thing she's worked so hard to protect? (978-1-63555-873-9)

Love's Truth by C.A. Popovich. Can Lynette and Barb make love work when unhealed wounds of betrayed trust and a secret could change everything? (978-1-63555-755-8)

Next Exit Home by Dena Blake. Home may be where the heart is, but for Harper Sims and Addison Foster, is the journey back worth the pain? (978-1-63555-727-5)

Not Broken by Lyn Hemphill. Falling in love is hard enough—even more so for Rose who's carrying her ex's baby. (978-1-63555-869-2)

The Noble and the Nightingale by Barbara Ann Wright. Two women on opposite sides of empires at war risk all for a chance at love. (978-1-63555-812-8)

What a Tangled Web by Melissa Brayden. Clementine Monroe has the chance to buy the café she's managed for years, but Madison LeGrange swoops in and buys it first. Now Clementine is forced to work for the enemy and ignore her former crush. (978-1-63555-749-7)

A Far Better Thing by JD Wilburn. When needs of her family and wants of her heart clash, Cass Halliburton is faced with the ultimate sacrifice. (978-1-63555-834-0)

Body Language by Renee Roman. When Mika offers to provide Jen erotic tutoring, will sex drive them into a deeper relationship or tear them apart? (978-1-63555-800-5)

Carrie and Hope by Joy Argento. For Carrie and Hope loss brings them together but secrets and fear may tear them apart. (978-1-63555-827-2)

Death's Prelude by David S. Pederson. In this prequel to the Detective Heath Barrington Mystery series, Heath discovers that first love changes you forever and drives you to become the person you're destined to be. (978-1-63555-786-2)

Ice Queen by Gun Brooke. School counselor Aislin Kennedy wants to help standoffish CEO Susanna Durr and her troubled teenage daughter become closer—even if it means risking her own heart in the process. (978-1-63555-721-3)

Masquerade by Anne Shade. In 1925 Harlem, New York, a notorious gangster sets her sights on seducing Celine, and new lovers Dinah and Celine are forced to risk their hearts, and lives, for love. (978-1-63555-831-9)

Royal Family by Jenny Frame. Loss has defined both Clay's and Katya's lives, but guarding their hearts may prove to be the biggest heartbreak of all. (978-1-63555-745-9)

Share the Moon by Toni Logan. Three best friends, an inherited vineyard and a resident ghost come together for fun, romance and a touch of magic. (978-1-63555-844-9)

Spirit of the Law by Carsen Taite. Attorney Owen Lassiter will do almost anything to put a murderer behind bars, but can she get past her reluctance to rely on unconventional help from the alluring Summer Byrne and keep from falling in love in the process? (978-1-63555-766-4)

The Devil Incarnate by Ali Vali. Cain Casey has so much to live for, but enemies who lurk in the shadows threaten to unravel it all. (978-1-63555-534-9)